(c)

Also by Pam Lewis

Speak Softly, She Can Hear

PERFECT FAMILY

PAM LEWIS

Simon & Schuster
New York London Toronto Sydney

Simon & Schuster
1230 Avenue of the Americas
New York, NY 10020

First Simon & Schuster hardcover edition April 2008

SIMON & SCHUSTER and colophon are registered trademarks of Simon & Schuster, Inc.

For information about special discounts for bulk purchases, please contact Simon & Schuster Special Sales at 1-800-456-6798 or business@simonandschuster.com.

Designed by Davina Mock-Maniscalco

Manufactured in the United States of America

10 9 8 7 6 5 4 3 2 1

Library of Congress Cataloging-in-Publication Data

Lewis, Pam, 1943–
Perfect family / by Pam Lewis.
p. cm.
1. Rich people—Fiction. 2. Family secrets—Fiction. 3. Deception—Fiction.
4. Connecticut—Fiction. 5. Psychological fiction. I. Title.

PS3612.E974P47 2008
813'.6—dc22   2007033538

ISBN-13: 978-0-7432-9145-3
ISBN-10:   0-7432-9145-X

For Robert Haskins Funk

"How can we live without our lives?
How will we know it's us without our past?"

—John Steinbeck, *The Grapes of Wrath*

PERFECT FAMILY

Chapter 1

William

Fond du Lac, Lake Aral, Vermont

At exactly three-thirty William Carteret parked beside his sister Pony's car at the lake house. He'd been driving since two, and now the sun was falling behind the mountain, and everything—the house, the lawn, the shore, and half the lake—was in shadow. A stiff wind was kicking up whitecaps on the water. A handful of sailboats scudded quickly, their small white sails crowded together as they headed for the last race buoy.

William stretched and walked down to the water, as he always did first thing. Someone was still on the beach on the opposite shore, where they had the afternoon sun. He envied them over there, the Nicelys, the Garners, the Wrights, and their neighbors, for the long slow afternoons filled with late light and the lazy wane of day. Here on the Carteret side, they had the early-morning sun, and if you asked William's father, Jasper Carteret III, he'd say they were better off because of it, that being on the western shore meant being early

1

risers; it meant being industrious, disciplined, and, although this was not spoken, superior.

William turned and headed toward the house, a big old gray dowager of a place, three stories tall. The house looked tired. It needed a new roof, a thought that depressed him because it would mean an assessment from his father. He and his sisters—Pony, Tinker, and Mira—would all have to pitch in to help pay for it. Pony wouldn't be able to come up with her share, so he and his other two sisters would have to carry her again. Maybe he'd bring it up with her while he was up here, or maybe not. Probably not. There was no getting blood from a stone.

Something in one of the upper windows caught his attention, an orange shape moving to one side of the pane. "Pony?" he shouted, and immediately she was plainly in view, waving to him. Had she been there all along? Watching him? Something was going on. She'd called him that morning and told him in that rapid-fire way she had that he needed to come up to the lake, and it had to be today. She had the place all to herself. Well, she and her son, Andrew, who was only a baby. But the point was, no Daddy, no Tinker, no Mira. Pony had just come up and let herself in, and they didn't even know about it. "So there!" she'd said, meaning she'd blown off the whole sign-up sheet, the careful summer schedule that Tinker had come up with after their mother died.

She vanished from the window. A moment later, the screen door flew open, banged against the side of the house, and slammed shut. Pony came at a run, a blur of bright orange T-shirt and white shorts across the lawn, her long dark red hair streaming behind.

"Oh, Jesus, William," she said, wrapping her arms around his neck. "You came."

She was the youngest of his three sisters, his hands-down favorite. She was lean and tall, and she had the kind of energy that made her light as air. She hugged him, freed herself, hugged him again. She had a broad face, high cheekbones, and a perfectly straight and slightly prominent nose; it was the kind of nose, their father said,

2

that came from generations of breeding. Her eyes, though, those were the main thing about Pony. Big hazel eyes always alert, always taking everything in, eyes that darted quickly and constantly.

"Wouldn't not." He glanced about, looking for evidence of someone else, but saw nothing.

She took a step back, taking him in, grinning. "Come inside. Andrew's taking a nap." She dragged him by the hand across the lawn to the porch and into the cavernous living room with its three big faded blue couches arranged around a massive stone fireplace where the last coals of a fire still burned. The baby's toys were scattered across the floor. William recognized the orange Tonka truck that had once been his, and Matchbox cars, also his from childhood. Even some of the girls' dolls were in evidence. Andrew's clothes and diapers were stacked in piles on the furniture; the room held the dismal smell of baby and sour milk.

"Looks like a tornado came through," he said.

"Voice down." Pony pointed to a crib in the corner, where the baby was sound asleep.

"I'll put my stuff upstairs," William said in a whisper.

The upstairs was like the downstairs: Pony's hair dryer lay in the sink, still plugged into the wall. Andrew's rubber toys were piled in the tub, and towels lay on the floor. William checked among the items on the vanity to see if there was a guy's razor or aftershave. He was 90 percent sure this was about a new boyfriend. But there was nothing belonging to an adult male on the whole second floor. He could hear Pony singing downstairs. An Elvis Costello tune, "Alison."

When he went back down, she was banging things around in the kitchen. She switched to whistling. The baby was awake now in his crib, looking blankly up at William, his face creased and moist from sleeping on his blanket. He was a cheerful little guy with very blond hair. When he saw William, he opened his mouth and wailed.

"What should I do?" William called out.

"Nothing. He's just hungry." Pony hoisted the baby out of the crib and went back into the kitchen, where she gave him a bottle, then blitzed around, the baby on one hip, making sandwiches with her free hand.

"So what's the deal?" William said. "Why am I up here?"

She stopped what she was doing and turned to look at him, cocking her head as if she saw something surprising in him. "All in good time," she said.

William went to the porch. A wind was blowing up the lake from the south. Overhead, the trees rustled, and from the lake came the hollow clank of the barrels under the raft as they were lifted and dropped.

A shout from next door caused William to look over at the Bells' place, partly visible through the trees. William's father still resented Dennis Bell (Dennis *père*, Jasper called him snidely) for buying the land from him eight years earlier and for the house Bell put up. William's father had sold only seventeen feet of water frontage, which was intended to force the Bells into building farther back, where the lot widened and where the house would be hidden among the trees. But Bell had put up an A-frame tight to the shore. It was a big triangle of a house with kelly-green trim, the only one of its kind on the lake, its cedar shake roof sloping all the way to the ground.

Every spring the Bells talked to William's father about blacktopping the right-of-way they shared, and every year William's father said no. The year before, a crew of guys had shown up and paved the private section of road that forked off the right-of-way to the Bells' house. William's family had contempt for the pristine condition in which the Bells kept their driveway, as if their own eroded two-track were a cut above.

Two shiny SUVs, a silver and a red, were visible through the trees. The Bell kids had Daisy rifles, and William thought he saw Denny, the youngest (Dennis *fils*), in the woods between the two houses. He was probably shooting squirrels. When Andrew got older, that would be a problem. Just as when William had been a kid up here, Andrew would have too much time on his hands by the time he hit eleven or twelve, and if the Bell kids or grandkids were shooting, Andrew would want to shoot, too. But that would be later. Nothing to worry about now. If William's mother were still alive, she'd be over there right now talking to Mrs. Bell, asking politely if she would please keep the boy from shooting off his gun. And then she'd come back to the house, distressed because Anita Bell would have said something like "Oh, what's the harm?" That was how the Bells were, casual about important things. William's father had called the police on them once, which had done no good. It wasn't against the law to shoot off a Daisy rifle on your own land.

The door creaked behind William, and Pony was there with Andrew still slung on one jutted hip. She lowered him to the floor in front of William. "Watch him for a sec, will you?"

Driving up from Connecticut, he had felt sanguine. That was the only word for it. The day was clear. The road was empty. He'd done eighty, sometimes ninety, all the way up 91 and not a single cop, not even north of Greenfield, where there were almost always speed traps. He'd had this idea that he would sit on the porch at Fond du Lac and work, something he'd seen in *The New York Times Magazine* once, an ad for booze showing a guy with bare feet propped on a railing looking out at the ocean, laptop open, rum drink at the ready. William eyed the baby, who sat on the floor like a lump, staring up at him. He was apparently easy as kids went, or so Tinker, the eldest of William's three sisters, always said. Tinker said Andrew would sit wherever he was put and stare at something until something else—his toes or a piece of lint on the floor—got his attention, and then he'd stare at that for the next half hour. She always followed that up by talking about how her own daughter, Isabel, who was eight now, had been lithe and quick at Andrew's age, the implication being that a restless child was brighter. It was another way for Tinker to cut Pony down to size. Tinker needed to step on Pony just to feel even.

William had been six when Tinker was born. Mira had come a

year later and Pony a year after that. Three damp little animals. Their mother was always attending to them—feeding them, burping them, changing their diapers. The house smelled all the time. He stopped having his friends over because of the blast of steamy baby smell that always hit him when he opened the front door. As his sisters grew older, Tinker, an officious, chubby little girl, rode herd on the others, parroting their mother about what they were allowed to do or not do. Their rooms were down the hall from his, and he could always hear her bullying her little sisters.

But then Pony had broken off and sought out William's company. She used to hang out in his room and lie on his bed while he struggled through his homework. She had questions for him. Lots of questions. *Are God and Santa Claus the same person?* Yes. *Is our family poor because we don't have a dishwasher?* No. *What's on the other side of the stars?* Not a clue. In their very careful family she was the one he admired. She once jumped from the garage roof. When their mother wasn't there, she did the forbidden: she swam across the lake without a boat. Once, when their mother had had a bunch of women to the house, Pony had taken small bills from each of the purses left in their parents' bedroom and spent it on candy.

Pony came back to the porch with a beer for William in one hand and a real drink in the other, something amber-colored with ice, letting the screen door slam behind her; the ghost of their mother's voice echoed in William's ears: *Do not let the screen door slam.* It didn't seem like a good idea to be drinking with the baby right there. If Pony got lit, and she could, William would be stuck with Andrew. She read him. "Don't worry," she said, putting the drinks on the table between them. "I'll be fine."

"I thought you quit." There'd been a time, before she had Andrew, when the family had worried about her.

"I did," she said, taking a long swallow.

The phone rang in the living room. Pony grabbed her glass and went inside to answer it. "Hello. Hi. Yes. Uh-huh. Shit," she said,

and then "Yeah, well, not much you can do about that, I guess."
After a few moments, the door banged again and she was back. She
sank into the chair opposite. "I thought you'd be here later."

"Is that a problem?"

She shrugged. She handed him a blistered strip of four photographs, taken in one of those old-fashioned photo booths, of a girl
and boy in perhaps their late teens. The girl was blond and wore a
feathered headdress. Her long hair hung like curtains on either side
of her face. The boy was partly hidden behind her. He had dark hair
swept back like Nixon's. It took a moment for William to understand
the girl was their mother. "Where did this come from?" he asked. He
turned the strip over. The words *Livvy, 1968* were written on the
back. "Nobody ever called her Livvy."

"I know. Isn't that a riot? Daddy always called her Olivia."

"But where did you get this thing?" he asked again. The family albums were full of pictures, but none of their mother as a girl. "Lost,"
their mother always said vaguely when William asked, and she would
allude to a flooded basement in which photos were destroyed or to a
move in which they were lost. It was always one incomplete explanation or the other.

"Cool your jets," Pony said.

"Who's the boy?"

"Not now, okay? Later."

Andrew let out a wail. Pony put her drink on the rail, and
William noticed it was fuller than before; she must have added to it.
She dragged Andrew's playpen from the corner of the porch, and
bumped it down the stairs to the lawn. It was a big expandable circle
she could put down anywhere, and it kept Andrew in pretty much
the same place for a while. She pulled it open as far as it would go.
Then she lowered Andrew into it.

William's good mood from driving up earlier was shot. He felt
uneasy; anxious, even. Pony was up. She was down. In and out of the
house. He wished she'd just sit still and tell him what was up. He
looked out at the water. The surface was still alive with tiny white-

caps. The cold water would calm him down. It would suck the annoyance right out of him.

"I'm taking a refresher lifesaving course at the town beach. I figured I'd better, what with Andrew," Pony said.

He was so glad to hear this. Everybody would be glad to hear it. Pony was a great mother, if you asked him, but anything that made her more conventional as a mother was going to make the rest of the family happy. "That's just great," he said.

"I haven't forgotten much."

"Like riding a bicycle," he said. All the Carteret kids had taken the lifesaving and water-safety-instructor courses over at the town beach the summer they were old enough. Their mother had insisted on it because she herself hadn't learned to swim until she was an adult, and she was a very nervous swimmer. She didn't care if they ever used it, if they ever got lifesaving jobs or saved anybody. No, she just wanted them to know how. The town beach lessons were famous for something called the drowning game. It should be illegal, William thought, but it was part of the Lake Aral program. The way it worked? Everybody swam into deep water at once, the whole class of twenty or thirty kids. They'd tread water for a minute or so, adrenaline going, and at the signal, each of them was to attack someone else, get the person into a hold, and swim him to shallow water. The object was to drag as many people to shore as you could. If somebody dragged you in, you lost and had to get out of the water. The last one in the water was the winner. William won it his year. He'd been fifteen, and he'd spent the winter building his upper body with weights, standing before his mirror. He'd put on twenty-three pounds that year, all muscle. Pony had won the drowning game her year, too. His sister Mira had allowed herself to be rescued right away so she could sit the whole thing out. Tinker had tried, but she had been one of the early ones to be pulled out.

"I'll go change," he said.

While he was up in his room, pulling on his trunks, he saw Pony down on the beach, toeing the sand, her head bowed. She'd stuffed her hair into her shirt, and it gave her back a kind of hump. She paced. She chewed a fingernail. She walked up the lawn, stepped into the baby's playpen, and sat down cross-legged in front of him. William heard the baby laugh. They were alike that way, Pony and Andrew. Their first reaction to each other was always laughter, no matter what. She kissed him, and he giggled again. She put a little yellow jacket on him and a hat because of the breeze.

"I need to tell you something," she had said over the telephone two years earlier. They'd met in Elizabeth Park in Hartford and taken a walk. It had been a mild November day. They'd walked through the dormant rose garden and sat on a bench. "I'm pregnant," Pony had said. He'd accepted the news quietly and waited for her to say more. "It's perfect, actually," she'd said. "The father won't ever know. He's long gone. A one-night stand, if memory serves." She'd smiled almost radiantly. "You're the only one I'm telling who the father is. Let them go crazy guessing. Tinker especially."

"People will think it was Seth," William said, referring to Pony's on-again-off-again boyfriend.

"Let them. He got married last year and moved to Canada."

When the family found out, things had fallen apart. Their father sank into one of his weekend-in-the-chair depressions. Tinker set up conference calls with Mira and William. Pony needed to be married to whomever the father was, she said. Or someone needed to approach Pony on the subject of an abortion, and she thought William was the one; Pony might listen to him. William had stopped taking Tinker's calls until Pony was safely into her second trimester. And then Andrew was born and the family laid down arms for a period. He was the first grandson, and what could anybody do? But Andrew was a year old now, and Pony had a job in an art supply store that paid nothing. They'd all have to pitch in, which raised yet another problem, in Tinker's view—how Pony would handle any money they gave her. She wasn't exactly a financial genius, and if the family ponied up—excuse the expression—some money for Andrew's care, how could they be sure Pony wouldn't spend it on art supplies or give it away to charity? Mira didn't see what was the matter with Pony buying art supplies. "She *is* an artist, Tinker," she said.

There had been some more e-mails about that lately, which William hadn't answered. He gave Pony money whenever he had it, but he didn't want to be part of the organized charity that Tinker was trying to set up. He didn't want to be bound to Tinker, didn't want to be ordered around. What was more, the others still believed the baby had a regular father someplace, a real guy who'd come out of hiding and take responsibility or, worst-case scenario, Pony would have somebody to sue for child support if things got bad. Nobody in the family but William knew how on her own Pony was with this one.

She stepped back over Andrew's playpen and went down to the water's edge, where she pulled off her shirt and stepped out of her shorts and then her underwear. William watched her, feeling lousy about it but watching anyway. She stood on the shore, hands on her hips, looking out at the water. Instinctively, he went to the other window to see if anybody was watching over at the Bells', but no. Nobody was outside over there now, as far as he could see.

He was annoyed that she would skinny-dip in the daytime. They didn't do that. Only at night. But then a lot had changed. Their mother's death had been the opening salvo, and ever since, the family had been caving in. Pony would not have had Andrew if their mother were still alive. William was sure of it. She would not have come up here without asking, and neither would he. Mira would have gone to graduate school. Their father would have had Fond du Lac painted. He would have contracted out the new roof. And William would still be working a nine-to-five at Aetna, a job he hated, because it was one thing to disappoint his mother but another to disappoint his father, who had, when you came down to it, pulled the rug out from under William in the first place.

Ever since childhood, William had assumed he would follow in his father's footsteps. He'd had the summer jobs at Carteret Ball Bearings—working the mail room, the advertising department, and—his best summer because it had kept him out-of-doors—working with the grounds crew. He'd gone to Trinity College in Hartford, the alma mater of all the Carterets, and studied history and economics, as they had. Unlike them, however, William had been a disappointing C student in everything but English.

But when William was in his junior year, his father sold the company. It had happened without warning, only an explanation after the fact. Advancement in manufacture and technology had made labor almost obsolete. Ball bearings could be produced by machine twenty-four hours a day: manufactured, assembled, packaged, shipped, and distributed without ever being touched by a human hand. The competition was revving up; upgrades needed to be made. The sale had gone quickly. The whole plant was knocked down and shipped to Finland, where it was reconstructed and producing within the month. The buildings were sold to a community college.

And so just out of college, William had gone to work at Aetna in a public relations job. It involved sitting in a cubicle most days and making incremental steps up the corporate ladder every year at performance-review time. When his mother died, he'd quit and started his own freelance business. The work suited him brilliantly, and he was good at it. When he worked, he earned money. When he didn't, he could go hiking. He would never be the chief executive officer of anything.

He caught sight of his reflection in the full-length mirror and leaned in to see his dark eyes and the long black lashes he'd cut down to the root in eighth grade after Amber Alexander had said she envied him. He turned sideways to see the musculature of his chest. Leonine, his girlfriend, Ruth, called him. He moved like a lion, she said; it was in his build, long in the torso and narrow through the hips and with the smooth gait of a cat. And his skin was olive, unlike that of his sisters, who all had fair, easily freckled skin and fine pale hairs on their arms and cheeks. William ran a hand over his hair, which was dark and cut very short. He had a high forehead and wide-set eyes, and he had the same strong nose as Pony.

She was in the water when he came back outside, swimming out toward the raft, doing the six-beat crawl he'd taught her, three kicks to each arm for power and endurance. She still liked to swim across the lake in midsummer, and if he was around, he'd row the safety boat for her, synchronizing his oars to the rhythm of her stroke. Now she paused and did a surface dive, her bare ass rising white and glistening before disappearing.

He and Pony often skinny-dipped during long family parties. The game was to make sure Tinker knew—a dropped shoe, a slammed door, something to alert their uptight sister that they were headed outside to the lake, to make her charge down to the water and stand there waving her flashlight and calling in a stage whisper to them: *This is so inappropriate.* Pony said that if Tinker were happy with her body, she'd be in there with them every time.

William entered the lake quickly, feeling the cold against his shins and thighs, the sudden shock to his groin. He did a quick immersion. He swam underwater, his eyes open to the black haze, and took a few strokes to get warm, then surfaced. He looked about for Pony. The choppy water everywhere made it difficult to see. He listened over the wind for a splash.

Something brushed his feet, coming up from a deeper place. He tucked on instinct, but her hands clamped fast around his ankles and pulled him down. He tried to buck, to kick her away, but she had him tight. She gripped his lower legs with both arms from behind. She shinnied up his body, arm over arm, to his knees and his thighs, pulling him down as she moved deeper underwater. He thrashed and tried to pry himself free, but of all the holds, this was the surest, the safest, for the rescuer. She was solidly behind, out of his reach and in control.

But he was ripped. Worse than ripped. He was scared. There hadn't been time to take in a breath. *Use your head,* he told himself. There was no breaking that hold. The only option was to stop fighting. He forced himself to let go, to surrender and feel immediately the soft warmth of her body along the length of him. On instinct, he

12

tried to twist away again, but she was too strong. *Jesus, Pony.* They broke the surface, and he hauled in a deep breath, then another. "What the fuck!" he shouted.

She kept him in her grip. "Like riding a bicycle," she said, and laughed. "You said so yourself. I've still got it."

"Let go." He could hardly breathe. He was hyperventilating, forcing himself to slow down, take in the breaths deep and slow. Nausea was setting in.

"Not on your life," she said. "You'll get me back. I know you will."

"God Almighty, I'm not going to do anything. Cut this out!"

But she kept sidestroking, her upper leg pulling up, thrusting away, lurching the two of them toward shore. "I didn't forget any of this stuff," she said. "We have the drowning game coming up in class. I plan to win. If I can take you, I can take anybody."

He couldn't speak. He had to think about breathing. The warmth of her body against his back unnerved him. He made a vain attempt to twist away again. They were in shallow water, and she loosened her grip. He crouched, swam away from her. She plopped down on the sand at the water's edge, totally at ease with her nakedness. Behind her, Andrew shook his pen with his fists.

"Put some clothes on," William said.

"Nobody's even up here now," she said. "Except a couple of Bells, and they don't count." Her skin was a weave of gooseflesh.

"*I'm* up here." He felt too shaky to stand. He dove underwater and swam the distance to the raft, as if it were possible to cleanse himself. He pulled himself up on the raft. The wind chilled him quickly, a new discomfort. He focused on the water and on the opposite shore. He forced himself to resist shivering. He'd panicked. She'd taken him by surprise, and he'd panicked.

He lay down to get out of the wind, pressing his chest against the warmer boards of the raft. She was at the water's edge, playing peekaboo with Andrew as if nothing had happened. William stared down through the slats below, a thin-line glimpse at the dark water under the raft, aware of exactly what had happened physiologically in his body. In the instant Pony had attacked him, his nervous system had kicked his heart into overdrive and sent blood to his limbs, where it was needed. Now came the aftermath. He felt dizzy and light-headed. His hands trembled. He pressed his cheek against the raft. He was furious at himself. He felt nauseated. He felt ashamed.

There was a trip on the Yucatan Peninsula he'd heard about. A week in a jungle so dense a person could advance only a mile a day toward Mayan ruins that might be there and might not. The ruins had never been found. The point of the expedition was the jour-ney. Every step had to be taken slowly, calculated. A snake in that jungle had a bite that disintegrated the vascular system and caused a person to bleed to death from his pores. There were venomous spiders and no way out. Sometimes William thought about that: what it would be like to be so trapped, forced to overcome panic or surely die.

That was the whole thing about panic. You had to use your head, not your instinct. As soon as the body got its way, you were in trou-ble. He sat up and watched Pony. She waved and smiled at him. She was still buck-naked. He lowered himself into the water and swam to shore. She was lying on her back on the sand, resting on her elbows, her breasts sloping to either side.

"What the fuck was that about?" he asked her. Without waiting for an answer, he headed up the lawn toward the house. Andrew stared as if William were an alien creature. William stared back. An-drew was the alien creature. Cute, but hey. William went upstairs, toweled off, and, as he changed into his clothes, watched Pony from the window. She stood at water's edge, stretching, arms over her head, leaning one way, then the other. He couldn't take his eyes off her, and she probably knew it. He felt the flutter of fear, the residual fear of a near-miss, a dangerous swerve on the highway, a stumble while hiking a knife-edge. It was lousy, the heavy sensation and feel-ing ashamed. She was his sister.

Years earlier, when Pony was about nine or ten, William had been in the bathroom of the West Hartford house, shaving. It was afternoon, and it was winter. The mirror on the medicine cabinet was spotted where the tin had eaten through, so shaving was a pain. Pony had banged on the door, demanding to be let in. William wrapped a towel around himself and opened the door a crack, but his little sister barged in and sat down on the commode, crossing her arms over her chest in fury. He went back to shaving. "So what's the problem?" he said.

"Mom," she said. "I'm coming out of my room, and she says, 'Pony, dear, I need to tell you about the birds and the bees.' " She looked at William and crossed her eyes. "Birds and bees? What planet is she on, anyway?"

"I'll bet she showed you that book," he said. "The one she keeps in the closet."

"It is so lame. She said that I am not allowed ever ever ever to let a boy put his hands below my waist." Pony grinned up at William. "I said, 'Maybe no boy will ever ever ever try.' She said, 'Oh, yes, they will.' She said it happens to every single girl in every city and every country and that it will happen to me, and the minute it does, I need to remember what she said."

William went on shaving.

"Well?"

"Well what?"

"Is it true?"

William nodded. "Yup," he said. "It's true."

"You think it'll even happen to Tinker?"

"Even Tinker."

"So I can be famous."

"How's that?" he asked.

"I'll be the only girl it *doesn't* happen to. I'll be on talk shows. I'll be on *Oprah*."

"You'll make us all so proud," William said.

"Here's what I don't get," Pony said. "I've seen your penis, right? And Daddy's and this kid Eddie's in my class, and what I want to know is how is one of those ever going to poke itself into a woman like Mom says? Like hello?"

"Ask Mom," William said. "Ask Tinker. Jeez, Pony."

"I'm asking you," Pony said. "Because you've got one."

"Under certain circumstances, it gets hard, " William said, trying for equilibrium. She deserved an answer.

"Can I see?"

"No," he said. But he felt it start to happen. Back then, just talking about it could make it happen. He turned back to the mirror to hide it from her. "Let me finish shaving," he said. "Get out of here."

"Why can't you show me? What's the big deal?"

He leaned against the cool sink to stop it from happening. "Scram."

"Why does everybody always have to get so mad about this stuff? Honestly!" she said, and left the room, slamming the door.

He kept watching her. She was back in the water, breaststroking in circles. The wind rippled across the water. She looked so white, frog-kicking, her black-looking hair fanning out, obscuring her shoulders. She surface-dove, emerged closer to shore, and said something to Andrew. Those two were the team now. Pony and Andrew. William felt like an intruder coming in today, stumbling over Andrew's toys, smelling his baby smells. The same lousy plug of loneliness in his gut as when the girls started being born.

Pony climbed the ladder to the raft and lay down on her back. William turned away. He gathered up his things, repacked, and made up his mind to head up to Phoenicia in the Catskills, maybe do North Dome. He couldn't remember if Ruth had done that one. They were doing the Catskill 3500s—thirty-five peaks, all over thirty-five hundred feet high; the task was to climb them all once in the good months and four of them again in the winter. William wanted the freedom of the mountains, the strain on his body, the exhaustion of a day climbing. The even exchange of effort and payoff.

Downstairs, he checked to see if he'd left anything, first the living room and then the kitchen. The two sandwiches Pony had made for their dinner were still sitting on a plate on the kitchen table. He took one for the drive home and laid a dish towel over the other. In the living room, he picked up the picture of their mother again. She was about seventeen in it, he guessed. He considered taking it but decided not to. It was Pony's. Her half-full glass of bourbon or whatever was on the porch rail, and he tossed the contents. He went back down to the water holding his duffel. The minute she saw him, she understood. "Oh, for God's sake, William," she shouted. She dove in and began to swim to shore.

"Adios," he shouted.

"You can't leave," she shouted to him.

What was he even doing here? Whatever she wanted to tell him would have to wait. He wasn't going to be a pawn in any of her stuff again. He threw his duffel into the backseat of his car. Pony was out of the water, coming up the sand. She picked up the orange shirt and covered herself.

"Look, I'm sorry, okay?" she said.

"Tell me what's going on."

"Can't. I promised."

"Promised who?"

She shook her head. "Just stay, William."

"What the hell is with you?" He gestured toward the house, toward Andrew, the lake, the whole thing. Then he got into his car. He backed onto the drive and stopped to look one more time. In the rearview mirror, he saw her turn away, throw the shirt back onto the grass, and head back toward the water. The baby, in his pen on the lawn, reached for her, but she must not have noticed. She walked past him and back into Lake Aral.

Chapter 2

Tinker

Daddy spoke in a slow, controlled voice. "Tinker. It's Dad." He drew a long breath. "Anita Bell called. No one seems to know where Pony is. Andrew is at Anita's. I need to go up there right away. Can you drive me?"

Tinker sat down at the kitchen table, the telephone cord stretching long. "Of course I will," she said.

Her husband, Mark, looked up over his newspaper, frowning. "Will what?" he mouthed.

"The police are involved, Tinker," her father said. "I'll explain in the car. Just come as soon as you can. I'll be waiting for you."

"You mean right now?"

"Of course now."

She replaced the receiver in the cradle. She tried to get her thoughts around this. All she could think was that Pony must have left Andrew with Anita and then not come back when she said she would. But the weird part was—*Anita?* Why would Pony leave the baby with Anita? The family had nothing to do with the Bells. She went into the living room and sat on the hassock opposite Mark. He dropped the newspaper on the floor. "Now what?" he said.

"Pony's missing. Daddy wants me to drive him up to the lake."

Mark shook his head as if to clear it. "Missing how?"

She explained again, as much as she knew, which was next to nothing. Mark had questions. What time did Pony leave the baby with Anita? Where did she go? Was she with anybody?

Tinker hated this feeling of being interrogated when she had no answers. She felt the weight of Mark's judgment. "You should call Anita yourself," Mark said. "And get the story firsthand."

"I told Daddy I'd be right over."

"I know you did," Mark said. "I'm just trying to get a handle on it. What if it's nothing?"

"What if it's something? They called the police."

"You didn't say that," Mark said.

"Pony never would have left Andrew with Anita unless something was wrong."

Mark leaned back in the chair, raised his shoulders and then lowered them.

"I can't exactly refuse," she said.

He didn't respond.

Sometimes it felt as if she was in the middle of a tug-of-war between Mark and her father. But what was she supposed to do? Blow Daddy off? In Mark's family, people hardly ever called one another, let alone asked for help. Her family was different. She went upstairs and hauled out a suitcase. She slammed it open and filled it. In her family, people went out of their way for one another. If there really was something the matter with Pony—and part of Tinker hoped there would be—Mark would be sorry.

She drove the mile to her father's house on Steele Road in West Hartford, where they'd all grown up. She was there fifteen minutes after he called. He was waiting on the front walk, a great hulking shape pacing in semidarkness, his bag and briefcase at the curb. He wore a trench coat even though it was a warm evening. The minute he saw her car, he flagged her down the way you flag down a taxi, as though she might drive by without stopping.

He got into the car, but he didn't speak. He was disheveled, his reddish-gray hair uncombed, and he had a slightly unpleasant smell. Anxiety. It caused the wings of fear to flutter for real inside her. He held a red notebook, the accounting kind he always used, a columnar book with numbered lines. There were dozens of them in his closet.

He opened the red book and flipped a few pages. "I'll read to you what I wrote. The facts," he said. She wished he'd wait until they were out of Hartford. She needed to watch for signs to the overpass that connected Interstate 84 to Interstate 91, a tricky place. If she missed the exit, she'd be headed south without a clue as to how to get back on going north.

"At 7:46 P.M. Officer Martine of the Hillsboro Barracks called JC. Martine had received a call from Anita Bell. Baby abandoned on lawn of Fond du Lac. Must be Andrew. Baby hysterical, wet. PC not there. Martine arrived at FdL 7:57 P.M. JC called Anita Bell. Andrew safe. 8:02, JC informed Martine will drive up. Called Tinker.' " He shut his book.

Tinker was sitting forward, chin over the wheel, hands gripping tightly, trying to understand as she navigated a lane change. It took her a moment to realize the PC was Pony and JC was Daddy. "Abandoned? I thought Pony left Andrew with Anita." She had to move a lane to the right to make the exit. She never trusted the mirrors and twisted around to see if there was a car in her blind spot.

"I never said that," her father said with annoyance.

She wished her father would put on his seat belt, but he didn't believe in them. "Okay, I'm sorry," she said. "Go on." She was safely through the interchange, doing seventy up I-91, a clear shot until they hit more traffic in Springfield.

Her father struggled with his coat, finally got it off, and threw it into the backseat. He settled back down and spoke again. "Anita heard Andrew at the house. Crying. She went to see if there was a problem." He spoke deliberately, as if to a child. Tinker imagined Anita charging through the woods in her Bermuda shorts, Ohio State sweatshirt, and flip-flops. "You know, that big expandable playpen Pony uses for Andrew," her father said.

"I never thought that playpen was a good idea," Tinker said. You didn't see them anymore. They weren't safe. Kids could pinch their fingers in them. "I never would have used that for Isabel," she said. Maybe this had something to do with the playpen. Maybe Andrew had hurt himself.

"Pony had left him in the playpen on the lawn. He was frantic. Anita took him inside and got him into some dry clothes. She looked all over for Pony. She thought perhaps Pony had fallen or had an accident. Pony wasn't there."

"What time was this? Was it dark?"

"Anita heard Andrew around seven-thirty," her father snapped. "I just told you that."

Tinker racked her brain for an explanation. Pony had been kidnapped. She'd run away. She'd left for a few minutes on an errand and had an accident. "Was her car there?"

"Of course it was, Tinker. She would not have taken her car, leaving Andrew outside," her father said.

"Daddy, I'm just trying to understand. Please don't snap at me."

"Her clothing was on the beach," he said.

"Oh God." They were passing the exit to the airport, cars peeling off, people going on trips. She wished she were one of them. She wished she were anywhere else but here. "You said you called the cops?"

"The police. Officer Martine is there right now with some of his men."

She couldn't say out loud what she was thinking. That Pony could have drowned. But that was impossible, wasn't it? Pony was the best swimmer in the family. Pony was strong. This worrying would all amount to a hill of beans. There was a great thought. They'd get there and Pony would be like, "What's *with* you guys?"

21

"Tell me, Tinker, would your sister have attempted a distance swim under the circumstances? With the baby outside?"

"She wouldn't swim across the lake naked," she said. Not even Pony would do that.

They rode in silence after that, theirs the only car on the highway for mile after mile of darkness. At White River Junction, she was going to suggest stopping for a bite, but her father's head was back and his mouth was open, so she kept driving. Let him sleep. She reached for the radio and turned the dial a few times, but they were in that long corridor without reception. *There will be a reasonable explanation for Pony's absence,* she kept telling herself. There always was.

She felt the first stirring of anger. There had been other times like this, other times of following up on Pony and even Mira. When Tinker was little, the rules had been clear and strict. There were bedtimes, ridiculous limits on the amount of TV she could watch, no eating between meals except for fruit, and a whole weekly schedule of chores. But it always seemed to Tinker that the rules were only for her. Pony and Mira just blew them off. Maybe they were chalk and cheese when it came to personality—Pony broke the rules out loud, while Mira was always secretive. Even so, they were usually in cahoots. Pony did Mira's chores in return for Mira's weekly hour of TV.

Mira the disappearance artist, Tinker thought. "Where did Mira go?" Tinker used to say whenever there was work to be done. Mira would always drift off to the bathroom while Tinker and Pony did the dishes. She would putz around in the garage while the others raked leaves. And when they were putting in the float at Fond du Lac, Mira was always around but never actually doing anything, not if you watched her closely, as Tinker had on many occasions. Mira would take up a paintbrush, do a few strokes with it, and then look out across the lake and start daydreaming. One summer Tinker decided to tell. Enough was enough. And it wasn't really tattling, it was about the injustice of the arrangement. Her mother was lying on a chaise, drying her long fair hair in the sun. It was draped over the back of her chair like a curtain, almost to the ground, and glistening. Her mother had on large dark glasses and a flowered two-piece. "What is it, sweetheart?" her mother said. Tinker was close to tears under the weight of what she was about to do. Tattling was the worst sin.

"Pony does Mira's chores," Tinker said.

Her mother sat up, raised her hair in both hands, and did that thing she could do, slowly twisting the hair behind her neck into a loose knot. Then she reached over and took Tinker's hand. "You just take care of Tinker."

Just outside the village of Hillsboro, there was a long downward sweep of road. The night was black, with bright stars. Tinker slowed at the crest and looked down at Lake Aral in the distance. A halo of bright light hovered over the near side of the lake. She wondered what was going on that would require all that light and then realized it was coming from their house and felt sick to her stomach. She nudged her father. "Daddy," she whispered. "We're almost there."

She was moving relentlessly into something terrible. There was no going back. She turned at the mailboxes onto the dirt road to their and the Bells' houses. Light filtered through the trees and became brighter as she approached the house. She slowed to a stop on the driveway between a police cruiser and Pony's car. The headlights from the police car lit up the wooded stretch between the Carterets' and the Bells'. Another cruiser sat partly on the grass closer to the water. There were two big halogen power lamps, one on the lawn and another down at the water. It hurt her eyes to look at them. Her father blinked in confusion. He looked shockingly old.

Randy Martine leaned in her window. "Tinker," he said. "Sir. Mr. Carteret. I'm afraid we haven't found anything. We've got a man out on the water. Mr. Bell from next door went out, too, in his rowboat. Dive team was here. They'll be back at first light. We need to search the lake, given the circumstances. The child left on the lawn, her clothing on the beach."

Her father got out of the car, grabbed his coat and threw it on, said something to Randy, and walked down to the water.

The first thing Tinker saw was an orange T-shirt on the grass by itself, and then maybe ten feet away and closer to the playpen, a pair of shorts, panties, and a bra on the sand, all bright white. To Tinker it looked as though Pony had thrown off the shirt on the run and then stopped to remove the rest before she ran into the water. Tinker's heart sank. People said that all the time, but it was accurate now. Her heart felt like a leaden object drilling down.

Randy, her father, and Anita Bell were clustered at the water's edge. Anita had on a white bathrobe and was barefoot. When Tinker approached, Anita gave her a hug that Tinker accepted stiffly, wishing she would just please go home. "Andrew's just fine now," Anita said. "He's asleep. I finally got him down, poor thing. I hope I did the right thing."

Her father patted Anita's shoulder. "Of course you did," he said.

"I took his temp, just to be sure." Anita pursed her lips. "Right as rain." She frowned. "I knew one of you Carterets was here, but I never saw who. I was out most of the day today, right through dinnertime. Denny was here, but you know kids. Sleep until noon, and the rest of the time with the CD stuck in his ear. Right, Denny?" Anita turned toward the woods that separated the two houses. Denny was there. Tall, skinny, hair in his eyes. He nodded and shoved his hands into his pockets.

"Was Pony here alone?" Randy asked Tinker.

"I didn't know she was here at all," Tinker said. "Usually we sign up."

"Mr. Carteret, sir, did you know she was here?"

"I did not," her father said.

"Does she ever leave the child alone? Is it customary behavior for her to perhaps duck out for a few minutes?"

"Absolutely not," her father said.

"Has she said anything to indicate she was depressed? Worried?"

"My daughter is not depressed."

24

"Sometimes," Randy said, "after the birth of a baby—"

"Pony is not depressed," her father said.

"Is Pony married?" Randy asked. "A husband we should contact?"

Her father shook his head.

"Boyfriend? Ex-husband? The baby's father? Somebody who might know why she was here? Somebody who might have spoken to her?"

"No, no," her father said. "Pony is a single mother."

"Sorry, but I do need to ask who the father is, sir," Randy said. "We need that information."

"No need to concern yourself there. Pony is raising Andrew on her own."

"But—"

"We don't know who the father is," Tinker said. She stole a glance at Anita.

Randy did a little double take. He'd been Tinker's boyfriend for a summer during high school, and she still loved the look of him. He was what you'd call fresh-faced.

"One of our men is asking around the lake houses to see if anybody knows anything. I'm afraid that's all we can do tonight," Randy said. "We'll have the divers come back here first thing in the morning. You all try to get some sleep. Try not to disturb anything."

It hit Tinker hard inside the house. Andrew's toys were everywhere. Pony had been sketching him; there were some drawings of him and bits of charcoal on the couch. There was a sandwich on a plate in the kitchen, covered with a dish towel, as though Pony planned to eat it later. Has she said anything to indicate she was depressed? Randy had asked. Didn't that sandwich say no? Wasn't the sandwich a sign of hope? You wouldn't make yourself a sandwich and then go outside and kill yourself. You wouldn't leave your son on the beach.

"Was Pony taking drugs?" Her father had come into the kitchen behind her, along with Anita and Denny.

"No." Tinker wasn't about to have that discussion with Anita and Denny present. Not that she knew the answer one way or another, but still.

Anita kept pulling the flaps of her bathrobe tighter across herself.

"We need to get Andrew," Tinker said. She felt panicked at the thought of him over at the Bells', where he didn't belong. He should be here with them.

Her father shook his head. "Let him sleep." He appealed to Anita. "If you don't mind."

"Oh, no," Anita said. "Anything we can do—"

"But Daddy—"

Her father put his arm around Anita's shoulders. "Do you need one of us to see you back to the house?" Tinker watched her father work the old charm on Anita, the Carteret grace.

Anita shook her head. "I'm sure everything will turn out just fine in the end, Jasper. I'm sure. It's what they say in these missing-persons cases. Ninety-nine times out of a hundred, it's nothing."

Anita shut the front door behind her, sealing in the silence. Pony was somewhere out there in that deep lake, Tinker was sure. "I'll make us some tea," Tinker said, thinking that the clink of cups and saucers, the whistle of the kettle, would be calming, normal. Her father sat on the sofa staring at the floor. He took the tea without looking up. He set it down. He reached for the telephone and began dialing.

He tried William, but there was no answer. Then Mira. In the quiet of the night, Tinker could hear Mira's alarmed voice filling the room. Mira hadn't seen Pony since Memorial Day, when they'd all been together. She hadn't spoken to Pony. Her father said he'd call as soon as they knew anything and then hung up. He kept calling. He went house by house around the lake. He'd dial the number, let it ring, hang up when no one answered, and go on to the next. So few people were there. It was too early; summer didn't begin for real at Lake Aral until the Fourth of July. He awakened a few people, apologized for the late hour, explained that Pony was missing, and asked if they had seen her. Out of a dozen calls, only one person had seen her—buying a newspaper at the general store that morning, carrying Andrew in one arm. She'd said hello. Nothing more. And no, no one had been with her.

Her father lay down on the couch and closed his eyes. He still had his overcoat on. Tinker stared at him the way you do at a sleeping child. His pale, freckled forehead relaxed in sleep, making him look younger, his face uncreased. Tinker waited until his breathing became slow and regular. She tiptoed to the kitchen. Randy had said not to disturb things, and she supposed that included the sandwich on the counter. She opened the refrigerator. There was some beer, some bottles for Andrew, and a few jars of baby food. Tinker shut the refrigerator and opened the cupboard. Cans of tuna fish. A jar of mayonnaise. She opened another cupboard. A bag of marshmallows and a box of Ritz crackers.

She pulled open the bag of marshmallows, removed one, and pressed it with her tongue to the roof of her mouth. The confectioners' sugar felt cool and lovely. She read the calorie warning on the side. A serving was six marshmallows, 138 calories, or 23 in each one. She put another one in her mouth and then several more, pushing them in, sucking on them, squeezing them flat, turning them to slime, sucking them down. She hadn't eaten since dinner. She checked on her father. He was still asleep on the couch, his breathing a near snore. She opened the box of crackers, careful to keep the paper from rustling, the way you open candy in a movie theater. She ate the crackers in stacks of four, putting them whole into her mouth. Her stomach felt taut and uncomfortable. She was at the point of no return. It didn't matter how many she ate now. When she finished, she stuffed the empty marshmallow bag into the pocket of her sweatpants. She folded down the paper in the box of crackers, closed the box, and put it back in the cupboard. She wiped the white powder and crumbs from the table, then wiped her sleeve across her mouth.

She covered her father with a blanket, switched off the living room light, and went outside to the porch, aware of the crackers still in the cupboard and the inevitability that sometime tonight she would slip back into the kitchen and eat them. Eat them all. It was her comfort, this hiatus, this period before she finished the food.

When she and Mark were first married and living in a small apartment in the south end of Hartford, Mark sometimes had to attend dinners at downtown hotels. The dinners always ran late and involved martinis. Tinker used to sit at the window, waiting for him and making frequent trips to the kitchen. Eating stilled her thoughts. It kept her from thinking of his car smashed into a streetlight. *He'll be the fourteenth car*, she'd tell herself so she could count off the time slowly and not worry for thirteen cars. When the fourteenth car went by, she'd start all over again.

Now she watched the water. *In half an hour Pony will come along in a canoe*, she told herself. *At two-forty-five she'll come swimming back across the lake.* The time ticked away. She went back to the kitchen for the crackers. She kept thinking about Pony's muscular thinness. Pony never could float. She was densely built, like a guy. She'd had to cheat in swimming tests to keep herself afloat, finning secretly so the instructor couldn't see.

If Pony were at the bottom of the lake, it could be days before she was found. Aral was the deepest lake in Vermont, so far down it hadn't even been measured. At three o'clock, Tinker took two Tylenol PMs and went up to her room. Her father was no longer on the couch. He must have gone to bed.

She woke up, groggy, to the sounds of voices. It was early. Six o'clock. She got up and went to the window. She felt thickheaded and bloated. Two Hillsboro police cars were in the drive next to Pony's car, as well as a gray sedan. There was a plain black van parked on the grass.

She knocked on her father's door, cracked it, and saw that he was lying on the bed, still in his trench coat, wide awake. "They're back," she said.

Four men were on the beach in black scuba gear, with tanks on their backs and hoods over their heads. She felt sick to her stomach. She went back inside to the upstairs bathroom before anyone noticed her, and sat on the edge of the tub. She looked at herself in the full-length mirror, hating what she saw—her heavy body, her hair frizzed from the night's humidity and bushing out to either side. A deep crease ran vertically between her fair eyebrows. She pressed at the crease out of habit, as if she could make it go away. She had circles beneath her eyes.

She splashed cold water on her face. Her mouth was open. She closed it, but it fell slack again. This must be what shock looked like. She wanted to stay where she was and not go out there again. But she had to. Daddy would need her.

Her father was standing next to Randy. Tinker joined them. "Tinker," Randy said.

She tried to get Randy to look her in the eye, but he was concentrating on the divers. All four of them waded into the water to their knees, crouched, and disappeared. A few big bubbles erupted at the surface where they entered, and then here and there, so she knew their locations. Randy said they were using the spiral pattern, starting with small loops and going to larger ones so they could cover the area thoroughly. "The longer they stay in the water, the better," he said. "Let's hope for the best."

How long did she watch? A long time? No time at all? There wasn't a ripple on the whole lake except for the circling disturbance of the divers. Tinker knew the lake bottom very well. They all did. "Fond du Lac" meant exactly that. Bottom of the lake. There were whole towns in the Midwest called Fond du Lac, but in those cases it meant the southernmost point of a lake.

Lake Aral was sandy right off the shore, but about fifteen feet out, the bottom fell away precipitously. You could swim underwater, your belly skimming the sandy bottom in the shallow part, and then follow the contour deeper and deeper, where the plant life began. Maybe a hundred feet beyond that was the raft, anchored in deep water by a chain that connected to a large concrete slab with an iron hook countersunk into it. She had always thought of the space between the shore and the anchor as a deepening triangle, theirs to use, their play area, well delineated. Safe.

One of the divers surfaced and signaled. Randy walked down to the water's edge to talk to the diver. Then the diver returned to the water. "I'm afraid he's found something," Randy said to Tinker and her father.

Her father's face had a hard set to it, and he was biting his lip for courage. Randy went to the van and talked to a man Tinker hadn't noticed earlier. She heard the crackling of a police radio. She could hear voices but not what they were saying. She felt so scared, she thought her legs might collapse. The rest of it happened in slow motion. All four divers came to the surface. Her father fell to the ground. Randy helped him to his feet and waved smelling salts under his nose. Her father refused the chair they brought over. Tinker sat in it. She had no strength in her legs.

The divers had something with them, were swimming it slowly toward shore. It was Pony. She lay facedown, her back and shoulders breaking the surface. Her skin was gray. Her hair looked almost black, and for a moment Tinker hoped it was somebody else. Somebody with black hair. From somewhere a stretcher had come. They moved it out onto the water. They lifted Pony onto it. The air felt painful on Tinker's skin. Her perceptions felt fractured. The water too black, the sky too bright.

The men moved in the slow motion of a dream. Pony was naked. Her head was bent. *Fix it,* Tinker wanted to say. *Fix her head.* Her father was up to his waist in the water now, in his clothes. He must have gone in. Then the men were lifting him up, as if in a baptism. He had collapsed again and gone under. One of the men had him by the elbow. Her father's coat was plastered to his body. Tinker still couldn't move. She was in the dream where you want to run but can't. They carried the stretcher to the beach and laid it on the grass. Her father said, "Yes." Tinker stood up. And the next thing she knew, she was there, looking down at Pony. They'd put a blanket over Pony's body but left her face exposed. Tinker dropped to her knees on the sand. Pony was so wet. She blotted Pony's face with the sleeve of her shirt. Water was pooled in Pony's mouth. The side of her head was raw red.

"What happened?" Tinker looked up at Randy, at the divers, and then down again. Pony's eyes were open. A milky color, not their usual brownish green. Her hair was sheared off on the left side where the skin was red.

Randy said something to one of the divers, who stepped up. "I'm sorry, ma'am. Sir." He looked down at his feet. "She was pretty deep," he said. "Her hair was caught on the chain for the anchor, pretty deep. We had to cut her hair to free her."

"But she wasn't allowed," Tinker shouted. *The rule, the rule, the rule*, she kept thinking. *Mother's rule.* They had to wear swim caps if they were doing anything with the raft. Their mother insisted. Long hair can become wrapped around things. *Why can't you ever listen, Pony?* Tinker thought. *Why don't you ever bloody listen?*

Randy helped her to her feet and across the lawn. There seemed to be men everywhere. Two more cars had arrived. People were in the house. Others were going through the sand on the beach. Somebody was talking to her father. They waved her over. The man was a cop.

"There will be an autopsy," her father said to her. "In Burlington. This is Officer Rivers."

Officer Rivers said that the medical examiner would determine the cause of death. He had some questions. He knew this was very difficult, but would they mind?

"No," Tinker said. "I mean, no, I don't mind."

"Was she in the habit of leaving the child while she went for a swim?" Officer Rivers asked. He had a round, pink face, fair eyebrows like hers.

"He's not even a year old." Tinker shrugged. "There were no habits."

"Was she a careful mother?"

"Yes," her father said.

"I'm sorry. Of course." Officer Rivers had a Vermont accent. "Do you know why she might have been"—he lifted his shoulders, opened his pudgy hands—"exploring the anchor?"

"Pony always attaches it on Memorial Day. But nobody ever goes down there other than that. It's dark, slimy," Tinker said.

"Something wrong with it, perhaps? Something she might have been checking?"

"I don't know why she'd have thought she needed to check it," her father said. "We just checked it a few weeks ago—" He broke down, regained his composure. "It had a repair, but the repair was fine."

"Did she have any trouble with anyone that you know of?"

"Oh God, you think somebody *did* this?" The thought took Tinker's breath away.

Officer Rivers pushed his glasses up so they rested on his forehead. "We have to consider the possibility."

"Pony had no enemies," her father said.

"Was anybody here with her?" the officer asked.

Tinker shook her head.

Officer Rivers put away his notebook and pen. He thanked them. He said there'd be a preliminary report in a day or two and a full report later on.

Then they were all gone. It was just Tinker and her father standing side by side on the grass looking out at the water, the enemy, sparkling brilliantly in the early-morning sun. The day was very still. It would be a hot one.

She could think of nothing to say. She glanced at her father. Tears glazed his eyes. "Oh God. Andrew. I'll go to the Bells'," she said.

They entered the Bells' house by the back door. Andrew was in a high chair in the crowded kitchen. The counter space was covered with small appliances, a tangle of cords behind them. Sayings adorned the walls in heart-shaped frames. Anita, grim-faced, was feeding Andrew; she got to her feet. She hugged Tinker's father and then Tinker. "I'm so sorry, Jasper." She had put on makeup that morning—eye shadow and very red lipstick, but her uncombed hair stuck out in stiff peaks.

The minute Andrew saw Tinker and her father, he recognized them and banged his fists on the metal tray of the high chair. Tinker raised the tray and picked him up. The weight of that baby was everything just then. Solid, stable, warm. She wanted to hold him longer, but he was restless, so she put him back and took the jar of baby food from Anita. Her hand shook as she raised the spoon to his mouth, but he opened wide.

They all watched Andrew eat. Everybody had to be thinking the same thing: This was what they had of Pony. He opened his mouth for spoon after spoon, enjoying their fixed attention, and then he caught on. He looked in alarm at Anita, at Tinker, at her father, then wildly around. "Mama," he wailed, looking about. His face drained when he couldn't find her.

Just then Denny slouched in and leaned against the doorjamb, half in and half out of the kitchen. All Tinker knew about the Bell kids was that there were several, mostly girls. She didn't know names or ages, just that every summer, there they were in some new incarnation of themselves, a year older, a year louder. She thought this one, Denny, might be the youngest. He was a sullen, caved-in-looking kid with an expression that was both frightened and belligerent. All the attention shifted to him. He shot a look at his mother. "They find out who did it?" he said.

"Oh my," Anita said. "Oh, Denny. Nobody did anything. I mean, they don't know anything yet. Right, Jasper?" She was all apologetic and flustered.

Tinker's father approached the boy. "What makes you think someone did this? Why did you ask us that question?"

Denny's face bleached of color. "No." He whined the word like a much younger child. He shook his head. "I just thought— Shit."

"Dennis!" Anita said. "Your mouth."

"Oh, man," Denny said.

Tinker's father put a hand on the boy's shoulder. "If you know something, son, tell us."

"No, man. I'm sorry. Honest." Denny squirmed away. Anita scowled, and Tinker had the feeling his mother was going to read him the riot act once they left. "He's been watching too much TV," Anita said. "I am very sorry."

Andrew continued to cry after they brought him back to Fond du Lac. He cried himself to exhaustion and finally fell asleep on the living room floor. Tinker didn't dare move him in case he woke again. It killed her not to be able to tidy up. At least to fold Pony's clothing. Anything. But Randy had said not to move things.

Her father was sitting at the telephone table, his clothes still damp. He called Mira. Tinker heard him say, "It's Pony. Sweetie, I have very bad news." Tinker pictured Mira in her sparse apartment in that three-decker, still in bed, still half asleep. There would be books stacked on the bed, a cluttered night table, and dead plants on the windowsill. Mira would be naked. She never wore a nightgown, even in winter. She said it was unhealthy, that it was warmer to sleep skin to the sheets. "There's been an accident here at Fond du Lac. Pony was found this morning. She drowned." Her father squeezed his eyes, listening to Mira. He was weeping. He explained about the night before, the call from Anita. It was the story he and Tinker would have to tell over and over again. After he hung up, he tried William. "Are you there? William. For God's sake, if you're listening to this, pick up the telephone now. It's about your sister. It's about Pony. I'm up at the lake house."

Tinker waited until her father was finished, and then she used the phone to call Mark at work. His secretary answered. "Donna," she said. "I need to talk to Mark. It's Tinker calling."

"Mrs. Bradshaw," Donna said. "I'm afraid he's in a meeting."

"Get him out." Tinker had a history with Donna.

"I'll see if I can," Donna said. "He's in with Mr. Hendrix."

"I don't care who he's in with, Donna." She had to wait a long time before Mark came on the line.

"What happened?" he said.

"Pony drowned," Tinker said, her voice brimming with justification before she realized it. "They found her this morning. Her hair got tangled under the raft."

"Jesus, Tinker."

"We don't know how it happened." Tinker burst out crying. Hearing herself say this made it true. "There's going to be an autopsy. It looks like she drowned, but just in case it was something else."

"But she's the best swimmer. What do you mean, 'something else'?"

"If she hit her head or something. She left Andrew on the lawn, and the police think that was odd. They'll do a tox screen."

"Drugs?"

"Daddy's a wreck. Nobody knows where William is."

"When will you be back?"

"It's up to Daddy," she said.

"And up to you," he said.

"This is much worse for him, Mark. A parent should never lose a child."

"You've lost your sister, Tink."

Her father drove her car, and she followed in Pony's because it had the baby seat. She felt like a criminal, stealing the car, kidnapping the baby, as though at any minute there would be sirens behind her. They stopped in White River Junction so she could change Andrew's diaper and they could get something to eat. It was the first ordinary situation they'd been in, surrounded by people going along in their lives. It seemed unreal to Tinker that people in the restaurant could look at her and her father and not know what had happened. The waitress made a big cheerful deal of how cute Andrew was, as though everything were normal.

Instead of heading straight to West Hartford, her father took the I-291 bypass to Manchester, and Tinker followed. He was taking them to Pony's apartment, which was just up from the main street. It wasn't much, one of those brick complexes, two stories high, low rent. Pony's one-bedroom was on the ground floor.

Tinker parked behind her father on the street. He walked to the front door and motioned to her to come, too. He was impatient, waiting for the key that would be with Pony's car keys. She wanted him to slow down, to let her get her bearings before she went into Pony's apartment, but he didn't hesitate. He opened the door and entered.

It smelled of Pony. Nothing Tinker could put her finger on, but if she was blindfolded, she'd know exactly where she was. Andrew fought to get out of her arms. She set him down on the floor, where he twisted every which way looking for his mother. When he couldn't find her, he started rocking on his hands and knees and then dropped his face against the carpet in despair.

Her father was riffling through the top of Pony's desk, keeping up a running commentary. "Nothing here. No. Maybe in one of the drawers." He scanned papers and put them aside, sometimes stopping to read further. "Bank statements," he said. "Letters. Bill from the electric company. I wonder if you'd take over this end of things, Tinker. Get these things paid? Reimburse you, of course." He paused over something, then kept on going. "If she hasn't named a guardian," he said, "we'll need to act quickly." He turned in his chair and faced her. "Tinker, just who is Andrew's father?"

"She never said."

"You don't *know*?"

"No."

"You're her sister," he said, as though it were more her job than his to know these things.

"William might know," she said.

"The main thing is to find some sort of documentation," he said. She took Andrew with her to the bedroom. Again, he looked everywhere for his mother, his soft hair brushing against her neck, his hope back in full force. When he didn't find her, she felt his whole body lose its will again. She put him down. He buried his face in a pile of Pony's clothing.

Pony's bed was in the middle of the room, unmade. Andrew's crib was against the wall, and there was a small bureau. Tinker sorted through the items on the bed table—bits of charcoal, small scraps of paper with line drawings, mostly of Andrew, who was still sobbing. Tinker's grief felt different. Not suffering, like Andrew, but a kind of vertigo that cut her thoughts in half. Pony was dead.

"Tinker," her father called. She went to the door. Her father was at the desk holding a tiny red packet, one of those little envelopes a bank provides for safe-deposit-box keys. He opened it and took out the key and a slip of paper that he read from: " 'SD key. Will. Mother's pearls. William Carteret is co-signer.' " He reached for the telephone, punched in William's number, then slammed down the receiver when he got the answering machine.

"I'll get him," Tinker said. "Don't worry."

"You do that," he said.

"I can keep Andrew with me until we know." It needed to be said out loud. "Mark can set up the crib, but I need baby things." Her father nodded. She found a canvas bag under the kitchen table and went about Pony's apartment, filling it with Andrew's things. His sippy cup, some toys and clothes, boxes of Pampers, and in the bathroom his rash cream, shampoo. There was so much a baby needed.

They locked up Pony's apartment. Tinker followed her father to his house and parked Pony's car in the garage. Andrew had fallen asleep from the motion of the car, and she was able to release the buckles of his car seat before he realized again she wasn't his mother and he began screaming. She entered the house through the back door, which opened to the kitchen. Her father was sitting in the dark.

"Oh, Daddy," she said. She turned on the light, and a hard fluorescence flooded the kitchen. She turned up the heat, but her father said to turn it back down. They never put up the thermostat after the first of May, no matter how cold it was. Tinker fixed her father a sandwich of avocado and cheese and poured a glass of orange juice. His answering machine light was blinking nonstop. The news must have spread, and people were already calling.

It had been under twenty-four hours since she'd picked her father up in front of the house, but it was forever. Her father was broken, as though parts of him had collapsed inside and he could no longer hold himself straight. She looked into the refrigerator again to see what else was there for his supper, but he told her not to bother. "This is no time for food," he said, and she felt the burn of his criticism. She warmed a bottle of milk for Andrew and gave it to him. He lay on the kitchen floor on his back, guzzling the milk, causing bubbles to swish up the sides of the bottle.

"If you find out who the father is, don't call him under any circumstances," her father said before she left. "Get the name and number and let me know, but don't call him."

"What about Andrew?"

"That's exactly the point," he said. "Our objective needs to be keeping Andrew in the family."

Tinker was home with a half hour to spare before Isabel's bus. Her house looked dirty in the afternoon light. Untended. She would have to clean just to get even, she realized. Tidy up. Clean the house before she could think what to do about Andrew. She carried him in one arm and the portable crib in the other. She set up the crib and put him down. He woke slightly but went back to sleep. Tinker opened the cupboard under the kitchen sink, where she kept the Baker's semisweet chocolate. She sat on the living room couch and unwrapped a square. She should take a shower. She hadn't had one since the day before yesterday. She should change her clothes. She should prepare for Isabel. Instead, she broke off a piece and put it into her mouth. As the chocolate warmed, she sucked it down her throat. When it was soft, she chewed it. She broke off another piece.

She imagined her father, rattling around in that big cold house all by himself, with his grief. The thought was unbearable. She checked her watch. Ten minutes before Isabel got home. Too late to shower now. She'd wait for the sound of the school bus down at the corner. She would have to watch for her from the house. She didn't dare leave Andrew alone, not even for the time it took to walk the hundred yards to the bus stop.

She was thinking about the last time she'd seen Pony, alive. Memorial Day weekend. She felt a stab under her solar plexus.

It was Memorial Day weekend just what, two, three weeks ago? The whole family had been there. It was tradition to go up and open camp on Memorial Day and close it on Labor Day. They'd turned on the water to the house. They'd swept the house clean of mouse droppings and cobwebs. They'd removed the bedsheets that protected the furniture from dust over the winter. Mark and William had mowed the grass, cleaned up the driftwood on the beach, and raked the sand. Tinker, Mira, and Pony had painted the barrels and the wooden part of the raft in a fresh coat of gunmetal gray. Pony had been outrageous, in Tinker's opinion, dancing around in short shorts. Too short. Why did she have to be that way? She was a mother now. Those days were over. Pony acted as though Andrew were a toy, a plaything, something to amuse her. She wasn't taking her responsibility seriously enough. Pony had brought him into the water even though it was very cold. She'd let him paint the raft, not that he could. He held the brush while Pony guided his hand, sloshing the brush in the bucket and spewing it over the grass and over himself. Tinker had made a point of checking the label for lead. No one said anything, as usual. It was always up to Tinker to be the bad cop. When they were upstairs, Tinker went into Pony's room. Pony was in her bikini, bent over at the waist, twisting her long hair into a thick rope. She stood when Tinker came in and shut the door and finished securing her hair. "What up?" she said.

"I need to talk to you about Andrew," Tinker said.

Pony grinned. "Sure. What about him?"

"When Isabel was a baby, I had Mother to help me. To, you know, give me advice."

Pony cocked her head. "Yeah?"

"It's not healthy for him to go into such cold water," Tinker said. "He's only a baby."

"He loved it."

"I just worry that you're perhaps a little—"

Pony stuck her hands on her hips. Her bikini was so small she might as well have been naked. She took a step forward. She was a little taller than Tinker, and very strong. "A little what?"

"A little casual with him."

"Look, Tinker. I don't interfere with the way you raise Isabel. I'd appreciate the same courtesy from you. I'm doing just fine."

As if Pony *could* interfere. That had been a shock; that Pony might disapprove of the way Tinker was raising Isabel had irritated Tinker enough to let the other shoe drop. "It's not appropriate to go around with your fanny hanging out of your shorts, Pony. It attracts the wrong kind of attention. You're a mother now."

"Wrong kind of attention?" Pony laughed. "Get real, Tinker. Anyway, it's just family up here."

"You know what I mean."

"Oh, fuck you, Tinker." Pony snapped the strings on her bikini bottom and left the room.

And those were the last words Pony had spoken to her. Tinker felt her insides tighten at this thought. She strained to remember the rest of the weekend. Had she and Pony said anything further? Had they hugged when they were all taking their leave? Tinker knew damn well they hadn't.

She thought she heard the hydraulic hiss of the school bus down at the corner. She waited for the second, louder hiss of the doors closing, but it didn't come. She checked her watch. Must have been something else. It was still a few minutes early for the bus, and she wanted to remember the rest, to fix a better memory of Pony in her mind, something to hang on to.

They'd let the paint on the raft and the barrels dry overnight, and on Sunday afternoon they'd rolled the barrels down to the beach, carried the wooden raft down, set it on the barrels, and rolled the whole thing into the water. The water was fiercely cold. But it was a badge of honor in their family not to complain and certainly not to pussyfoot in like you saw people doing at the town beach. Tinker had plunged right in. They'd all gasped at the cold and laughed.

It was a ritual. They did it the same way every year. Pony stood on the raft like the captain of a ship in her red bikini, her hair stuffed into a white rubber swim cap, while William and Mira and Tinker pushed the thing out into deep water. Tinker and William did most of the work. Mira was pretty worthless. She was too vain to be any help. She more hung on the raft than pushed, keeping her shoulders well out of the water so her gelled hair would stay dry and her polished black fingernails wouldn't break.

"God forbid you should flatten your spikes," Tinker said.

"God forbid you should lighten up," Mira said.

Pony's first job was to keep a line of sight to the shore, the water, and some set of indicators she used to approximate where the anchor hook was. "Stop!" she called out, and they stopped while Pony peered down. Tinker thought she couldn't see a thing in that dark water, but Pony had her ways. "Okay," she said. She waved at the rest of the family on the shore—Mark and their father, Andrew and Isabel. Tinker wished she'd just hurry up. It was so cold. The anchor chain was coiled high in one corner. Pony pushed it over with her foot. She let it play out and then she slipped into the water and was gone. She had to find the eye down there and hook the chain to it. They waited. After perhaps a minute, she burst to the surface and everybody cheered.

After the raft was secured, they swam to shore, and this was the part that rankled, even now, when it was so wrong of Tinker to think this way. It was the way her father wrapped a big towel around Pony as though she was the only one who'd done anything, as though none of the rest of them were cold and wet and miserable from being in the water so long.

Tinker checked her watch. She went into the kitchen to double-check the time on the stove clock. Ten past. The bus should have come by now. Why hadn't she heard it? She felt alarm, the panicky vision of something terrible happening to Isabel. She went outside. Their house was set sideways to the road, so the front door opened onto the driveway. She was barefoot and had to step carefully along the drive to the point where she could see down to the bus stop. Down at the corner, the Vance kids were playing on their lawn. Isabel always came right home. It was the rule. No loitering.

"Isabel?" she called. The kids stopped playing. "Is Isabel with you?" she shouted.

One of the kids shook his head.

"Did she get off the bus?"

She was seized by terror. Those damn kids weren't listening. She screamed louder. "Did Isabel get off the bus with you?"

The same boy nodded and went back to playing.

Now Tinker had to scream Isabel's name at the top of her lungs. The neighbor across the street came to her door and looked out.

"I'm here, Mama." Isabel was suddenly, miraculously, on the sidewalk on the opposite side of the street, several houses up from theirs. Just standing calmly in her yellow dress, holding her book bag by one strap. Why hadn't Tinker *seen* her? A car was parked close to where Isabel stood. A man was in it. He was looking out his window at Tinker, his face obscured by a baseball cap and sunglasses. She stared at him. He stared back for a fleeting second. She tried to put it together. Had Isabel been talking to him? Tinker charged toward the car. "Hey!" she said. "You!" The man rolled up his window. He took off at a high speed before she even thought to look at the license plate.

"Who was that?" Tinker shouted at Isabel. She didn't care who heard her. "Were you talking to him?"

"No," Isabel said.

"Did he do something?"

Isabel's eyes were huge. She was frightened, backing away from Tinker as if her mother might hit her, but Tinker had never hit her daughter, ever.

"Answer me!"

"No," Isabel said again, petulance creeping in.

"Who was he? What did he want?" Tinker was still shouting.

"Nothing," Isabel said. Tinker had to take a breath. *Calm down.* A couple of neighbors had come out on their front lawns, drawn by the commotion. She waved at them to say it was okay. *Slow down,* she told herself. *Stay in control.* Isabel was okay.

"He didn't want anything." Isabel stuck out her lower lip, fighting back tears.

"How many times do you have to be told to come right home? Not to talk to strangers."

"But I *didn't*," Isabel said, and stalked off toward the house, dragging her book bag behind her.

Oh God, Tinker thought too late. Isabel would see Andrew sleeping in the living room. She'd want to know why. Tinker would have to explain about Pony. What would she say? She should have thought this through earlier. She hadn't thought it out at all. She had never felt so afraid.

Chapter 3

William

It took William and Ruth two and a half hours to reach the summit of North Dome, and the blackflies were thick around their faces. Before they could head back down, they needed to find the true summit. In the Catskills, mountaintops were wide and flat, the actual summit points only slightly more elevated than the rest. They had to find the canister, open it, sign the register, and put it back. Someone from the Catskill 3500 Club collected the signatures and entered them. It was how you proved you'd done the peak. If you didn't sign the register, you'd have to come up again some other time and find it then.

The truth was that in spite of the blackflies, William felt great. At peace. Since leaving Fond du Lac the evening before, he'd mulled over the experience with Pony. He'd put himself first for once by leaving. She could be reckless as hell sometimes. She could think something was funny when it wasn't. It wasn't funny to attack somebody in the water. She knew that from lifesaving. From their whole lives up there. There was no excuse for what she'd done. The blinding terror of that moment had gone to the core of him. And she knew it. He'd been right to leave. Whatever she had to tell him could wait.

He watched Ruth's small compact shape thrashing through the brush. Ruth would never pull a stunt like that. Ruth had respect for things. That being said, she reminded him of Pony. They shared a quality—energy, zest, something. But Ruth was smaller and had that very cool white crew cut. She had to roll up the bottoms of her pants because she was too short for regular sizes. William saw blackfly welts on the back of her neck. "Put on some more bug stuff," he said. "Here." He sprayed deet into his hand and wiped it along the back of her neck. She wore a bandana over her face to protect her nose and cheeks. He wiped some more on her forehead. She hated the stuff. It was toxic. It was carcinogenic. But she let him do it anyway, because otherwise she'd lose her mind.

"There!" she shouted. He looked, and sure enough, the canister was nailed at eye level to a tree not twenty feet from where they stood. They signed it quickly and immediately headed back down, stopping at an overlook for a few minutes to drink some water and look at the view from the southeast corner of the summit plateau. They kept going, Ruth in the lead to set the pace because William was too fast. He'd wait for her to climb down the steep parts until she was clear, and then he'd go quickly, scrambling over the stone like a mountain goat.

He'd met Ruth the autumn before on a group hike along a section of the Appalachian Trail in Salisbury, Connecticut. There had been nine of them that day. William noticed Ruth right away. All the guys had. She was cute, small, with a world-class smile.

The leader was a lanky guy named Chris. He gathered them into a circle and explained a little about the hike. They'd all introduced themselves. Ruth said she was from West Hartford, same as William. Chris asked for a volunteer to be the sweep, and a heavyset older guy raised his hand. Then Chris took off up the trail at a near run, and by the time William had zipped his pack and locked his car, he was caught behind two women who were moving slowly. It was good trail etiquette to stand aside and let the faster people pass, but the two women didn't seem to know about that, and he didn't have the heart to race past. They lumbered along talking about the fact that the hike had been advertised as a B-pace when in fact it felt like a double-A. When the trail widened, he shot ahead, making his apologies. A gap had formed in the middle of the hike, and he had the trail to himself for about ten minutes, something he liked on big hikes, being alone and not alone. He caught up at a trail junction where Chris had stopped to wait. Ruth was there, and so was a guy named Alan.

Ruth gave William a lovely smile, and he returned it.

"I see *you* finally made it," Alan said with a husky laugh and a quick sidelong glance at Ruth. He hopped from foot to foot the way joggers do at red lights so they don't break their momentum. He had on a new-looking shirt and pants and one of those microfiber French Foreign Legion–looking hats with a long bill and a flap on the back to protect his neck from the sun. Several gadgets dangled from buckles at his waist—a pedometer, an altimeter, a compass, and a digital camera in a holster. Asshole.

It took a while for the two women to catch up, and after them a couple from Mystic. The sweep finally hove into view, smacking at mosquitoes.

"Okay." Alan slung on his pack and buckled it up. "Everybody's here. Let's go."

William had to hand it to Chris—he didn't let himself be pressured into taking off right away. He let the sweep drop his pack, sit on a rock, and take out his water bottle. The guy's face was red. "You okay back there?" Chris called out. The sweep raised a hand in return.

"He's fine," Alan said. "Let's go."

They waited another five minutes for the sweep to rest, then took off again. William moved easily to the front of the line, just behind Ruth. He kept his eyes on the trail ahead of him, but they strayed to watch Ruth's muscular calves and dynamite ass.

After a half hour, they came to a ridge that looked out over a valley to the east. They were admiring the view, pointing out landmarks, when they heard a shout. Chris told them to stay put while he made his way back. William wondered if it was the sweep. The guy was seriously out of shape.

"People come on these hikes who shouldn't, you know what I'm saying?" Alan said, looking to Ruth for confirmation. She gave him a polite smile. "In Tibet last year," he continued, "we had a guy—you could hear him wheezing a mile away."

William looked off across the valley, trying to tune Alan out. He knew what was coming, the whole let-me-tell-you-where-I've-been routine. Alan had the skeevy back-door gig nailed, beginning his stories with "When I was in . . ." Fill in the blanks. The Dolomites, Bhutan, Torres del Paine, always told as if the place was a detail and not the main point. "Is that so?" Ruth asked with all the interest of a clam.

The man of the couple from Mystic came back up the trail. The poor guy's face was white. He said the sweep had collapsed. A heart attack, maybe.

"Jesus H. Christ," Alan said.

They made their way back to find the man lying on his back across the trail, exactly where he must have fallen. The trees on either side pressed in, leaving no room to maneuver. Chris was crouched over the man. Everyone was talking at once about CPR. Who knew how to do it? Alan started hauling pieces of wood onto the trail, saying they should rig up a litter of some sort and get him down. He'd seen it done in the Whites.

William asked the couple from Mystic how long they thought it had been since they saw the man. The husband said a half hour, at least. The woman nodded agreement. William knelt and lifted the guy's eyelids; the pupils were huge and fixed. The guy was dead, beyond CPR. William took Chris aside. "You want my help?"

Chris said yes. He was shaking.

"Walk people back to their cars and get help. I can stay here. I need one other person to stay with me."

Chris called for two volunteers. Alan's hand shot up. Chris explained that he and Alan would take the group back to the trailhead
and to their cars. He said William would wait with the body. He
needed one other person to stay, too.

Which was how Ruth and William ended up on the Appalachian
Trail, watching over the corpse of a stranger as light drained from the
sky and the air became chill. After a time, Ruth said, "There's a wife
somewhere, or kids, parents, friends who don't know yet. Their lives
are about to fall apart."

William had been thinking the same thing.

"That was good you helped Chris out," she said.

They heard the helicopter just before the last of the daylight vanished. It set down out of sight. Chris and the EMTs broke through
the woods with a folded stretcher and flashlights.

After the helicopter left, Ruth took the lead and William followed her back out, lighting their path from behind with his
flashlight. At the car, she surprised him. She put her arms around
his neck and kissed him. He held her tightly to himself, feeling
how small she was and how strong. Their kiss was filled with something ancient and delicious. Being so close to death. Feeling so
alive.

William followed Ruth to her apartment. She lived not far from
William on the third floor of a house belonging to a man who wrote
books about medicine. She made them some tea, and they talked for
a long time about the man who had died. It was late, and by then his
family must know of his death. They made love. William fell into a
deep, exhausted sleep but woke often during the night to find Ruth
wide awake and staring at the ceiling. She couldn't get the family off
her mind. She kept imagining the way the news would be rolling out,
the midnight telephone calls, the dark hours of grief. She imagined a
great sad network spreading over the world, the information about
this man making its way to the people he'd loved. She just couldn't
get over it.

* * *

Now, from the shower in their motel, William watched Ruth in the bedroom. She was sitting naked on the bed with her cell phone to her ear, checking for any messages on her home phone, just in case. She had a big job coming up in the next few weeks: A woman in Glastonbury needed landscaping and gardens put in at a new house. Ruth was lining up some people to work, getting her orders straight. She made notes on a small pad of paper as she listened to her messages. He was toweling off when she came into the bathroom, her face somber. "You'd better listen to this one," she said.

He took the cell from her. "Ruth?" The voice belonged to his sister Tinker. "This is Tinker Bradshaw, William's sister. I got your number from information." Her voice broke. "I'm looking for William. It's an emergency. I keep getting his machine. Do you know where he is? Is he with you? If you see him, have him call me right away. Day or night."

William punched in Tinker's number. Isabel answered. "Hi, Isabel," he said. "Sweetheart. It's Uncle William calling. Is your mom there?"

"Aunt Pony died," Isabel whispered. "She drowned."

He couldn't have heard that right. There were a lot of other voices in the background. Tinker came on the line. "William?" she said. "Is that you?"

He lowered himself carefully to the bed. He felt Ruth's close presence. "What's going on?"

Tinker spoke between sobs. "Pony was missing. Anita Bell called Daddy. We went up there, oh man, when? Two nights ago. I can't think. Where have you been? We've been looking for you for two days. The police—Randy—found her yesterday morning. She drowned, William. Her hair got caught in that chain." Tinker broke into a wail. "Nobody knew she was even up there."

There wasn't enough air in the room.

"Are you there, William?"

"I was there," he said. "I just was there."

"Daddy passed out in the water. She looked so awful."

"Tinker, slow it down."

"There were footprints on the sand besides hers. Somebody else was there. Randy Martine saw them last night before the ambulance this morning and all those people. Somebody was with her."

William leaned over, reached for the wastepaper basket. He thought he'd throw up. "The other footprints are mine. I was there."

"You were *what*?"

"Where's Andrew?" William reeled with shock.

"What do you mean, you were there?"

"Is Andrew okay?"

"Yes. What were you doing up there?"

"She can't be dead," William said.

"She is. I *saw* her, William."

He couldn't believe it. He couldn't take it in at all. "It can't be."

Mark's voice came on the line. "Hey, man," he said.

"Mark," William said.

"We think maybe she was trying to fix the anchor. Was something wrong with it?"

"I don't know."

"Your dad wants us all at the house on Sunday at three. Family meeting."

"I have to hang up," William said.

"Okay, I understand," Mark said.

"Wait." Tinker again. "Is Seth Andrew's father?"

"I have to hang up, Tinker," William said.

"Don't call Seth," Tinker said.

"Why would I?" William asked. Keeping Pony's secrets was a habit with him.

"Just don't. Daddy said."

William gave the phone to Ruth. He pressed his hands to his face.

"This is Ruth. He can't talk anymore." She listened for a moment before saying, "I'm so sorry. Yes. Okay. I will."

William took the phone. He called Vermont information and got the number for the Hartwick barracks. "Randy, it's William Carteret."

Randy Martine had been around every summer of William's life, a kid who lived at the lake year-round. A nice guy. A decent guy. "Oh, man, William. First let me say I'm so sorry."

"Where is she now?"

"Medical examiner."

"You think someone did this?"

"There were footprints. Possibly she had company."

"They were mine, Randy. I was there. Oh, man, she was fine. She was great. This whole thing—"

"What time was that?"

"Three-thirty. Left maybe five-thirty."

"Any reason you didn't stay?"

"The kid. The chaos. I thought I'd be able to work. I knew I couldn't."

"You notice anything unusual about her?" Randy asked.

"Like what?"

"Her mood. Something she might have said. Done. Anything that stands out. Was she expecting anyone?"

"She had something to tell me, but then she never did."

"Concerning?"

"Don't know. She showed me an old picture of my mother. She showed me a lifesaving move," William said. "Took me by surprise. Damn near—" He almost said "drowned me."

Randy cleared his throat. "There are unusual circumstances, William. The baby left unattended like that. It raises a red flag. What was her relationship to the child?"

"It was great," William said. "You should have seen the two of them together."

"So she was happy to be a mom."

"She didn't kill herself, Randy." William gave Ruth an exasperated look. She'd dressed and was putting things into the suitcase.

"You left on good terms?"

"Jesus, Randy. Of course. Yes."

51

"One more thing. Was there a problem with the chain to the raft?"

"No," William said. "Not as of Memorial Day. Here's the thing that bothers me. She went in without a cap. You knew my mom, right? She drilled that into us like nobody's business. So for Pony to go under the raft without a cap doesn't add up. But how could anybody kill her? I mean, that would take a person wrapping her hair around the bottom of the chain, and how could anybody drag her down there? She was too strong for that. So none of it makes sense."

"We'll check all the possibilities," Randy said.

"Like what?"

"It's possible she drowned before becoming caught in the chain. It's possible she hit her head. As I said, we'll know when the autopsy comes in."

Chapter 4

William

The point of Carteret family meetings was to keep everybody in the loop all the time. No secrets. "We're a democracy," Jasper liked to say. "Rumor and misinformation can wreak havoc on families. The democratic way is to hold meetings and require full attendance so everybody can hear the same thing at the same time in the same words."

In theory, it made sense. Sure. But real truths ricocheted around the family via a well-oiled partisan network, a whole crosshatch of allegiances. William entered the family house on Steele Road through the kitchen pantry at the back. No one had turned on any lights, and the kitchen, with its fading linoleum and old soapstone sink, was dark. He heard voices coming from the dining room.

They were already seated at the table, his father at the head. Jasper Carteret III was tall and broad, with fair, freckled skin, once-red hair now shot through with white, and heavy eyebrows that nearly obscured pale hazel eyes. Pony's empty chair was to his right, and then Mira. Mira was an enigma to William—the cerebral sister, the one he knew least. She gave him a wan smile, her eyes huge under heavy black makeup. She'd dyed the ends of her hair a bright blue.

Tinker, hands folded on the table, nodded at William. Even in grief, she was letting him know he was late. The buffet was covered with pictures of Pony, some propped up, others in piles. Andrew stood in his portable crib beside the buffet, slapping the rim and smiling.

After William sat, Jasper began. "This may well be the most difficult thing we've ever faced as a family. More difficult even than when your mother died, because your sister's death, your youngest sister, is outside the natural order of things." He paused to let that sink in. "But we are a family, and we shall get through this together. We are strong."

"You're right, Daddy. We will." Tinker blew her nose and wiped her eyes with a handkerchief.

"What we all must have, before we go further, is a firm understanding—to the best of our ability—of exactly what happened." Jasper opened one of those red journals he kept. William noticed a tremor in his father's hand. The old man was fighting back tears. "Here's what we know. The autopsy has been ruled negative." He glanced at his three children from beneath those big eyebrows. "In other words, nothing was found to indicate foul play. She was alive when her hair caught on the chain." He looked at Tinker. "The lacerations we saw along the side of her face were the result of her effort to pull free. The cause of death was drowning."

Mira groaned. "Do we have to do this now?"

"The toxicology screen ruled out poison and drugs," Jasper continued. "Pony's blood alcohol level was point-oh-four. That's considered a trace amount. Pony was not drunk. Do not allow yourselves to think that she was. Do not allow anyone to suggest otherwise. We must be together on this point. She must have had a beer in the afternoon. Well before she elected to swim. I'm told it takes an hour to metabolize a drink."

William remembered the amber liquid in Pony's glass. Almost two drinks. Plus the half before he'd thrown the rest out. An hour for each drink. Two and a half hours? He'd left at five-thirty. Her last drink had been at about five. So, what? Six-thirty? Unless she'd had more to drink after he left and then went in much later. But with Andrew still on the grass? It was such a disconnect. The whole thing.

"Pony drowned," Jasper said again. "It was an accident. A terrible accident. But Andrew was safely in his playpen. Pony must have gone in only for a quick swim. Nothing irresponsible in that at all. Not at all. Your mother used to do it, settle you children on the lawn and go for a swim, watching, always watching, of course." William glanced at Tinker and then at Mira to see if they had any reaction. Tinker ignored the look, but he could count on Mira, the way he used to count on Pony, to acknowledge his surprise; their mother got wet, but she certainly didn't swim.

"We believe Pony meant to check the anchor. Perhaps to make sure she'd attached it correctly on Memorial Day."

Mira sat up, reached into her purse, took out a small prescription bottle, and popped one into her mouth.

"God, Mira," Tinker whispered.

"Relax," Mira said.

"The police believe her hair caught on the chain where the extension—those extra links—had been added. It happened quickly. Suffering was minimal. William, I understand you were there the day she died."

William nodded. The spotlight was on. Here it came.

"Without a word to anyone," Jasper said.

William felt the judgment against him. He was six, eight, thirteen years old again, a kid cowering tongue-tied before the great man. In trouble again for breaking some rule he didn't even know about. The story of his life. Just then Andrew reached up to the buffet and pulled one of the pictures, and a whole slew of them cascaded into his crib. Tinker swatted his little hand. "Must not touch."

"He wants his mother," William said. "Cut him a break."

"You were the last person to see your sister alive, William," Jasper said. "We need to know about that."

William's heart picked up speed, thrumming in his chest. He felt so guilty, so responsible, even though he hadn't done anything wrong. The three of them were watching, waiting. Maybe this was the big show, the whole reason for the meeting. Get William. Pin it on William. He stared at his hands. "She called me. Said she had the place to herself and did I want to come up. I said sure. I can work anywhere now." Jasper tapped a pencil; it was a sore subject between them. William raised his eyes to Mira. She looked like a panda. "I couldn't work with the baby there. I realized that. And Pony was hyper."

"Hyper?" Jasper said.

"She kept jumping up to get things. Sitting down, taking care of the baby."

"Babies require a lot of care," Tinker said.

"Was she expecting anyone?" Jasper asked.

"She got a phone call while I was there, but she didn't say who it was. She didn't say anybody else was coming. I don't think so."

"And you didn't think to ask?"

"Well, no, Dad. I didn't think to ask. I realize now I should have. I should have said, 'Hey, Pone, who was that?' and not given up until she told me, and I should have asked what the person wanted and where he lived and how he knew her and what the hell was his phone number. But then hey, I didn't know she was going to die, Dad. Now, if I'd only known that, why, then—"

"Don't be spurious with us, William."

William tipped his chair back, something his father hated to see him do.

"That call was made from a pay phone in Burlington," Jasper said. "The police checked the line."

"People still use pay phones?" Mira looked around, wide-eyed. Apparently, it was a serious question. When no one answered, she

56

sighed dramatically, tucked her bare feet under her, and laid her head on the table.

"So you know more than I do, Dad," William said.

"An hour later, she was dead," His father's tone caused William to look up sharply.

"An hour? They set a time?"

"Was she down?" Mira asked, alert again. "Was she depressed or anything?"

"Were the two of you drinking?" Jasper barked out.

"I had a beer, Dad," William said.

"And what about your little sister?"

"She had a drink. You already know that. But she wasn't drunk. You said so yourself."

"Was Pony clothed when you and she swam? Was she wearing her swimsuit?" Jasper was spitting out the questions fast. Under those merciless eyebrows, his eyes bored into William's.

William had a flash of Pony's bare white ass breaking the water, the whitecaps in the distance. He ran a hand over his face. "Why does it matter?" he said.

"Everything matters."

"For whatever it's worth, no," William said.

"And were you?"

"Was I what?" William rocked back in his chair, hitting the wall.

"Wearing trunks."

"God Almighty." William slammed the chair forward. "Where are you going with this, anyway? Say it."

"You guys *were* always skinny-dipping," Tinker said. "It's a fair question."

"Oh, big deal," Mira said. "The Gleves go in as a whole family. Emily told me. We're lightweights compared to them."

"Did anything happen between you that might have contributed to her death?" Jasper asked.

The question knocked the wind out of William. "I can't believe you'd ask me that."

"I would ask the same of anyone who was with her so shortly before her death."

"No, you wouldn't. You'd ask me. You think I did something."

"William." His father dropped his head, rubbed his temples with his palms. "Nothing of the sort, William."

They glared at each other. William felt so guilty. It had to show. A nagging voice shouted, *He's right, and you know it. If you hadn't left, Pony would be alive. All you had to do was sit her down and say, "Come on, what's this about?"*

Tinker took Andrew in her lap and sat back down at the table next to William. "What about Denny Bell?" she asked.

"What about him?"

"You didn't *know?*" Mira said. "He asked Daddy and Tinker if they'd caught the guy who did it or something, right, Tinker? It was the morning after, and it freaked everybody out."

"Mira, enough. Pony's death was accidental. I don't want to encourage rumors." Jasper cleared his throat. "Young Dennis spoke out of turn."

"Maybe he did something," Mira said.

"There's no evidence to suggest that anyone did anything," Jasper said. "There's a great deal more to cover, so if I can have your attention." He said he'd called Becker's Mortuary on Farmington Avenue and spoken to Ralph Becker personally. The wake was scheduled for Monday evening at the home. The funeral would be on Tuesday at the Congregational church on Main Street.

"Becker's?" William said.

"We used Becker's for your mother's service. They did a good job."

"Pony hated Becker's," William said.

"Nonsense," Jasper said. But William remembered the day of their mother's funeral, sitting in the car with Pony. How she'd dreaded going in there. She'd said it was contaminated with all those other people passing through there on their way to the great beyond, and it creeped her out. "She would hate this, Dad," William said. "She'd really hate having Becker's do the deed." He let his hands drop onto the table.

"Do you have a better idea?" His father's tone of voice said what William had heard all his life: *It's always easier to second-guess than to take action oneself.*

"If there was a way," William said. "A pine box. Burial overlooking the lake somewhere."

"I'd like you to be practical, William," Jasper said.

"Tinker? Mira?" William said. "Somebody want to help me out here?"

Mira's Xanax or whatever must have kicked in. She had a half-mast expression. "Pony would definitely want a green burial," she said. "You know what that is, Daddy? Or an air burial, like in Tibet, where the birds—" She clapped a hand over her mouth. "Sorry," she said.

Tinker frowned at her. "I think we should let Daddy take the lead on this." Her mouth was full.

Jasper continued. Everything would be as it had been for their mother's service.

The viewing would be in the morning; the funeral would follow. The notice had already gone into the paper. Jasper had written it himself and sent it to all of them as an e-mail attachment for comment the day before, and since no one had responded with any changes, he'd gone ahead and sent it in. William hadn't checked his e-mail.

Everything was moving ahead rocket-fast. Jasper removed a yellow legal pad from the manila folder, closed the folder, and squared it on the table with the tips of his fingers. He passed the pad to Tinker, who passed it to Mira and then to William. It was a single sentence in Pony's handwriting:

> *If anything ever happens and I can't take care of Andrew, I would like my brother, William Carteret, to act as guardian. Pony Carteret.*

"Did you know about this?" Jasper asked William.

"No," William said. Oh, man. He stared at Pony's familiar uneven

59

handwriting, a nervous-looking mix of print and cursive. He had to get up, away from his father and sisters. He needed to move around. "Excuse me," he said. He went through the kitchen and out the side door, taking deep breaths. The air pressed down on him as though it had weight. Could Pony have been making arrangements for Andrew because she knew she would die? She'd been watching William from the window that day, which had been odd, but then she'd been joyous, running into his arms. He'd heard that when people decided to kill themselves, they felt great. It was one of the warning signs—a depressed person who's abruptly happy. But Pony hadn't been depressed. When they'd all been at the lake to open camp on Memorial Day, she'd been fine, her usual funny, offbeat self. Could she have asked him up to Fond du Lac to say goodbye and he'd left before she had the chance? Was she planning to tell him after Andrew was asleep, like in that play *'Night, Mother*, where the daughter explains why she's going to kill herself to her own mother and there's nothing the mother can do to stop her? Had that been it? William sat on the back step. *Don't be an asshole,* he told himself. Pony couldn't have wrapped her own hair around the chain. "Huh," he said out loud, feeling relief. *And she would have never left Andrew on the beach. Never. Okay?* He wiped his mouth on the hem of his shirt and took some deep breaths. He went back to the dining room.

"Is Andrew something you feel you can manage?" Jasper asked without breaking stride.

William opened his hands. "It's what she wanted, Dad," he said.

"It's not binding, not notarized. It won't hold up."

"Like in court?" William pulled out his chair and let it drop loudly. "Why would it need to? We all know she wrote this."

"I'm saying you don't have to take it on. It's not required by law."

"It's what she wanted," William repeated, and sat down.

"There's the matter of the baby's father," Jasper said. "It might not be as simple as that."

"Do you know Seth's last name?" Tinker asked William. "It has to be Seth."

"We are not going to contact Seth," Jasper said. "If Seth is indeed the father, he'll have to take it upon himself to take action. I have no intention of making it easy for him."

"It isn't Seth," William said.

"Who is it?" Mira asked.

"This isn't a game any longer," Jasper said.

"It never was a game, Dad," William said. "Pony slept with a guy she met. She didn't even know his name."

"No way," Tinker said.

"Get a life," Mira said.

"And your source on this, William?" Jasper asked.

"Pony," William said.

"Did she tell either of you differently?" Jasper asked Mira and Tinker.

"Jesus, Dad," William said.

"She told me it didn't matter who the father was," Mira said.

"It matters." Jasper tapped the table with a pencil. "It matters a great deal."

"She didn't want to have to share Andrew with anybody else. You have to admit that it simplifies things," William said.

They all turned to look at Andrew in his crib. With the sudden attention on him, Andrew smiled happily.

"How is Andrew faring, Tinker?"

"Oh, he has his moments, Daddy. Isabel adores him."

"Perhaps it would be best if Andrew continued to stay with Tinker and Mark. It's certainly a stable environment."

"Oh," Tinker said. "Well—"

William tapped the legal pad. "All due respect, Dad, but—"

"You'll agree, William, you're not set up for a child," Jasper said. He'd already prepared this; he'd had all day to figure out what he'd say. He forged ahead. "Your hours. Your capriciousness. Having a child would change all that. You need to be fully prepared to take on a baby. It's an enormous change in a person's life. Tinker will vouch for that." The son of a bitch smiled at Tinker. "Tinker and

61

Mark's is an established home, and I think Andrew needs continuity." He glanced at the girls. "I'd like us to come to an agreement about what's best for the baby, as a family. I have to say I'm more than relieved to learn there's no father out there who will make a claim on him."

"We can keep him," Tinker said. "It's no trouble. And consult with William about decisions and stuff. I mean, if that's what William wants, too."

"Who does Andrew like best?" Mira asked.

"He's calmer when he's held by women," Tinker said. "Mark noticed it, too. When Mark holds him, he cries."

"I imagine," Jasper said, "a court might rule it was in Andrew's best interest to live with Tinker and Mark. All else being equal."

The train had left the station. William was back in that lousy old familiar territory where, either way, he'd lose. Could he raise a baby? No. He didn't know the first thing about kids. Kids got sick. Kids had accidents. He didn't like kids much. But did he want to agree that he couldn't? Hell, no. Not that, either.

Jasper and Tinker were passing the legal pad back and forth, looking it over again as if they could make it say more than it did. Mira crossed her legs, sat up straight, raised her arms over her head, and stretched. "Guardian," she said. "Isn't that like William has to approve of stuff?" She opened her eyes and poked Tinker. "Like, you can't send him to a military academy without running it by William first?"

"He's not going to any military academy," Tinker said.

"I'm kidding, Tinker." Mira rolled her eyes at William.

"There's nothing funny about this," Tinker said.

"We'll all be involved." Jasper looked at William, Mira, and Tinker in turn. "So we're in agreement?"

William looked across to Pony's chair and ached for her like a missing limb. She was his phantom pain. He said something affirmative. He was beat. Jasper ran the show. He always had and he always would.

* * *

When William was a child, the sun had risen and set on his father. William would get up early for school just for the chance to join his father at breakfast. His father wore wonderful black suits, crisp white shirts, and darkly striped neckties. He smelled powerfully of aftershave. He carried a leather briefcase, cracked with age. His shoes were always highly polished. At exactly eight A.M. his father walked to a large black Buick, William right behind him, copying his father's head-down, long-stride gait, one hand pretending to hold a briefcase, the other behind his back, palm out.

William was mystified by what his father did all day—where he went and what he did. He must have asked his mother this question, because on his tenth birthday, he was given permission to skip a day of school and accompany his father to the office. He'd seen Carteret Ball Bearings a few times, but only from the outside. It was a large collection of ancient brick buildings surrounded by an expanse of patchy lawn, several asphalt parking lots, the whole thing enclosed by a tall chain-link fence.

They rode in silence that morning. William assumed his father had serious matters on his mind. They slowed at the gate and were waved through by a guard. They parked directly in front of the main building, which was grand compared to the others and in much better repair. William held his father's hand as they walked down the glistening corridors. He felt lifted, adored. He was the crown prince, pretender to the throne. Everywhere, people said good morning to his father. They made a fuss over William, the beloved son of the beloved man.

They rode the elevator to the penthouse. Two secretaries sat at large desks facing each other: frowning Miss Falconer and plump, smiling Mrs. Casey. They crossed to his father's office, a huge room with plush silver-colored carpeting, floor-to-ceiling emerald-green draperies, and a modern-looking desk. William's father told him to sit on the couch. He gave him some paper and pencils, then he took one phone call after the other, swiveling in his chair, hoisting his feet onto his desk. After a while, William leaned back against the sofa and raised his feet to the coffee table, letting them down with a thunk. His father swung around to see what had made the noise, scowled at William, and made a dusting motion with one hand that said, *Remove your feet.*

His father left the room for a time, saying only that he'd be back in a bit. While he was gone, William sat in his father's chair. He opened the long desk drawers and tried out the pens and scissors and stapler. He hit pay dirt with a package of playing cards that featured pictures of women naked from the waist up, wearing Santa hats, their nipples adorned with tiny wreaths. William separated out his favorites, slipped them into his pocket, then returned the rest of the pack to the drawer. He studied the three photographs that sat on the desk, all in silver frames. They were the Christmas photos taken in the years when his three sisters had been born. In each photo his parents sat in the center, his mother holding the newest baby. In all of them William stood to the left, apart, a hand on his mother's shoulder, like a little soldier.

He made the rounds of the walls and the portraits of his dour ancestors. The first Jasper W. Carteret, with his off-center beard and hard stare. Jasper Junior, Jasper II, and finally, William's father, Jasper III, clean-shaven and in color. There were other photos, too. Some had been taken at picnics in the great yard behind the house on Steele Road, a hundred years ago, William thought. And parties at Fond du Lac. Both houses had been in the Carteret family for generations. There were so many people in the pictures, the women in long white dresses, the men in suits standing at long tables covered in flowers and serving dishes. Life seemed happier then. The parties were enormous, everything decorated in streamers and bunting, even the trees.

His father returned and took him to lunch in the executive dining room. With a slight tip of his head, he indicated men at other tables. Joe Donaldson, a patent attorney; Irving Sykes, marketing. William had no idea what any of it meant.

After lunch his father's office filled with men. Even at his age,

William understood that these men both admired and feared his father. William was filled with an eye-watering pride in his father. The men all shook William's hand and clapped him on the back, anxious to be liked by a little boy. William knew he was being indulged because he was his father's son. He understood that it had nothing to do with him, he hadn't earned it. He basked in it anyway.

They adjourned to a conference room off his father's office where the chairs were upholstered in leather and had heavy wooden arms. The meeting began with banter, punctuated with laughter. Mrs. Casey served coffee in small cups and saucers to the men, a glass of milk to William. At some unheard signal, the meeting changed. His father cleared his throat and began to direct a series of questions at a young man who sat opposite William. Again, William didn't understand the content. What he understood was the crescendo of accusation and the ratcheting up of questions afterward until the young man, red-faced and sweating, faltered over his answers.

Then William's father fired him.

It was as though all the air had been sucked from the room. The men were silent, looking down at their hands. The young man sat stunned for a moment and then pushed his chair back. He stood and left the room. There was a pause, a shifting of chairs, a clearing of throats, and the meeting continued as before. When it was adjourned, the heavyset man beside William, whom people called Sully, said, "You okay, son?" William nodded. "Your old man sure put on a show for you," he said. "But don't tell him I said so." And William didn't. For years he kept that remark a secret until one night at the lake, heavy with alcohol, he told his father what Sully had said all those years earlier, expecting his father to laugh about it. Instead, his father had become angry. "He had no right" was all he said.

Chapter 5

William

Becker's was a spanking-white colonial-style funeral home with stately columns in the front, a broad circular driveway, and a bright, chemical-green lawn. A sign, white plastic letters on black, just inside the front door said ANGELA CARTERET—SALON B. William stared at it. Angela? She'd never been Angela. She'd been Pony since the day she was born, and William had given her the name. At the age of eight, he'd wanted a pony, not another sister. So he'd called the new one Pony and kept on calling her Pony until Tinker and Mira and, finally, even their mother started calling her Pony, too. After that the name stuck. It was the right name for her. Even as a very little girl, she had long legs. She could outrun anybody.

William felt Ruth at his side, pressing close against him. She'd surprised him by wearing a dress. It was outdated; even he knew that the loose-fitting dark blue print with puffy sleeves was from some other time. But Ruth wasn't a girl to own many dresses, and he was touched that she'd done this.

He felt as if he were walking through water, as if he were pushing his way through the sea to move past the sign and join the line for the guest book, where he could stop and catch his breath. He and Ruth were behind a group of kids all in black, tattoos snaking up the backs of their necks, sliding from under their cuffs onto their wrists. His father's neighbors were among them, the women in veiled hats, strings of pearls at their throats. The men in dark suits. Death was the great leveler. He spotted Tinker heading toward him, large and important in some black tentlike dress, her flyaway hair held in place by combs and barrettes.

She gave him a long hug, pressing her body against his. Her eyes were red. She pointed across the salon to an alcove where Pony's white coffin lay, lit savagely. Beyond the coffin, his family was standing in a line. Salon B had gold carpets, red brocade drapes, small gold chairs in rows. It was the same room, he was sure. His mother's wake had been here. He felt sick.

"Daddy thinks you should come now." Tinker gave Ruth an imploring look. *Make him*, it said. Then she turned and went back to the alcove. The line inched forward. When it was William's turn, he was unable to write because his hands were shaking too badly. Ruth wrote out their names—William Carteret and Ruth Czapinski. He couldn't believe this. He couldn't believe he was here. And yet he knew he had to keep moving forward, right into it.

The coffin lid was raised, showing the white tufted party-dress lining. And his family, what was left of his family, stood off to one side, shoulder to shoulder, in a line against the wall.

William was on automatic. All at once he was looking down into the face of his little sister. His beloved Pony. Her skin was dotted with copper freckles, like thrown confetti. Her lips were parted slightly so that a trace of white teeth showed between them, and her closed eyes made two perfect crescents, the lashes long and resting on the tops of her full cheeks.

"Oh, Pone," he whispered, taking her in greedily. Somebody had pulled her hair back so tightly that it tugged at the corners of her eyes, pulling them up. Her eyes appeared almost Asian. All wrong.

He kept staring. And saw, on closer inspection, that her hair had been bluntly cut on one side. The fibers of his grief gathered into a rope at the base of his throat as understanding spread. He remembered what he'd been told: The divers had had to cut it to free her. He made himself look into her face and imagine what might have happened. He felt compelled to picture everything. If she had experienced that torturous cruel death, then he could damn well stay here, standing on two feet and breathing air. It was the least he could do. And maybe, by seeing the scene in his mind's eye, he would understand more of what happened. Maybe he would see a detail that would explain what the hell had happened to her, because the more he thought about it, the less he understood. It didn't make sense. Hair could snag. Sure it could. But wouldn't she have to be right up next to the chain for that? Cheek to metal? Yes. Then her hair could snag. Just a few strands at first. She would have jerked away in annoyance, but more hair could have wrapped around and become tangled with the first. If she reached up to yank the hair free, she might have inadvertently pushed more hair into the tangle. Panic would have set in for real. She would have been thrashing and in that act catching a great deal more of it, like a glue trap where the greater the struggle, the tighter the snare.

The room swayed under the reality of the image. *Stay with it*, he told himself. Because the central question remained: Why? His father had speculated that she had been trying to fix the chain or inspect it. But the chain was fine. Maybe she hadn't been trying to get to that broken link. Not *to* anything at all but from something. Or someone. Someone had called her from a pay phone in Burlington. Who the hell had it been?

The mourners kept coming with hands to be shaken and cheeks to be offered. He caught glimpses of Pony, her pale profile sleeping through all this. Everything was surreal. The sounds, the murmurs, the muted colors. Pony's friends were coming toward him. Lulu Garner, Carolla Lyon, and Katherine Nicely. The three little kittens.

68

Summer after summer they'd practically lived at Fond du Lac, sleeping over many nights, giggling into the wee hours, spying on William. Now they were dressed in black and drained of color, their cheeks cool as they leaned up to accept his kiss.

Katherine lingered. She was a square-faced girl with long pale hair, the kindest and smartest of Pony's friends, a second-year med student at Columbia, he'd heard. She pressed her face into his chest. "William, I need to see you later. There's something I want to show you. I'll be at the lake most of the summer."

His father's loud voice erupted from the other room, cutting through the reverential quiet. At the same time, he saw Tinker bearing down on him, her face twisted in dismay. "Do something," she hissed at him. "It's Minerva!"

In the larger room, his aunt Minerva seemed to be hanging from his father's arm, like a brightly feathered bird attacking much larger prey. His father stood head and shoulders above her, trying to shake her off.

"This is *exactly* the time and the place, Jasper." Minerva was tiny, dressed in layers and layers, more clothes than person. She had a theatrical voice, one that carried. She and his father were in a cleared space like a pair of dancers. His father said something. "I will *not* keep my voice down," she said, louder than before, seeming to give him a small push. William's father dusted his sleeve and shot his cuffs. He said something else to her angrily and walked off.

William smiled. He hadn't known Minerva was here, and her presence lifted his spirits. She was his mother's much older sister, eccentric and wonderful. She used to come up to the lake in a taxi from New York, and there was always great fanfare when she arrived, the bright yellow cab appearing through the trees and Minerva stepping out in her weird attire, laden down with ancient luggage and gifts for all the children. And always the expectation that something would happen. Each evening during her visit, Minerva and William's mother had walked arm in arm along the dirt road, his mother leaning down, their heads together, talking. When Minerva was around, William's mother seemed to have new energy. The sisters adored each other.

Upon seeing William now, Minerva broke into a wide smile, rushed toward him, and tipped her papery cheek up for a kiss. "William, my dear," she said.

He was struck by her scent. *Gardenia.* He guided her to some chairs nearby. She took his hand. Hers were cold and delicate. "I've been watching you," she said.

"I hope I've behaved." He grinned at her.

She squeezed his hand. "You never do."

"What was that all about with Dad?" he asked.

"Your father being your father." She gave him a conspiratorial smile. "He's a stubborn man."

"He sounded angry."

"I'm sure he was," she said. Her skin was whitened with powder, her mouth a shock of red lipstick. Her watery blue eyes were rimmed darkly in black. She was wearing blouses in pale and ruffled fabrics with various frilled necklines and cuffs. And she had on many skirts in frothy pastels, shrouding her legs and feet, like a peony. Pony had always defended Minerva. "It's her style," she would say. "Her flair." But Minerva exasperated Tinker. "If she has enough money to live on the Upper East Side in New York City, she has enough money to dress decently. She looks like a bag lady," Tinker would say.

"This would have killed your mother," Minerva said. "You and Pony were her great loves, you know."

William felt tears push at the back of his eyes. He looked away.

"You go right ahead and cry," Minerva said. "Don't hold it back."

But he couldn't. Not here. Not with his father watching them from across the room.

"Life is a web, William," she said. "Everything is connected."

He had no idea what she meant, but he felt reassured. He put an arm around her and held her for a minute or two before she pulled away.

"Your mother would forgive me," she said. "I'm sure of it."

"For what?" William had to smile. What sin had she committed?

In a much stronger voice, she said, "My loyalty is to you, William. It is not to Jasper Carteret. You must come see me in New York. After all this." She waved a pale hand at the room. William scanned the crowd for Ruth and found her behind Isabel. He motioned them over.

"Is that lovely creature yours?" Minerva asked him.

William smiled. "So far," he said.

"Take good care of her." She clutched at William's wrist. "You will come and see me. You must promise."

"I promise," William said.

"Soon." She glanced over William's shoulder. "Oh dear, Jasper again."

"Tell me what this is about."

"I've said too much," she said.

"Minerva, you haven't said anything."

His father was gliding toward them, tapping his watch impatiently, a practiced smile on his face. The room was filling quickly. The service was about to begin. William took his place in the front row. A minister began to speak. He had a narcotic voice, droning and self-important. Pony would have wanted a poet. A weatherman. A drill sergeant. Anything but this. William concentrated on the gleaming white coffin, now draped in roses and irises, which had been moved to the front room.

He heard his name and started. It was his turn. He stood and went to the podium. Before him was a sea of faces. The room was full. People were standing at the back. He was stopped by the size of the crowd. He hadn't realized.

In the front row were his father, Tinker holding Andrew, Mira, Mark, and Isabel. In the row behind his family sat Ruth. She was sitting with Mark's family, who had turned out in force, all of them big like Mark, with broad, honest faces. He scanned the rows beyond. Katherine Nicely and a few other girls from the lake were there. The

Bells, too. That threw him off. They must have driven down. He hadn't seen them earlier.

William hadn't prepared anything. "We're here today because of our love for Pony. We are united in our love and our grief."

"Amen," someone said.

"Amen," William repeated, taking strength. "'Pony,' I want to say to her, 'you had a standing-room-only crowd.'" A murmur came back to him from the congregation. He wiped his eyes. Ruth smiled up at him. "Her spirit was so big, too damn big to reduce to a few statements, you know?" In the front row, his father crossed his arms tightly over his chest, a sharp gesture that showed his displeasure. William addressed the people farther back. He found Katherine Nicely's upturned face, shiny with tears. "She was a generous person. A kind person. Right, Katherine?" People turned to see.

"She was always moving," William went on. "You all remember how she never sat still. How she was always moving, always doing something. Engaged. Whatever it was, she did it to the max."

The Bells were a few rows behind Katherine. Anita and Dennis sat side by side in dark nylon windbreakers. Denny, the youngest of the kids—the one who'd been shooting his BB gun that day—slouched at the end of the row, his long legs extending into the aisle, his head lowered as though he were studying something on the floor. William spoke right to him. He wanted the kid to sit up and be respectful. "Every summer, there's a swimming race across the lake. Pony took it the last four years. By a long shot." Denny's sneakers were untied, the white laces loose on the carpet. Now the kid was examining his fingernails. William let the silence fall. Maybe ten seconds or so, enough to be uncomfortable. Anita reached across and must have given Denny the sit-up-straight signal, because he hauled in his feet and swung the hair out of his face.

"Pony could swim better than she could walk." William couldn't take his eyes off Denny. The kid knew something. He'd wanted to know if they'd found who did it, a very odd question, if you asked

William. "How could this have happened?" William directed the question to Denny.

Anita looked from William to Denny and back, like, *What's going on?* A few people turned to see whom William was speaking to.

William paused, then continued. "If anyone knows anything that would help us, please come forward. Or call me. There must be something else." His voice broke. The sea of people looked back with empty faces or with tears streaming down. He had their pity. He didn't want that. He pressed his hands together and forced a smile. "She'd hate all these tears. You know she would. She'd want us to celebrate her life, not mourn her death. So that's what we'll do." William stepped down and took his seat. Ruth laid a hand on his shoulder from behind and squeezed. The minister invited people to speak if they wished. His father leaned forward to get a full look at William and glowered. William supposed it was for suggesting Pony's death had been anything other than an accident, for not toeing the family line. He held his father's gaze until the old man looked away.

Katherine Nicely stood. "Pony e-mailed me last week. She was so happy with Andrew. She was such a good mom." She choked up and sat down. The room was quiet for a time before Lulu Garner stood and whispered about how she would miss Pony. A few other people spoke, including a woman who had worked with Pony at the art store and a man with a deep voice who had bought one of her paintings.

Mira swiveled around to see. "Good-looking guy," she whispered to William.

William couldn't believe her sometimes. Was she for real?

After the service, William looked everywhere for Denny Bell, but people kept stopping him, tugging at him, telling him how sorry they were. He was thwarted, as in one of those dreams where you can't make any progress. His legs felt like lead.

The limos were lined up on Farmington Avenue. Ralph Becker himself was holding the door open. "Immediate family only in this one," Tinker said, emerging from somewhere and taking William's arm. In that dress she looked like a bat, operatic, hems fluttering. "Just you, me, Daddy, Mira, and Isabel in the limo. Ralph said."

"What about Ruth?" William said.

"If Mark can't, Ruth can't."

He wanted to smack her one sometimes, the way she had everything organized. Even now she couldn't let it go. A big red SUV with Massachusetts plates backed out of a space nearby. The Bells. "Hey," William shouted. "Wait!" They were leaving. They couldn't leave. He ran down the block, calling to them to stop, but the SUV pulled into the street and hung a right. Through its tinted windows, William saw the sullen moon of Denny Bell's face watching him from the backseat. When William turned back, Tinker had shown Ruth to another car. Ruth gave him a little what-can-you-do wave.

In the limo, his father asked, scowling, what all the yelling was about.

William didn't answer. He looked out the window, holding his tongue. Holding his temper. The procession went down Trout Brook to Fern Street. Past the Morley school they'd all gone to as kids. Left on Steele Road, past their house, toward the cemetery.

William braced his feet to keep from sliding off the small seat when the limo took the turn onto Asylum. Everything rushed past backward. He had to focus to keep from becoming carsick. His father slouched against the side of the limo, his eyes shut. Isabel laid her head in Mira's lap. Mira stroked the child's hair.

"What were you arguing with Minerva about at the wake, Dad?" William asked his father.

"There was no argument," his father said, still with his eyes shut.

"This is Pony's *funeral*, William. Give it a rest," Tinker said.

"I hadn't noticed," William said.

"Stop it, both of you," Mira said.

Now the limo turned sharply, entering the cemetery through narrow iron gates, then to the Carteret family plot at the crest of the hill.

A hole had been dug. The earth looked dark and rich along the sides. People arrived and walked slowly up the hill.

The minister spoke again. William's attention was fixed on the coffin, which lay suspended on heavy gray straps over the grave. He didn't want to see it lowered. He didn't want to hear the sound of earth being thrown on top of it. He didn't want to be here for the end, so he turned away and walked down the expanse of green, among the monuments, to the point where the hill curved steeply down and gave onto a view in the distance of Hartford and the Connecticut River glistening in the sun. It was a perfectly clear day, and he thought how many Carteret funerals must have been held in that very spot. How many of his ancestors, being unable to watch the earth swallow up someone they loved, had come and stood exactly where William stood.

He became aware of a voice very much like his mother's singing a familiar hymn. He walked partway back up the hill toward the gathering to hear it better. Mira stood there, her arms at her sides, her face lifted, the blue tips of her hair catching the sun. She had a huge voice for such a small person.

Help of the helpless, O abide with me.

People tried to join in on the chorus, but she wouldn't slow for them. This was her moment. *Damn*, he thought, and came closer. Mira winked at him. She was headed into the last verse, the one they never sang in church, Pony's favorite. The wicked verse, she used to call it. "You know what it means?" Pony had told him. "It means you can get away with anything as long as you're decent about it. You can go do your thing in life, and when you die, pfft! It's all forgiven. Isn't that cool? I mean, if you believe in that stuff. But even if you don't."

William joined in. He stepped up and joined Mira in singing it, startling people with his baritone.

Thou on my head in early youth didst smile;
And, though rebellious and perverse meanwhile,

Thou hast not left me, oft as I left Thee,
On to the close, O Lord, abide with me.

"I wish I'd known you were going to do that," Tinker said in the limo going back to the house. "I would have had the words for people. Right, Daddy?"

"We all know the words," William said.

"Other people didn't."

"I didn't know I was going to," Mira said. "I just decided to do it. For Pony."

William shut his eyes and thought of Fond du Lac, and it occurred to him that the house would still be warm from Pony. It would still hold the last of her presence. He'd go up there. He'd ask Ruth. Before the family started their regular summer visits there, before they contaminated everything and the remaining threads of his sister were lost forever.

Chapter 6

Mira

The letter was addressed to Ms. Miranda Carteret. Give the man credit for getting that right. Mira was short for Miranda and not a name unto itself, as some believed, because of the actress Mira Sorvino. Mira had told guys in bars that it was short for Miracle. Or she'd say Mirage, if she was about to leave them cold. Or hot, as the case may be.

He also got the address right. 14 Maplewood Avenue, West Hartford, CT 06119. Even the apartment number: #2. He'd done his homework.

He'd spoken at Pony's service, and she'd liked that, and then he was at the house after, which she found ballsy, given his thin connection to the family. She'd caught glimpses of him now and then. At one point she was in the dining room, off by herself, watching Mark pouring wine for Pony's friends, the cute ones from the lake—Katherine and those other two she always got mixed up. They were laughing at something, and Tinker must have heard the laughter, because she came out of the kitchen and made a beeline for them. She slid an arm around Mark's waist, as if saying, *Hands off*. She leaned over to kiss each of the girls, who were as thin as birds and with lustrous, swinging hair, the polar opposite of poor old Tinker. But what Tinker didn't know was that she had a puss full of powdered sugar from eating something sweet in the kitchen by herself. Mark wiped it away with his thumb in full view of the three goddesses. Tinker just fled for the hall and up the stairs. Poor Tinker. But anyway, that was when Mira spotted the man from the funeral, the one who'd spoken, the writer of the letter she was holding. He was observing William at a distance, as if he wanted to introduce himself. Then the doorbell rang, and she was the only one near enough to answer it.

Aunt Minerva walked in, looking anorectic, like one of those skinny girls who wear tons of clothes to cover up their thinness. A taxi was waiting on the street with its interior lights on. Oh, that taxi was going to vex Tinker. A taxi from Manhattan to Hartford and back. Tinker would tally it. She would know exactly how much money Minerva was wasting.

Mira hadn't spoken to Minerva yet. There'd been an argument or something between Minerva and her father, so Mira had steered clear. Anyway, William was so obviously her favorite. Minerva and William had been talking at Pony's funeral, their heads bowed together, whispering. Minerva made William laugh. She would reach out and touch his cheek or his arm in an affectionate way. Mira didn't mind at all that William was the favorite, but Tinker! Mira had heard more than once how when Tinker was five and William was eleven, Minerva had invited William to stay with her in New York for a week. They'd gone to the theater, to restaurants. They'd stayed up all night playing monopoly and then went outside and roamed around the New York streets at three in the morning. Tinker had assumed she would take her turn when she was William's age, and then Mira and Pony would have their turns after her. Everything fair and square. But the invitation never came. Only William was ever asked. That year and others. It absolutely frosted Tinker.

"Mira, sweetheart." Minerva glanced about. "So many people!"
Mira took her aunt's coat.

"Are you terribly overwhelmed?" Minerva asked her.

"Yes," Mira said. "As a matter of fact." It came as a relief to be asked this question. She loved it when she didn't have to explain herself.

"You must duck out," Minerva said. "You're not a person to take solace in crowds."

So she had. She'd gone out into the backyard, away from that numbing sound, away from all those people. She'd pulled a lawn chair out beyond the patio to the dark at the far end of the yard.

When their mother had died, well, she could admit that to herself. She was good at identifying feelings. Her mother's death had come as a shock. But she'd also felt a certain excitement. It had been out of the blue, and of course it was awful. But there had been an almost delicious edge to it, too, because it was the fulfillment of a promise once made and now kept. Mira had occasionally imagined the day her mother would die; her father, too. She supposed everyone did that. How old would Mira be? How would it happen? Where? How would she get the news? She had both dreaded and anticipated it. And then all of a sudden there it was. Her mother was dead. She'd felt intensely the removal of a protection. While her parents were alive, they were the barrier between her and her own death. Now one was gone.

But this? Pony?

The back door to the house opened behind her, and she'd turned to see the man from the funeral. "Nice out here." He dragged a chair across the grass toward her. "You're one of the sisters, right?" He extended a hand. "Keith Brink."

She knew who he was. She didn't take the hand right away. She wanted to see what he'd do.

"Maybe you want to be alone out here."

"You can stay." She took his hand. She liked to know how a guy's hands felt, the way dogs saw with their noses. She'd know about a guy once she'd touched his hand. Keith's was large and warm, a little rough. Comforting.

He sat down and leaned forward, resting his elbows on his knees. It felt private, being with him. "This must be pretty hard for you."

She took him in. The dark stranger. "Who are you, anyway?"

"Nobody," he said with a grin. He leaned back in the chair. "What I mean is, I'm not from around here. I'm from Iowa, here on a job. Your sister was such a nice girl, and I wanted to pay my respects."

She studied his face for longer than was usually comfortable. "Nice girl," she repeated.

"You can talk to me if you want," he said.

"I'm a year older. I rode a bike before her. I learned to read before her. Got my driver's license first. Everything. Then she goes and bloody dies before me. It's like impossible to take it in."

He studied her. "You feel cheated, is that it?"

That was exactly it. She watched his face for disapproval and found none. "She got there first. I keep thinking, *How could she do that to me?*"

"Sounds like you think she did it on purpose."

"How well did you know her?" Mira asked.

"Hardly at all, really. I saw her paintings at a bank in East Hartford. I liked them. The bank had her number. I called, went over to her place, and bought one of the ones she had there."

"What did it cost you?"

"A hundred and fifty."

She whistled. She put her head back and shut her eyes.

"Too much?" He waited for her to answer, but she didn't. After a few moments more, he gave up and left. She watched him through half-open eyes. Just at the back door, he turned, as she'd known he would. She smiled privately to herself. He'd be back. He'd lift her spirits. The things she'd told him might have shocked other people. After he left, she felt more relaxed.

He was nothing like Peter Cassidy. He was a lot older than Peter was back then. Darker, too, but he brought Peter to mind in spades. Certain guys always did. Peter was her best friend Judy's older brother, and one afternoon when Mira was thirteen, she had gone to their house on Foxcroft Road, a few blocks away. Judy wasn't there. Neither were Mr. and Mrs. Cassidy. But Peter had been there. They hadn't spoken a word to each other. He'd taken her down to the basement, where they had a pool table with a bare bulb hanging over it so the light was bright in the center of the room, dark all around the sides. They shot some pool, still without speaking. Mira had been wearing a skirt, and Peter had fooled with the hem of her skirt when she leaned over to take a shot. She'd liked the way that felt. She'd let him slip his finger into her. All with only the sound of their breathing and the slap of billiard balls to break the silence.

Mira had gone back to the Cassidys' a lot of times, and it was always the same. Always in the basement, always without speaking, always with Mira pretending to play pool.

Mira opened her knees slightly to the great black yard behind, pretended Peter Cassidy was out there, slipped her hand to her groin, and circled gently, insistently, waiting for the charge to shoot through her, waiting to feel good, to feel more, to feel anything at all. Finally, the sensation caught and built and then, unexpectedly, as if she'd been ripped wide open, the tears came and wouldn't stop. When it was over, she dried her cheeks with the sleeve of her shirt. It was then she heard the sound nearby of stones under the soles of someone's shoes. Somebody was out there. "Who's there?" she whispered into the darkness, but there was no answer.

The note said:

Dear Miranda,

I wanted to again express my condolences. My thoughts and prayers are with you. I wonder if we might meet for coffee sometime. I have thought of you since we met at your father's. Please

*meet me at the Readers' Feast on Farmington Avenue. I'll be there
at one o'clock on Saturday.*

Keith Brink

He'd printed it carefully—black ink in block letters on plain
notebook paper. His signature had a very large *K* and a very large *B.*
Would she go? Would she not? She remembered the feeling of his
hand, which she had liked, and she was sure he had been the one
she'd heard, the one who'd watched her that night. It was such a
nervy thing for a stranger to do in her father's house. It felt intimate.
She couldn't decide. She got to the Readers' Feast at one-fifteen and
spotted him near the window at a small table. He had already spotted her.

He pulled out the chair, something people never did anymore.
She sat down and there was a moment of silence. She might not have
recognized him on the street. He looked different. He was still good-
looking, but in a tumbled-around, nicked-by-life way. He had on
jeans and a plaid western shirt. He probably noticed her eye. She had
an abnormality, a keyhole-shaped iris. People either stared at it or
avoided looking. Keith did neither. The table was too small. Her
knees touched his. The effect on him was immediate. She never tired
of the way men responded so predictably to her touch, like puppies.
He smiled. "I'm glad you decided to come."

"Tell me who you are," she said.

"Keith Brink."

"Married?"

He shook his head.

"Girlfriend?"

"Not yet. What about you."

She shook her head.

"You look like her." He scanned her face. "You have her mouth.
Her skin."

Mira looked into his very blue eyes. *Keithie blue eyes.* He unnerved her a little. His hair was smooth as a seal's. He had that pull

she liked in a guy. Something she never wanted to analyze. Maybe a little dangerous, but nothing she couldn't handle. It was either there or it wasn't. And wide shoulders. "So you buy a painting from a total stranger, and then you go to her funeral."

His smiling blue eyes seemed to drill into her. "What can I say?"

"It wasn't a question."

"I bet you're one of those women who never know how beautiful they are."

"Oh, give me a break." She glanced around. She felt conspicuous.

He laughed. "You're like her, too. She didn't let people get away with much."

"Meaning she didn't let you get away with much. So as I was saying, you buy a painting from her, and what does that take? Twenty minutes?"

"I was there longer than that. A couple of hours. We hit it off, I guess. I don't remember all we talked about. I've tried to remember. Her boy, I guess. The family. She wanted to know about the Midwest."

"When was this, anyway?"

He ran a hand over his face. "A month ago. Maybe six weeks."

"And you never saw her again after that?"

He shook his head.

"How did you know she died?"

He didn't even break stride. "Teller at the bank."

"What do you do for a living?" she asked.

"Plumbing and heating systems. I move around the country, job to job."

"Let me see your hands." She liked blue-collar guys. He held them out. She felt the palms and the undersides of his fingertips, which were callused. She tapped one very lightly. "Can you feel that?"

He shook his head.

"A construction worker who's into bank art. A real Renaissance man." She sat back and crossed her legs. She'd worn a long skirt, almost to the floor, and a gauzy blue shirt. She knew she looked at home in the Readers' Feast, which was a little café attached to a bookstore. He didn't. He would look at home in a Taco Bell.

"I had bare walls," he said.

"Why did you ask me here?" The jury was out on him. He had very white teeth.

"Do I need a reason?"

She scanned his face, held his gaze for so long that she saw the threads of various blues in his eyes. "Yes."

"I think you're interesting."

"People like you don't find people like me interesting," she said.

"Then I'm the exception." He had been tipping back in his chair. He leaned forward with a dull thump. "I've had loss, too. I know what it's like, and I know what makes it—well, not better—nothing does that. Bearable, maybe. After my mother died, people I didn't know came up and told me things about her I never knew. It was nice."

"Like what?"

"What she was like when she was younger. Little things. I just saw her . . . differently."

"That sucks, though, doesn't it? In a metaphysical kind of way."

He had a great lopsided smile. "Pony said you were the thinker in the family."

"She did? No way. What else did she say?"

"That of all you kids, you were the one who was going to make it."

"Get out of here," Mira said.

"You asked me to tell you what she said. She liked you best."

"No. William was her favorite. They were like this." She held up her index and middle finger, twisted.

"She said William was an enigma."

"Wrong. William's the all-American guy. Into sports, C-student, baseball-cap kind of a guy. Pony idolized him."

"Can I ask you something?

"Shoot."

"What happened? It's hard to believe anybody like her could drown."

84

Her father had practically wet his pants telling the family what to think. "It was an accident. Her hair got hooked around a broken link in a chain. The police don't know why."

"It's a criminal investigation?"

"Between you and me?" She loved the intimacy a person could have with strangers, and Keith Brink was just passing through. "Pony would try anything. Nothing ever scared her."

"So what are you saying?"

"I'm saying there are ways to brush up against death and then go too far."

"Suicide?"

"With Pony, it was more like she was always flirting with danger. She didn't stop when she should." Mira leaned toward him. "She didn't like to take precautions, that's all. She drove too fast. Fucked without protection. Skied out of control. Risk is more fun, no question, but hey, it's risk. It gets you closer to death. That's the definition."

"What about you?" he asked. "Are you like that?"

Her eyes traveled all over his face. He had a tiny hairline scar over his eyebrow, the faint beginnings of crow's-feet. She felt breathless. *Yes,* she thought. *Sure. Like right now.* "Not in the water. I would never take the chances Pony took in the water." She showed him with her hand how Pony did the forbidden jackknife off the raft, how she'd jump high and quick as a whip, then straighten so her front skimmed the side of the raft. "It's the straightest way to dive in, but you can break your neck. Maybe that's what she did, and she ran into the chain. Or maybe she hyperventilated. It wouldn't be the first time, by a long shot. She liked to hyperventilate so she could stay underwater longer. But you can black out."

"You tell anybody this stuff?"

"What's the point? She'll still be dead." Tears welled in her eyes.

He took out a perfectly white handkerchief and handed it to her.

"I need air," she said.

She and Keith walked to Elizabeth Park. She'd let herself get off

85

on Pony's freewheeling spirit, her refusal to follow rules. She'd been bragging about Pony as if she were alive and still full of it, and the realization that she wasn't had pulled the rug out from under her. They sat on a bench overlooking the Rose Garden, which was in full bloom and fragrant. A wedding party was being photographed; all the bridesmaids were in shocking pink. A line of white limos waited at the curb. "My mom once told me we don't have the stamina for hardship in our family," she said.

"Yeah?" he said. "Why'd she say that?"

"I have stamina," she said. "Nobody thinks so, but I do."

"What happened to her? To your mother?"

"Weren't we just talking about me?" she said.

"You're the one who brought her up," Keith said.

He had a point there. "A brain aneurysm. You know, a stroke. It was sudden."

"Those are two different things. Which was it?"

"What difference does it make?" Mira had been watching bright pink bridesmaids squeeze into one of the limos.

"So I guess all you girls look like your dad, and your brother favors your mom?"

She studied his face. She felt both brazen and entitled. He'd had acne as a kid; there were small pitted scars. "How old are you?" she asked.

"Thirty-six," he said.

"Twenty-seven." She tapped her chest. "That's a big difference."

"Meaning?"

"Meaning it's a big difference." She kept her eyes on his an extra beat, long enough to feel the familiar, sweet pull at her core. She touched his cheek lightly to feel the tiny marks.

"I never bought you that coffee. You up for it?"

They walked back without speaking, their bodies bumping from time to time. As they went into the restaurant, she felt Keith's hand at the small of her back, a reassuringly protective gesture. It melted her the way a man's touch usually did. It got her thinking about what she liked in him—the way he looked, sort of craggy; that he was from somewhere else and that he'd go back to wherever that was; that he was a little bit formal; that he'd taken the time to be so nice to her, to express his condolences; that he'd cared for Pony, too. There was just one thing, and the time had come to ask it. "So let's get this straight," she said after they'd sat down again in the restaurant. "Were you two an item? I say yes. But tell me I'm wrong."

"I never even touched her," he said. "It wasn't like that at all."

They sat in the window facing the street. He ordered a pot of tea. She ordered an iced coffee. They each had a salad. He smiled at her. Damn, but he had the bluest eyes. "So tell me more about yourself," he said.

Mira told him that she was adjunct faculty at the University of Hartford, enough to squeak by on financially; that she'd had a short story published in a literary magazine; and that someday she would write a novel, but her father would have to die first because she couldn't bear to have him read any of it. "I love my dad," she said. "It's nothing personal."

She told him she went to a lot of writers' conferences, which was where she should have been right then. She loved the feeling of sitting around after a reading. There would be wine and cheese. Sometimes somebody would make hash brownies. She usually got it on with the visiting writers, although she didn't tell Keith that part.

He listened attentively. She told him how the Carterets were high achievers and how it had been hard for all of them to come along after a company president like her father and a beauty like her mother. Hard to live up to either one of those ideals. And then, because she was on a roll and because he didn't stop her, she told him about the Christmas cards. How the whole family would line up in front of the fireplace at Thanksgiving for the official family portrait, all of them in new clothes, all smiling at the camera. "We were a very good-looking group," she said. "We were this perfect family," doing those little quote signs with her fingers to show that she was being ironic, that she knew perfectly well there was no such thing.

She was fourteen, and her mother was taking her to Halifax, Nova Scotia, for the abortion. Water everywhere, Mira remembered. Rivers and canals and bays in a gray city dominated by a fort that people told her repeatedly not to miss. The crown jewel of Halifax. And the rain came down. The sky held, dreary and gray, so that forevermore Mira would hate the rain.

The clinic was called Floris House, a large brick mansion that was once somebody's estate. The people were nice, but they dealt with her mother more than with Mira. She was led from room to room, told what to do, interrogated gently, but otherwise she might as well not have existed. She was the vessel containing the abomination. She was so ashamed of herself that she could barely speak above a whisper.

The night before the procedure, in her cell-like white room, she had asked her mother the most frightening of all questions: "Does Daddy know?"

"No," her mother said, and it was a small miracle, as far as Mira was concerned, the only bright spot in her world, that her shame was contained to the two of them. "He thinks we've gone to the lake for a few days." Indeed, it was to Fond du Lac that they would return after her "procedure" so Mira could rest. Mira went back to watching *The Simpsons* and *Whose Line Is It Anyway?* on a small black-and-white TV. She felt juvenile watching those shows, but they were familiar and comforting. Krusty the Klown was onstage when her mother aimed the remote, muted the television, and said, "Sweetheart, I'd like to know your thoughts."

At first Mira was confused because she thought her mother was asking about Krusty. Then she remembered where she was and what would happen in the morning. "I'm so sorry." She had been saying this for two weeks.

"Beyond that." Her mother was dressed in a flowery-print dress with short sleeves. She had goose bumps dotting her arms. It was cold in Floris House. "What are your thoughts about the procedure?"

Mira's mind went blank. She raised her shoulders and let them drop. "I don't know," she said, although she knew exactly what she thought. She was so relieved she could barely contain it. Her only concern was that something would happen between now and the abortion that would delay or even cancel it. The clinic would burn down, or the doctor would be killed in a car crash, and then it would be too late and she'd have to go to term. She could hardly wait to have it over with, to be rid of the terror she had felt every moment since she'd known she was late.

"Is it a life?" her mother asked.

"No," Mira said immediately. "Not yet."

"When does life begin?" her mother said.

They'd had this in school. Conception, birth, the third trimester? One of those. Her social studies teacher had posed the question one day, out of the blue. Mira couldn't remember the answer, if there even was an answer. She did not consider what was inside her a life. Not remotely. "When a baby is born, I guess," Mira said.

"So, and I don't mean to trivialize this, but you see this as something akin to an appendectomy? A tonsillectomy? Just the removal of something inside you?"

Mira nodded, feeling like whatever she said would be wrong. Was it possible her mother would change her mind, not let her go through with it? But her mother went back to her book, and Mira was glad the conversation was over. She stared at the muted TV screen. Bart and Lisa were in the audience, laughing at Krusty.

"We'll keep this between ourselves, shall we?" her mother said.

Fuckin' A, Mira thought, but said, "Okay," with the reverence she knew was expected.

"This is a very private thing," her mother said. "The most private thing."

Mira gave a solemn nod.

"Did you consider having the baby?" her mother said.

"No," Mira practically shouted. "God, no."

"I need to be sure," her mother said. "Absolutely sure. If you don't want to go through with this, you can change your mind right up to the last minute. I want you to be absolutely clear about that. It would be complicated to take this baby to term and to give birth, but if that's what you want, that's what you must do."

"I don't want that," Mira said. "I'm positive." She thought of school, of her friends, of being one of *those* girls—there had been exactly two—who came to class pregnant, bigger and bigger all the time, and then just disappeared. People made jokes about those girls. The boys call them cunts.

"Does the boy know?" her mother said.

"No," she said. She'd thought this part was over, where her mother kept asking and she kept refusing to say who it was. Peter Cassidy would be in so much trouble.

Her mother glanced down at her book, and Mira hoped the conversation was over. But her mother laid down the book again. "Something very similar happened to me," she said.

This was big news. "You had an abortion?" Mira said.

"No," her mother said. "That's the point. I didn't." She glanced at the window. Rain streamed down the panes. "Can you keep this to yourself, Mira?"

"Yes," Mira said. Was she ever. She was willing to keep anything to herself.

"I had the baby. That's why I've been asking all these questions. Things were very different for me." Her mother's chin trembled as she spoke.

"What happened to it?" All Mira could think was that one day someone would come to the door and say they were the baby. The way she'd seen on *Unsolved Mysteries*.

"The baby was William," her mother said.

"William!" Mira had been conned. Her mother's story collapsed. It was a lesser deal, a much lesser deal. Not the same at all. Nevertheless, she scrambled to understand so she could respond. "You and Daddy *had* to get married?" she said.

"The man was not your father," her mother said. "He was someone I knew many years ago."

"Wait a minute," Mira said. It was all happening way too fast. "William has a different father than us?"

"I'm telling you this because of what's happening to you, sweetheart, and what will happen tomorrow. You need to know that you're not alone. People handle these things in many ways. There's no one right answer. I simply want you to be sure. This is a big step. In the future, it will take on importance for you, whichever course of action you take. The abortion or having the baby."

"William has a different *father*?" Mira asked again.

"Yes."

"But who?" Mira wished her mother would just say.

"We weren't right for each other. It didn't last."

"But who?"

Her mother smiled. "His name was Lawrence."

"So William is like my half brother," Mira said. "Lawrence. What was he like?"

"Handsome, mercurial," her mother said. Months later, Mira would look up the word: *Lively, witty, and fast-talking*, the dictionary said. *Likely to do the unexpected.*

"What about me?" Mira asked her mother. "Am I Daddy's daughter?"

"Well, of course you are," her mother said, looking so surprised. Call her crazy, but it was a fair question.

"Does William ever see him?"

Her mother shook her head. "Please don't talk about this with either William or your sisters. I'm telling you for a purpose. I believe in sharing very private information when it bears on one of my children's lives. What I've told you was for your ears only, Mira."

"Okay," Mira said. And then an odd thing happened. She slept well that night, and in the morning, through the haze of anesthetic and afterward, the pain and cramps, she thought not at all of herself and what was happening to her but of her mother and William and Lawrence. In the car, driving from Halifax to Fond du Lac, she knew better than to bring up the subject, but it didn't matter. She felt content. She and her mother were bound to each other. Secret for secret, silence for silence.

Chapter 7

William

Ruth was out the door and to the car before William pulled to a stop. She'd been watching for him, just as Pony had been that day. She threw her duffel into the backseat, climbed in, and gave him a kiss. "How are you?"

"Fine," he said. The day was steamy, and the car was without air-conditioning, so they had to leave the windows down. Hot air rushed through as they drove, unrefreshing and loud.

After they got out of Hartford, Ruth poked him in the arm lightly. "'Fine' never means 'fine,'" she said. "What's up?"

He loved that in her, the way she didn't let him get away with things. "I want to ask around some more," he said. "I just have this feeling, you know?"

Ruth lifted her bare feet to the dashboard. "Like what?"

"Okay, Denny Bell asked my dad and Tinker if they found who did it. Why would he assume somebody did it?"

"Because he's a kid. Because he's addicted to *Law and Order*."

"Think about it. Your neighbor drowns in his backyard pool, and

93

the first thing you ask is if they found who did it? There's a disconnect there, and I'm going to find out what it is."

"What else?"

"Katherine Nicely wants to tell me something. She wouldn't say what."

"I like her," Ruth said. "I talked to her a little bit."

"And there was that fight between my aunt and my dad that nobody will talk about. I'm supposed to go see Minerva, but I want to do this stuff first. So it's nothing and it's everything."

"See? You're not fine," she said.

"I'm not fine."

When he pulled to a stop in the driveway, Ruth bolted and cut across the grass down to the water, raising both arms overhead in a hard stretch. She wasn't a girl to sit still for long. *Like Pony*, he thought.

The intervening weeks had made a difference in Lake Aral—between abandoned preseason and flying high. Today distant shouts traveled over the water's surface. Boats dotted the lake. Bits of conversation could be heard. At the Bells' house, the dooryard was crammed with cars. Three girls sunned themselves in bright plastic floats on the water. *Don't think twice*, he told himself. He stripped down and went in. The water was cold, but he didn't hesitate. He swam to the raft and hung on to the ladder for a moment. The bite of cold water kept him in the moment. He slid from the raft into the water, dropped down, feeling his way around a barrel and coming up under the raft in that familiar cloacal chamber. He held on to the struts overhead. He'd shown all his sisters how to navigate the underbelly of the raft, because it mattered. If they ever wanted to explore the world under there, and they would, it was better to know how than to risk it solo.

He'd been a taskmaster. First Tinker, who'd been terrified to go under the raft. He'd had to bribe her with M&M's. Then Mira, thin, quiet, somber. She had done everything William said as if it was her duty, and then never did it again, as far as he knew. Pony had been the best, with her sloppy, twisted little dive and splayed feet. When

Pony was about twelve, she'd convinced their father one Memorial Day to give her the job of setting anchor. William had gone down there with her, swimming alongside, both of them in goggles and caps, the family watching from the shore. She'd done it every year since.

William felt his way back under the barrels. He located the chain, which was hooked to a ring bolted to one corner of the raft. He grasped the cold metal, took a deep breath, and pulled himself down headfirst, hand over hand into the pitch black. He felt the smooth links, each one as big as his palm and still easy to hold. By summer's end, the chain would be ribboned with algae.

He came to the knot of links. They'd had to reinforce the chain—the coronary bypass, Pony had called it. William felt for the jagged end where they'd hooked a two-foot length of chain above and below a rusted link, so that if the link gave, the new chain would take up the slack.

His lungs ached for air, but he hadn't finished. He felt for the loop of chain. He needed to understand by feel if there had been a problem, a reason for her to be there. Instead, his hand rested on something soft. He snatched his hand away, then reached again, this time letting his fingers slide through the mass. Pony's hair. A thick bloom of it was wrapped around the tangle of chain. He shot to the surface and gulped air. He hung on the ladder, panting.

But he still wasn't done. He went back down the chain, this time to find out what he needed to know. He felt around, concentrating on the chain itself, letting his fingers slide through the hair. The chain was fine. The old chain was still holding, the bypass solidly attached. If there wasn't a problem, what the hell had she been doing down there? And without a cap, which meant she hadn't planned to go down. If she'd planned it, she'd have protected herself. He knew she would have. It was the one rule she followed.

William hauled their luggage into the house. The living room was steaming hot and smelled of age and ash from the fireplace.

"Musty in here." Ruth was right behind him. "Mind?" And before he could answer, she was opening the windows, one after the other. She raised each sash and propped it with a stick kept on the sills for that purpose, since the roping was long since broken.

It was all going too fast. "I mind!" he said.

She stopped short and turned to look at him with a puzzled expression. "You're kidding, right?"

"Ask me before you go taking over."

"Taking over?" She cocked her head. "Taking *over*? This place has been shut up for weeks."

He should apologize. He knew that. But the house contained the last of Pony. It felt like Ruth was letting her out. When he didn't say anything, she went out onto the front porch, letting the screen door slam behind her. He followed. She was standing at the rail, looking out over the water.

"Okay, I'm sorry," he said. Barbecue smells came across the water from the Bells'. Smoke and charred beef. They were having a party over there; it would get bigger and louder tonight.

"You need to be here with Pony," she said. "Your memory of Pony, anyway. I don't see how I can help. Honest." Before he could say another thing, she pushed by him and went inside, letting the door slam again, and maybe he wasn't completely sorry. He could run after her, but he wasn't going to do that. He watched the lake in front of the Bells'. They had a blow-up toy the size of a garage out on the water, stairs on one side of it and a slide on the other. It was plastic, blue, yellow, and red. Some girls were pulling themselves up the chubby stairs and laughing. When Ruth came out again, she had changed clothes and carried her suitcase. "There's a bus for Hartford in an hour and a half. I want to be on that bus," she said.

"Oh, come on, Ruth," he said.

"Give me some credit here, William," she said. "You need to do this alone. You may not know it, but I do."

They drove to Springfield. He went inside with her and bought the ticket and waited the half hour, shoulder to shoulder with her on the wooden bench.

"Are you mad at me?" he asked her.

"No. It's just I should have known better," she said. Before she boarded the bus, she kissed him. "Take your time with all this. Just let it all come."

In the morning, he made his way through the wood toward the Bells'. The driveway was full of cars. The house had that silent hungover feel. He'd have to get to Denny later, he thought. He decided to start with Katherine, who lived directly across the lake.

In the Carteret family—in any Aral family—you didn't swim across the lake without a boat. You could get a cramp out there and sink like a stone. You could have a heart attack, a seizure. You could get too tired to keep going, and then what? There you'd be, the theory went, a spent piece of flesh and bone treading water a mile from the bottom. But the next morning, when William got up, there was no one around to ask.

He changed into his trunks and entered the water from the northernmost point of the property so he could cut the float a wide berth. He swam the six-beat crawl he'd learned at Trinity, the one skill he'd taken with him from that institute of higher learning that had paid off. He could swim for hours at that pace, a nice easy arm stroke, a slightly faster kick.

Swimming. He should have done this sooner. He could get lost in swimming. The world shrank to the small dark space he inhabited, to the evenness of breathing. The effort of moving, which at first came with difficulty, eventually smoothed out so he was only a machine pushing through the water, speeding up, slowing down, checking every so often to make sure he was on course, heading across to the other side. As he swam, he thought about a picture he'd noticed wedged into the frame of a mirror in the living room, a Polaroid from the summer before at Jasper's seventieth. They always gathered for Jasper's birthday. August 1, high summer, was the hottest time of the year up there, just as the leaves became that blackish-green before they colored in the fall. The picture showed a semicircle of chairs on the sand—Jasper holding Andrew, who was only a few weeks old, hefty Mark on Jasper's right, and William on the left, all of them squinting into the sun. "The men of Fond du Lac," Tinker had said before taking the shot. "Let's get one of just the men."

The usual houseful had been there, everyone present and accounted for. For the actual party, some neighbors came by. There was something feral about his sisters at those things. Their voices never stopped. They were always one-upping one another, fighting for attention, fighting to be the funny one, even Tinker. Mira had taken center stage, though, in her snake-patterned tights and black halter top. She'd woven among the guests, dancing to the music. William thought she must have been smoking pot to do that. He didn't remember seeing her after that, which wasn't unusual. Mira often did something memorable and then vanished.

Later that evening, when the coffee cups were gathered and the Scotch made its way out for the second time, Pony got William's attention and cocked her head toward the lake, which meant a late-night swim. They'd made their way down to the lakefront. The moon was almost full, a heavy golden globe hanging low. A harvest moon. Pony stripped down, dove in, and swam hard for the float. It took William longer. He stood in the water up to his knees, mesmerized by the wide swath of moonlight on the sultry lake. And then Mark was beside him. Big Mark, his skin fish-white in the moonlight. "Couldn't resist," he said. "What the hell, I've always wanted to do this."

It was a first, Mark coming with them. "Great," William said, pleased. He dove in, turned, and waited for Mark, who lowered himself with a shiver and a small yelp before he swam. The feeling of cold water on William's bare skin, his balls, always came as a surprise, that splayed, loose feeling he never had in trunks. He swam quietly, finning his hands, allowing his legs to dangle, to float behind him, the luxurious feeling of his sex free in cold water.

Ahead, he could see the pale round of Pony's face in the darkness. She was waiting at the ladder. He and Mark swam closer, and she disappeared. A moment later, she called, "Under here, guys," her voice echoing from the chamber between the barrels under the float. William dove down, his eyes open, feeling above for the opening between the barrels. He came up beside Pony. The barrels rolled and clanked. It smelled of decay and wet wood, the same secret smell from every summer of his life.

"Was that Mark on the beach with you?" Pony asked.

"Yeah," William said, and then called to Mark, "We're under here, man," and seconds later, he felt Mark at his legs. He reached to guide Mark up and into the small hollow. Their bodies brushed, their knees knocked, feet tangled.

"Bad boy, Marcus," Pony whispered to him. "Tinker's going to have your ass."

They might as well have been blind, it was so dark. But William felt their bodies against his, Mark frantically treading water beside him. "Hold on to the struts," William said to Mark. "Like this." He found Mark's shoulder, ran his hand the length of Mark's arm, and guided the hand overhead to one of the struts holding in the barrels.

Immediately, Mark's legs relaxed. William, Mark, and Pony held absolutely still. "You guys always do this," Mark breathed. "You always cut out before the Scotch comes out again."

"We do," Pony said. "Daddy's parties are like—well, you know. Enough is enough."

Mark laughed. "I guess," he said. "I wish Tinker would come. She used to love this."

"You're kidding," Pony said.

"No, she did," Mark said. "We used to skinny-dip up here all the time, but early in the morning. Five, six o'clock."

"It's nice then," Pony said.

"We get the early sun here on the Carteret side of the lake," William imitated his father's gravelly baritone, and they laughed.

Their breath was warm and regular on one another's faces. "I love you guys." Pony's face touched William's, and he felt her lips brush his cheek, then the swirl of water as she groped for Mark's face and kissed him, too. There was a silence of several seconds.

"Christ," Mark said.

Pony's ripple of a laugh echoed in the small space. "*Hasta la vista, kids.*" She took a quick breath and dropped into deeper water.

William felt the clumsy, hurried brush of Mark's feet and legs against his own as he angled down and under the raft to surface on the other side. In a minute or so, he heard their whispered voices and Pony's laugh again.

Now, at midlake, William stopped. He looked out in all directions. His arms appeared murky and green sculling under the water, reminding him of Denny Bell's face in the darkly tinted window of the family SUV as it pulled away after Pony's funeral. Denny Bell knew something. That skeevy, pathetic kid had information. William would talk to him this afternoon, no matter how many people were around.

He looked back to the shore he'd come from. Fond du Lac, the next-to-last house in a loose string of large houses with wide lawns and separated by thick clusters of tall pine trees. And to the left of that, the Bells' A-frame jutted up from the lake like an arrowhead. William turned and swam the breaststroke for a while. He was headed for the Nicelys' house, a white bungalow with a screened-in porch running the full width, close to the water. The houses on this side of the lake were newer, closer together, and more cheerful. There were several boats tied to the Nicelys' pier. A car was parked close beside the house.

He hoped Katherine would be home. He hoped her parents wouldn't be. The parents were okay. He was a lawyer, and she was some big deal in a software company in Boston. But he didn't want their pity, their very formal pity, which was what it would be. *William, darling, we're so terribly . . . and how is your family? How is Jasper? Poor dear man.*

Forget that.

When he could touch bottom, he saw Katherine heading down the path toward him at a near run, wearing a bright yellow sundress and a baseball cap facing sideways so the bill was on one side and her ponytail bobbed through the hole in the cap on the other. A goofy look on anybody else, cute on her. He had always thought of Katherine as a bandy-legged little tomboy; now she was a woman, and he was startled by it, as if time had zipped past without his noticing.

Before he was even out of the water, she threw herself at him and was embracing him and sobbing so hard he almost had to hold her up to keep her from slipping into the water. "Oh God," she kept saying, clutching at him. He held her while she heaved sobs into his shoulder. "I thought you were *her,*" she wailed. "It keeps happening. I see somebody swimming out in the middle of the lake. I hear a car in the driveway. The telephone rings, and I think, *Oh, it'll be Pony,* and then Jesus, it's this hit to the solar plexus all over again when I realize no, of course it isn't. It can't be. She's dead. She drowned. And then I can't believe it all over again."

She pulled away, shielded her eyes with one hand, and punched him in the shoulder with the flat of her other hand. "And what are you doing swimming the lake without a boat, William Carteret? You want us to lose you, too? Goddamn. When I realized it was you—" She pushed his shoulder again. "You *know* better."

The ghost of loss swept through him again. He couldn't remember being alone with Katherine. Where Katherine was, Pony was. He looked about as if he might find her. They were all doing that, it seemed. A personality as strong as Pony's took a while to leave this earth. Up at the house, on the screened porch, a young woman was watching them. Her arms crossed over her chest. He waved.

"She's watching, isn't she?" Katherine lowered her head.

"Who is she?"

"Annie." Katherine sounded weary.

"Annie who?" He had to smile. The drama. Everything about Katherine ran hot or cold, like Pony. Never an in between.

"She is jealous of everything. I had no idea. None at all. Now she'll be pissed about you. About the hug. You wait and see. Any minute she'll be down here." She flopped down on a wooden bench overlooking the lake. "She's jealous of Pony, for Christ's sake. Pony!"

William turned to take another look.

"Don't!" Katherine snapped. "She'll know I'm talking about her."

"Um, Katherine?" William said. "What's—"

"You do know I'm gay, right?"

"Didn't get that memo," he said.

She let out a whoop. "To hear Mom talk, my coming out was the shot heard round the lake." Katherine put her feet up on the fence. She had brown feet and long sinewy toes. "There are some e-mails you need to see." A door slammed. She looked beyond him up toward the house. "Oh, brother."

The girlfriend was heading down the path toward them.

"She'll be loaded for bear," Katherine said.

"Women," William said. "Can't live with 'em, can't—"

"And who might you be?" The girlfriend's voice was high-pitched. She also wore a baseball cap.

"I might be William, from across the lake." She was tall and lanky. "I'm an old friend of the family. And you?"

"Anne Foster." She had a dynamite handshake and was less pretty up close, which had to do with worry lines and a certain nervous, darting quality. "So what would the two of you be all in cahoots about?"

"William is Pony's brother," Katherine said.

"Oh." Anne brightened. "I'm so terribly sorry," she said.

"I need to show William some e-mails, Anne," Katherine said. "We'll be up at the house." She led the way past Anne, back up the path to the house. William followed. Halfway up the path, he turned to see what Anne was doing, and she was right behind him.

Katherine led the way to a small study off the living room where a laptop was set up. "Sit," she told William. Leaning over him, she hit buttons and scrolled down until she had a screen full of e-mails. "Read. They start three weeks before she died."

To: Nicekat@columbia.edu
From: ponycarteret@aol.com
Date: May 17, 2002
Subject: nipple damage

Dr. Nicely,

Andrew has teeth!!! Well, a tooth. And it's a stunner. Whiter than white. God, baby's teeth are almost blue. Eye whites too.

It's trying to get through his upper gum. Ouch! What should I do, kitcat? He fusses like a little madman. He took a bite of my nipple just for relief. His relief.

Tell me more about Anne.

Love,

P

To: ponycarteret@aol.com
From: Nicekat@columbia.edu
Date: May 20, 2002
Subject: RE: nipple damage

Pone,

Rub his little gums with your finger. He'll object at first, but they find it soothing. Worth a try. Two minutes or so. A cold teething ring is good too. I'm sure you have one. NO ASPIRIN! Acetaminophen or ibuprofen for babies if you must. It's called motherhood, so get used to the feeling of wanting to relieve his suffering but being unable. The teeth have to come in. You went through it yourself as a baby. We all did. And look how we turned out.

Anne is first-year med. Princeton undergrad. Comes

from a family of six kids. Raised in Oregon where the family still is. Got as far from them as she could so no one could spy on her. One downside. They don't know. When one of her family visits NYC (and they seem to a lot) I have to hide all my stuff in her apartment. I haven't even met them.

To: Nicekat@columbia.edu
From: ponycarteret@aol.com
Date: May 24, 2002
Subject: [none]

Kitcat,

Big Q for you. You know normal from not normal. So I need to ask you, and this is no joke, is Andrew normal? My doctor says he is, or at least he never said Andrew wasn't. But I depend on you. You'd tell me if there was anything wrong. And I mean it, if you've ever noticed anything, even the slightest of anything, you need to tell me ASAP. Don't call me. I'm not ready to talk yet. Email it, okay?

Love,

Pony

To: ponycarteret@aol.com
From: Nicekat@columbia.edu
Date: May 24, 2002
Subject: RE: [none]

What happened? Why that question? I've never noticed anything remotely wrong in all the times I've seen him, if that helps. What's this all about anyway? Why are you suddenly so worried about Andrew? Did something happen?

How is he otherwise?

K

To: Nicekat@columbia.edu
From: ponycarteret@aol.com
Date: May 28, 2002
Subject: RE: [none]

You have NO IDEA how much that helps.

Yes, something happened, but I can't tell you yet. I need to sort out things. I'm okay. Don't worry about me, please. I'll tell you when I can.

As to Anne, you need to love somebody who's enlightened. You're opting for convenience, I can tell. She probably lives down the hall, right? I hate to think of you playing that stupidass game. Just come right out and tell the family next time they're in town. Don't hide your relationship. It's way too important.

Andrew is like a puppy, to answer your question. Chewing on everything. He's found his own solution to teething. I paint and he chews on my shoes.

P.

To: ponycarteret@aol.com
From: Nicekat@columbia.edu
Date: June 1, 2002
Subject: RE: [none]

Pony,

Don't let him chew your shoes.

I told Anne about your suggestion and she went white as chalk. You're wrong. She would not thank me for it. She would poison me for it.

Annie will be up at the lake this summer. I want you to meet her.

I won't press you about whatever it is that's going on. Just remember, I'm here for you. 24/7.

To: Nicekat@columbia.edu
From: ponycarteret@aol.com
Date: June 7 , 2002
Subject: RE: [none]

Kitcat—I found this in Wikipedia. Does the medical community agree? Or is it just some sicko Wiki commentator?

Most social scientists believe that the primary purpose of the prohibition, often called the incest taboo, is to protect the nuclear family from the consequences of sexual rivalry and jealousy. The taboo is linked with the rule of exogamy (marriage outside of one's kinship group, usually for the purpose of social alliance between groups). Besides reinforcing the incest prohibition, this rule prevents families from becoming culturally ingrown through continuous endogamy (marriage within a kinship group). Highly inbred populations have diminished reproductive capacity and have higher risks for hereditary disorders. Marriage to relatives outside the nuclear family is common in a number of cultures, however, and it is no longer widely believed that the incest taboo serves principally to guard against inbreeding as a negative biological result of incest.

They're new shoes. Fresh out of the box. Don't worry so much.

Love,
Pone

To: ponycarteret@aol.com
From: Nicekat@columbia.edu
Date: June 8, 2002
Subject: RE: [none]

How can I answer this stuff when you're not telling me anything? I don't know. The Wiki passage sounds right in a sociological way. But what does any of it have to do with Andrew? (I'm making good on my promise not to call but it's killing me.) If there's some issue with incest, here's what I know. First, a problem would have shown up by now, in the first year, so you're home free. Second, if you have any reason to suspect a history of incest with the father, don't tell your pediatrician. In today's world of managed care there's no such thing as a secret. Schools, doctors, everybody could have access, believe me. Third, it takes a genetic miracle to create a problem, unlike what most people believe.

I don't know how it could be incest, but that's what you're suggesting, right?

Love,

K

To: Nicekat@columbia.edu
From: ponycarteret@aol.com
Date: June 8, 2002
Subject: RE: [none]

I can tell you next week. Promise. Everything's okay.

P

"That's the end," Katherine said. "Two days before she died. She was worried about the possibility of incest." She crouched beside him and looked up. "Does any of it ring a bell? Does it mean anything at all to you?"

"I'm not the father, if that's what you're thinking." William pushed his chair back sharply and stood. The chair clattered over. Anne was watching from the open door. "What are you looking at?" he said. Anne sighed in disgust and disappeared.

"I wasn't thinking that at all." Katherine got to her feet. "For some reason, she was worried about Andrew's father."

"I have to get going," he said.

"You can't walk home in bare feet, William."

But he left. He felt lousy. He thought of the way Pony had watched him from the turret when he'd first arrived. The whole cat-and-mouse feel that afternoon. He shivered. How could he help remembering what Pony had done that day? Her aggression had been disturbing as hell. *Face it,* he told himself. *She invited you up with seduction in mind, and you blew her off. You rejected her.* He stopped, feeling sick to his stomach. Was that it? *No way,* he thought. *No way. She was just being her usual self.* It had never bothered her to show her body. It was who she was. It was something else.

He strode up the short drive to the lake road, gravel pressing into his bare feet. So then why the big worry about incest? Unless she'd found out something about the father. The guy's mother was his sister. But later for that. Right now he wanted to tackle the Denny thing. That held more promise. Make the kid talk. At the very least, maybe he could find out what Pony had done after he left, and that would be something, wouldn't it?

He walked faster, breathed deeper. He was coming to a bend in the road, heading toward the town beach, past the general store, traffic picking up. People slowed and waved to him. He knew what they must be saying to one another. *Isn't that William Carteret? The one whose sister drowned?* He stopped waving back. Something nagged at him. Something he couldn't put a finger on. He left. She died. He kept seeing the way she'd looked coming up the beach toward him as he backed his car out of the drive.

And again the feeling that he was missing something. The phone call came to mind. The phone call and the photograph of his mother, of their mother. There was more to this. There had to be. Another car came from behind and slowed, then bumped along the shoulder. He turned. Katherine had pulled to the side of the road and stuck her head out the window. "William, get in," she said. "Honest to God, you can't walk all that way barefoot. You'll tear up your feet. Just get in."

She was a lousy driver. She stripped the gears, gave it too much gas, lurched. "I feel awful," she said. "I didn't realize it would upset you so."

"It wasn't you," he said.

"Mind if I sit on your porch awhile when we get to the house?" Katherine said. "I don't feel like going back just yet."

At Fond du Lac, William took the stairs two at a time to Pony's room. Her bed was tightly made—an iron bed, like something you'd see in an army barracks. Narrow, with a thin mattress covered in a pink bedspread tucked in tightly all the way around. In the corner of the room, folded away, was a portable crib for Andrew. Instead of her things on the shelves, Andrew's. His small T-shirts and shorts, little rolled pairs of socks.

The picture of their mother had to be there somewhere. It wasn't downstairs. Nobody had taken it. He checked the drawers of Pony's bureau and her desk, even under her mattress. Nothing. He went through the closet, through the pockets of jackets, and then checked the downstairs again, opening every drawer, pulling the cushions off the couches and chairs. The turret. Maybe the picture was in the turret. It was where she'd been when he arrived at the house that day.

He went to the third floor, the steep extra staircase to the turret. They used the room up there for storage—old boxes, racks of clothes, broken furniture. A new box sat near the wall, marked in Tinker's hand, PONY. William rummaged through it. The toys that had been out were back in the box. He went to the turret window and looked down at his car, over to the shiny green roof of the Bells' A-frame. In the woods between their two houses, something glinted in the sun and was gone. But there was nothing metal out there. He watched. And then he caught a glimpse of it again, and of something else, of a person.

He swung back downstairs, holding the rails to take the stairs two, three, at a time, and ran out across the lawn to the strip of woods separating the two houses. He figured he'd seen the flash thirty or forty feet into the woods. He stood quietly, listening. He was rewarded by a shifting, something creaking somewhere overhead. He followed the sound. At first he couldn't see anything, but then he made out a plywood platform with crude sides built in a sugar maple maybe ten or twelve feet off the ground. "Hey," he said. "Hey. I know you're up there."

Denny Bell's face appeared over the edge of the board. "I'm not doing anything," Denny said.

"Is that a tree house?" William asked.

"It's a blind," Denny said.

"Blind," William repeated. "What are you hunting?" The kid was pathetic. There was less than half an acre between the two houses.

"Deer," Denny said.

"Give me a break. I want to talk to you," William said.

"I'm busy."

"It looks like this thing is on our land." William stood directly under the blind and looked around. "Sure it is. The boundary isn't even close. Does your dad know about this?" William watched as Denny grabbed on to a limb, pulled himself out of the blind, and shinnied down the tree to the ground. He was barefoot, the ratty hem of his jeans hanging in limp folds at his ankles.

"This is our land," Denny said.

William laughed. "No, it isn't." He pointed into the woods, toward the Bells' property. "Your line is that stone wall over there."

"I can take it down," Denny said.

"You were watching my little sister go skinny-dipping the day she died, weren't you?"

"No."

"Sure you were. What normal kid your age wouldn't?" William gave the boy a gentle shove.

The boy reared back. "I'd never go skinny-dipping with *my* sister."

"So you *did* see."

Denny hiked his jeans.

"You like it up here?" William asked.

"It sucks," Denny said.

"Where's home for you guys, anyway?" William knew it was Massachusetts somewhere but wasn't sure where.

"Worcester," Denny said.

"Holy Cross is in Worcester, right?"

Denny shrugged.

"I used to hate it up here when I was your age," William said. Instinct told him to take it slow or he'd blow the whole thing. "I was bored out of my skull up here. I wanted to stay home in the summer and do stuff with my friends."

"You got that right. No place to go boarding. Back home I do rail slides at the Civic Center every night."

"Yeah?" William said. "You can do that?"

"Sure." Denny showed William with his hand how he took the stairs on a skateboard, crossed a plaza, hopped the railing down to a lower plaza. "It's easy," he said with a shrug. "When I get back home, I'll be fucking rusty."

"It'll come back, trust me," William said. He let the silence settle over them. He was determined to get information out of Denny but didn't want to scare him off. "You know where the Cushmans live?" he asked after a while.

"Next camp down, right? They got that German shepherd," Denny said.

William pointed with his thumb to the next house down. "There was a woman living in that house when I was about your age. She used to go in swimming every morning." He laughed. "My mom thought I was a real Boy Scout because I started getting up early. But what I did was, I got up at five-thirty because the woman over there went in swimming buck naked. Oh, man," he said, remembering. "She was a little fat, but she looked good to me."

"Yeah?" Denny said, sitting up. "How close could you get?"

"Closer than that tree house of yours," William said.

"Like what?"

"From here to the door."

"No shit," Denny said.

"She'd parade around before she went in."

"Like how?"

"She'd stretch, touch her toes bent over."

"Oh, man." Denny slapped his forehead. "Did she have big tits?"

"Biggest I ever saw," William said. "And you know what she did one day?"

"What?" Denny's eyes were huge.

"I used to hide down near the water. There's a boathouse with a dock over there, and I hid behind the boathouse. And she'd come down and go right out on the dock, do her thing, then sit down and slide into the water. And then she'd swim, and then she'd come back, and that was the best part, because she'd come up the ladder and back down the dock. Full-frontal."

"She have a towel?"

"Nope."

"Shit," Denny said. "So what happened? That day you said something happened."

"This one morning at the end of the summer, she comes out of the water as usual, but this time she doesn't go back toward her house, she comes right up to the boathouse and says, 'Is that you back there, William Carteret?' "

"No way!" Denny slapped his forehead. "Freakin' no way. What did you do?"

"I said, 'Yes, ma'am, it is.' And she says, 'Well, come on out of there and show yourself.' And so I did. And she's just standing there in front of me, dripping wet and starkers. Nothing but a smile. She was maybe as far from me as I am from you right now. So we're right up close. She just smiles, you know? She puts out her hands like she wants me to come closer. She beckons."

"Oh, man," Denny said.

"She hugged me."

"No way!" Denny said.

"Way," William said.

Denny slapped his forehead again and stamped his feet. "What did you do?"

"Let's just say I was speechless," William said. "She got her towel. She went back to her house."

"That's *all*?" Denny said. "She just hugs you?"

"It was plenty," William said.

"You should have *fucked* her!" Denny said. "She was asking for it."

"Oh?" William said. "You know that?"

"Sure," Denny said. "That's what I would have done."

William paused for a few beats. "The reason I'm telling you this is because it's normal to watch women. You don't have to be afraid to tell me. I swear. You were watching my sister that day, weren't you?"

"Yeah," Denny blurted out. He made a sour face, looked away. "I mean no."

"All I want to know is what Pony did after I left."

Denny looked away. "I wouldn't know."

"Why are you so scared?"

"I'm not scared of anything," Denny said.

William pointed in the direction of the tree house. "My father isn't going to like it that you guys built a tree house in one of our trees."

" 'Guys'? It was just me. My dad doesn't even know."

"You had it a long time?"

"My dad thinks I should be up at the club playing tennis with all those faggoty kids. He comes up here on weekends, and it's always, 'So, Dennis, how's the social scene going?' I could hurl."

"I know where you're coming from," William said.

"It was an accident," Denny said. "Isn't that what they're saying about her? That's what the paper said. It was an accidental drowning."

"That's right, but accidents don't happen in a vacuum. Something happens to cause an accident. You know, like somebody steps off a curb and a car comes tearing by. Circumstance, accident, sure, but there are events leading up to it. I just want to know what those were. Maybe she fell and hit her head. Or maybe she went down to the anchor a couple of times before her hair snagged. I don't know. I want to know what happened in the last five minutes of my sister's life. Did she go in and out of the water a couple of times? Did she play with the baby? Did she sing to him? Is that so much to ask?"

Denny pushed the hair off his face for the hundredth time. "Sorry, man," he said.

"I think you're scared."

"I'm scared of nothing."

Denny turned to watch as Katherine approached along the path through the woods.

"Hi Denny," she said when she reached them.

"You know my friend Katherine here? Lives across the lake? Katherine was my sister's best friend. I saw you outside that day," William said. "I know you were out here the day Pony died. I saw you."

Denny thrust his hands into his pockets.

"We'll be on our way as soon as you tell me what my sister did on the day she died. It's not so much to ask. It's nothing to ask. And I think you're being a little prick to hold out on us this way."

The kid was so thin his ribs were perfectly visible. You could practically see his heart beating hundreds of times a minute.

"William," Katherine said. "He's just a kid."

"A kid who's holding out on us."

"It was an accident. The cops said." Denny hugged his skinny chest and gripped his elbows.

"I only want to know what she did, what you saw," William said.

"Nothing happened, okay?"

"You've got 'liar' written all over you."

"I think my parents are home. I heard a car."

"Good," William said. "I can talk to them about the tree house."

"He never even *touched* her."

William wasn't sure he'd heard right. "What did you say? Who never touched her?" He approached.

"Guy was an asshole," Denny said with a quick glance at Katherine.

"*What* guy?" William came close to grabbing the kid by the throat. "What are you telling us? There was a guy? Why didn't you tell anybody this before? What is the matter with you?"

Denny backed away. Katherine was right behind William. She elbowed him hard in the side. "Denny," she said. She shot William a warning glance and spoke to Denny: "Look at me." The kid turned his face toward her, and she took his chin in her hand. "This is really important. And it's okay. You didn't do anything wrong. But we need to know everything that happened."

"I wasn't watching her because she was naked," Denny said sullenly to William. "I was just watching her. I had nothing better to do. That's all. Anyway, I couldn't see anything. She was in the water most of the time."

William tried to control his voice. "Okay. And a guy was there."

"No, that was later. She did laps or something." Denny's head was lowered, his face obscured by his hair. He was picking at his thumb. He looked up at William, waved a finger back and forth. "You know, out to the float, back to the shore. Boy, could she swim. Every time she'd come to shore, she'd, like walk on her elbows in the shallow part and talk to the baby from the water, and then she'd go back out and swim to the raft."

William could picture it. His little sister, her hair streaming behind, her smile. The sweetness of it.

"It was nice," Denny said.

"It must have been, Denny," Katherine said. "I'm glad you told us that. And Andrew was okay during this?"

Denny shrugged and sat back. "I guess," he said. "I mean, yeah, actually. Every time she came close, he'd kind of shake the playpen." He shook his fists as Andrew must have. "I stopped watching." He gave William a quick look and then concentrated again on picking at his thumb, which was red and raw-looking. "Well, I did. I don't care if you believe me or not. I came inside, and it was later I hear a car door slam over here and a radio going. I figured it was you, but there's this guy on the grass."

William's heart beat faster. "Who?"

"How am I supposed to know?"

"What did he look like?" William had to struggle to keep his voice level.

"He had on a blue shirt, I remember. Jeans, maybe. Baseball cap. I was pretty far away."

"Did she know him?"

"I don't know!" Denny heaved a big sigh. "How am I supposed to know all this?"

By the way she acted, idiot, William thought. "No way you could." He kept his voice calm. "So, the guy is on the grass and—"

"She waves at him." Denny waved a hand, the sort of wave a child gives going bye-bye. "Yup. She waved at him."

"Where was she?"

"In the water, by the raft." Denny met William's eyes.

William had to keep reminding himself that the only way to the truth was to keep a lid on it. "She waved at him. So it sounds like she knew him, then."

"Oh yeah," Denny said. "Maybe. She used to wave at me sometimes." He grinned at Katherine.

"You're doing fine, Denny," Katherine said. "Pony gave the man a wave. Good."

Denny, squinting, twisted his mouth to the side, trying to remember. "He left the car radio going. And it was windy, like, there was all this noise and shit in the trees. I thought she was, like, laughing. He starts doing this stupid bullfighter thing with her towel." Denny held his hands to the side, tucked his feet together, and raised his chin in imitation of the way a matador would wave a cape. The boy had grace.

"What time was this?" William asked.

"Sheesh." Danny seemed to deflate again and opened his arms wide. "How should I know?"

116

"Approximately," William said.

Katherine patted Denny as if to say, *Don't worry about him, he's just being dense.*

"I don't have to talk to you," Denny said

"You're right, Denny," Katherine said. "You don't, but it helps us so much to hear all this. Pony Carteret was my best friend. I knew her all my life. I'm so grateful that you saw anything at all and that you're willing to tell us. Every little bit of information is like a gift."

"Tell *him* that," Denny said.

"She was his sister. He's upset. Not at you, though." Katherine gave William a look Denny couldn't see that said, *Behave yourself.* She smiled at Denny. "You were telling us—Well, let me make sure I understand. The way I understand it is that Pony was in the water, swimming in the nude, and this man was onshore and seemed to be teasing her with the towel. Is that right? That's what it sounds like, like he was being funny."

Denny nodded but seemed uncertain. "Yeah. But maybe she was, like, telling him to cut the shit or whatever. She was in close to shore like she was doing with the kid, you know, on her elbows. I couldn't hear what she was saying, but hey. He was being a jerk. I would never have done that."

William felt the wrenching pull of grief, a stone on his heart. He could see it all too clearly. The matador. Pony scared. Or angry. It took a lot to scare Pony.

"Did he hurt her?" William asked. He couldn't stand not to know.

Katherine took William's hand, held it tight. *Courage,* she seemed to be saying.

Denny shook his head. "No. He never touched her. But he touched the kid. He picks up the kid." Denny held his arms straight out. "Like the kid's got a stinky diaper. And he says, 'Ha ha,' like that, not laughing but saying the words. And then she just does this weird thing, like that was what made me think it was okay again.

117

Like that woman you saw, that Mrs. Cushman, you know? She stands up in the water, and she's, you know, she's—"

"Yes?" Katherine said. "Naked."

"She's doing that thing with her hands, like *Come on in*." Denny imitated the way Pony must have beckoned the guy into the water with both hands to get him away from Andrew. "And the guy puts the kid down, strips down to his jockeys, and goes in the lake." Denny demonstrated someone on tiptoes, arms up, in cold water. "But he goes in like this. Like some girl who doesn't want to get her pussy wet."

"Hey," William said.

Denny looked at Katherine. "Sorry," he said.

"It's okay. Then what?"

"They get out to the raft. Or *he* gets out to the raft. I couldn't see her after that. The trees were in the way. They're blowing all over, and his radio in the car is still going. I don't know."

"Randy Martine needs to know all this," Katherine said to William.

"Aw, man," Denny said. "You promised."

"I didn't promise," William said. "How close were you? Where were you when this was going on?"

"In my—" Denny swung his head to one side. "You know."

"Tree house."

"What are you so worried about, Denny?" Katherine asked. "You're only telling what you saw."

"He's out on the raft, and where is she?" William said.

"I don't know. I told you. Maybe she was under it. He was talking to her, so she was somewhere."

"And then what?"

"Then nothing. The next thing I see is he's swimming back in. He's getting dressed."

"Does he mess with the baby?"

"No." Denny buried his head in his hands.

"What, Denny?" Katherine asked.

"Nothing."

"Did it occur to you Pony was in trouble out there?"

The kid shook his head.

"And you didn't tell the police any of this because . . . ?"

"It was an accident, man. I would have, but the cops said it was an accident. And I figure the cops know."

"And because you were frightened," Katherine said.

William used the phone in the kitchen to call Randy Martine at home. Randy arrived at the house in a squad car with the lights rolling, just ahead of Anita and Dennis Senior, who came in looking bewildered and then immediately assumed Denny had done something to cause the police to be there. Dennis *père* was a guy whose back was too long, as if his spine had grown too fast for the front of him, folding him forward over his large stomach. A guy with hair in his ears and a loud voice that soon had the rest of them talking too loud. "What the hell?" he said when he walked in. Katherine jumped to her feet, introduced herself, and told the Bells about the man Denny had seen at the Carterets' house the day Pony died.

They all crowded around the small kitchen with its depressing red, yellow, and green Tiffany light fixture casting a weak stained light over everything. William and Katherine sat on the countertops and the Bells at the kitchen table with Randy, who walked Denny through the whole thing again.

"What time?" Randy asked.

"Six?" Denny asked back.

"Did you see the car? The license?"

"Nope," Denny said.

"That's okay, Denny," Randy said. "Can you describe the man? Anything at all."

Denny looked at William, then at his father. "Average size, I guess."

"And what's that?"

"Like him." Denny swung his head in his father's direction.

"So," Randy said. "About six feet tall?"

"I'm six-one, son," said Dennis *père*. William had a thing about that, fathers addressing their sons as "son." It got under his skin, and he didn't know why.

"Age?" Randy asked Denny.

Again Denny looked at the men. "Like you, I guess. Like him." He indicated William.

"So in his thirties, you think."

"I guess."

"Were you able to see his face?"

Denny shrugged. "A little."

"You did?" William said. "You never told us."

"Can you identify him?" Randy asked.

"He had on a baseball cap. I'm not sure."

"Any mark on that cap?"

"I couldn't tell." Denny rolled his eyes.

"What was he wearing?"

"Jeans. Blue shirt."

"Anything else you can add?"

"He saw me," Denny said.

"Oh, dear God," Anita said.

"When?" Randy asked. William liked the way Randy was doing this, firing questions at the kid, getting more out of him.

"I was up in the, you know, blind and all. He must have gone in the house. I can't be sure. He was near where the baby was, and he saw me. He looked right at me."

"Did he say anything?"

"He didn't need to."

"What do you mean?" Anita shrieked.

Denny imitated the man. He stood with his feet planted, one hand on his hip, jabbing the air with a finger. Menacing as hell.

"Would you recognize him?" Randy asked.

"Maybe."

"Did he ever touch Pony?" Randy asked Denny. "That you saw."

Denny shook his head. "I wish I'd gone over there," he said, and looked at William and Katherine, appealing to them.

"Damn good thing you didn't, son," Dennis Senior said, and William could only stare at the man. Did he know what he was saying?

Chapter 8

Mira

Mira dyed the tips of her hair from electric blue to black.

She bought black lipstick.

She canceled Tucson.

She was looking at the brochure for the workshop in Tucson she would not attend. The brochure showed a desert garden, a small swimming pool, and an adobe house in the background. She was to get free room and board in return for a few workshops for the other five or six "guests," who would, Mira guessed, be middle-aged women, artsy suburban types, and perhaps one or two men. Mira's credentials were only a shade better than the students'—publication in a small-circulation literary magazine, a year as adjunct faculty at the University of Hartford, and one semester substituting as a creative writing teacher for someone who'd quit at the last minute.

How could she go to something like that? She couldn't concentrate anymore. She couldn't write. She couldn't even read. She'd get through half a page in a book and have no memory of what she'd read. She needed to keep moving, find ways to kill time.

She was leaning on the balcony rail of her apartment watching Sheila, the woman who lived on the first floor. Sheila had three mixed-breed dogs. She walked home from work twice a day to escort them the fifteen feet across the driveway to the backyard, where they peed burns in the grass in a pattern of large pale dots. Mira hadn't paid such close attention to Sheila until lately, until she herself was at home. She marveled at the way Sheila held to a routine. How did people get to that? Mira had a hard time doing anything twice. Right now, seeing the top of Sheila's square gray head, Mira wanted to drop something on her. An egg, perhaps. Get her to react. Change her trajectory.

Mira went back inside and checked the clock. She put on makeup. She'd taken to lining her eyes in black, a thick smudge of it all around. And whitening her already white skin with powder. Like Isak Dinesen. Like Joyce Carol Oates. Those women knew the power of the image. She looked into her blank face, round, like a clock with dark eyes at two and ten, red mouth at six. She parted her cropped hair. Black as spades but with auburn roots, like a woolly bear's. Nobody else had that. She would become just like Minerva one day. Eccentric as hell. She was sure of it.

The telephone rang, and she let the machine take it in case it was Tinker again, and it was. She'd been calling every few days for the past couple of weeks. Tinker sounded bone-weary. "Do you know where William is, Mira? Have you heard anything? We should all reach out to one another. But how can we? William isn't picking up. Where is he? We need to do something for Daddy's birthday. This year more than any other. We need to show solidarity. Isabel will be crushed if we don't." Tinker paused and drew in a long breath. "Mira, I know you're there. Pick up, dammit." Big sigh. "Okay, whatever. Look, I need your help. Daddy wants us to empty out Pony's apartment, and I'm not doing it alone."

Mira called Keith Brink. It had been three weeks since that first time at the Readers' Feast. He'd taken to calling her every few days, and they'd talk. He'd say, "Let's get together," and sometimes she'd say okay and come up with a plan. One time she'd suggested they take a tour of the Harriet Beecher Stowe house, which he'd claimed to enjoy although he'd never read *Uncle Tom's Cabin*, and how could anybody enjoy the house without that? Another time she'd invited him for a walk around the West Hartford reservoir. She liked being seen with him. She liked how they looked together, how people noticed his swagger and his cowboy hat. She still couldn't read him, though. That was the intriguing thing, the challenge. On that walk around the reservoir, he'd told her a joke. It was about two guys in the woods when a grizzly bear attacks. "I don't have to outrun the bear," one of them says in the punch line. "I'd only have to outrun you."

It was the kind of joke that made you laugh and then slap a hand over your mouth because it was so mean. "You have a sardonic sense of humor," she'd said, and he'd colored visibly, darkening as if she'd insulted or criticized him. It was possible he didn't know what the word meant, but then neither did she, not really; she wouldn't have been able to define it exactly, for example. The word had just slipped out the way words sometimes did, and she was pretty sure "sardonic" was close. Later she'd looked it up, and sure enough, it meant mocking, derisive, which wasn't necessarily a bad thing.

And sometimes she had this sneaking suspicion he felt sorry for her. *Poor little Mira*, he'd said more than once at something she'd told him. That always gave her pause, as if he saw something pitiable in her beyond just her suffering over Pony's death. She didn't like it, but she didn't correct it either. Let him go ahead and feel sorry for her if that was what he needed to do.

She thought it was time to ratchet things up a notch.

He didn't pick up at first. Well, of course not; it was a workday. But then he did. "Why are you at home today?" she asked without introducing herself. But she said it softly, not in a harsh way.

"Job site's not ready. They lost electricity."

"I'm coming over," she said.

He hesitated, probably because she hadn't taken the lead before. This was new. "My place isn't much," he said.

124

"I want to see it." It had occurred to her that he might be married or have a girlfriend. That was always a possibility with any guy who acted eager but also held himself a little at bay the way Keith did.

"Suit yourself," he said.

As she drove over, she thought again how she wasn't his type at all. He was midwestern, a Republican, probably a Rush Limbaugh listener to boot. His type was those women you saw in bars doing the Texas two-step or whatever it was called, women with teased hair and tight jeans. Women who were tougher-looking than Mira. And yet he dug her act; there was no question about that at all.

His motel was a large U-shaped structure with navy blue canopies over the windows. He'd been watching for her, and he opened the door before she was even out of the car. He stood there grinning, with his arms open as she approached. She poked him in the stomach lightly, instead of accepting the hug. He was a little soft there, the start of a gut. She slipped past him into the room, which was well lit and large. "This is nice," she said. "What do you mean, 'not much'?"

"It's not what you're used to," he said.

"And what would that be?" She wanted him to say it out loud.

"Just making conversation," he said.

She looked around the room. "So where's Pony's painting?"

"Out," he said.

Mira laughed. "Like out for a stroll? What do you mean it's out?"

"Being framed." He had an off-kilter smile, and there was something she'd been wanting to find out about his face. "Stand in the light," she said. He allowed himself to be taken by the hand and drawn to the window. "Okay, now." She covered half his face with her hand and looked at the half that was still exposed. Keith's left side had not one thread of emotion. It was blank. She switched to cover the other side and reared back. "Wow," she said. His right side was full to overflowing. A whole storm of a face. Should she tell him? He might be vain about his looks. He could be anything. "Pony taught me that," she said. "She did a series in art school where she would paint faces. Two left sides making up one portrait. Two rights the other. Some people have such different halves and you wouldn't even know they were the same person. People with two different faces are more interesting, Pony said. Like you." She ran her fingers down his cheek. She hadn't intended to do that, but she loved the feel of sharp stubble where a guy's sideburns end.

He took her hand and pressed it to his chest. With his other hand, he touched her eyelid. "Tit for tat," he said, peering into her eye.

"It's called a coloboma." She was used to explaining the condition that gave her pupil the shape of a keyhole.

"Coloboma," he repeated, and kissed her eyelid. In his voice, the word felt heavy and sensual.

"My ophthalmologist said it has no effect on my vision."

"How would he know?"

She'd wondered that herself, wondered if in fact she did see the world differently. She let Keith look closely. He tipped her head back for better light. His touch was light on her chin. He gently raised the eyelid to see it better. The gesture felt incredibly intimate.

"It's Greek for 'mutilated,' " she said.

"Aw," he said, and she felt his pity rain down again. This time she didn't let it go. She was sensitive about her eye.

"I want to drive up to the lake," she said.

He seemed to stop breathing, to freeze in place.

"What's the matter?" she asked.

"You're here five minutes and you want to leave. Are you fucking with me?"

"Say *what*?" She stepped away. "Where did *that* come from?"

"I can't just take off like you can. I have to work."

She didn't think that was it at all. He didn't like to be taken by surprise and he liked being the one in charge. Fine. "Who said anything about overnight? It's a little over an hour each way. I'd like to go up there."

He colored visibly and forced a smile. "Can't a guy make a joke around you?"

She studied him a moment and poked him gently in the stomach again. "Ha-ha," she said.

Keith drove fast, way over the speed limit. He really opened it up after Springfield, on 91. He wasn't a car-talker. Not many guys were. So she watched the countryside go by outside her window. This was something to do. Anything was better than sitting in her apartment and watching the neighbors.

It was past twilight when they arrived. All around the lake, lights glittered like an uneven string of tiny jewels. Mira was glad not to have to face the place in broad daylight. It was easier this way. She hadn't been there since Pony died. She walked down to the water. Keith was behind her.

"So that's it?" he asked.

"That's it," she said. It was still light enough to see the raft on the water.

"Lots of houses out there," he said. "I had the impression this was more secluded."

"It is and it isn't. The houses are all on the lake. Outside of that, nothing."

He walked up and down the beach, looking around. "What about the people over there? In that house?" He was pointing to the Bells' house.

"The Bells," she said.

"She's the one who heard the baby, right?"

"Right."

"Why did your brother leave that day?"

"I don't know."

"Why did he come up here in the first place?"

"Stop it," she said. "You're asking things I don't know the answers to. I hate that."

"But this is where it happened," he said. "Anybody would be curious."

"I need to see the raft," she said. "You want to come?"

He shook his head. "Rather not, actually."

She undressed on the beach and went into the water in her underwear. She swam quickly to the raft and went up the ladder. Underneath, the barrels clanged. She was trying to imagine what it had been like for Pony that day. The water now was warm, like the air. But that hadn't been the case the day Pony died. It had been June still, and the water would have been cold. Mira shivered at the thought, but no matter how hard she thought about Pony, no matter how she tried to feel it, Pony's death still hung separately. She felt as though she were wrapped in gauze and Pony's death was just outside it, waiting for her. Even here, just where she died. Keith was watching her from the shore, pacing. He checked his watch. *Bored*, she thought. *Not a guy to come in swimming.* She swam back and used the key under the shutter to let them into the house.

Once inside, Keith went from room to room, looking at everything. He put on his glasses to see the photographs on the walls better. She was touched again by his interest. He got close, squinting and running his fingers over them. He must have been looking for her in them the way her other boyfriends did, she thought. Trying to pick her out in all those scenes down at the beach, the picnics, wondering what she'd looked like as a kid. Was she fat or thin, happy or sad. He took one from the wall and brought it closer to the light. "Oh, man." He held it close and studied it. He ran his index finger over it. It was a shot of the whole family sitting on the steps to the porch at Fond du Lac. "Is this your mother?" he asked.

She looked over his shoulder. "Yes." In the picture, her mother sat in the front middle of the group, an arm around Pony on one side and Mira on the other. Her hair was pulled back, and she was smiling.

"Where was she born?"

"My mom? Why do you want to know?"

"She looks Scandinavian or something. She's so blond."

"California," she said.

"It's a big state."

Mira shrugged. "Some small town up north is all I know."

"What's with you people?" he asked with a laugh.

"Excuse me?" she said. That one had come out of left field.

He twisted around to see her and squeezed her hand. "Most people know where their mothers were born."

"Where was yours born?"

"Chicago," he said.

"It's a big city. What street?"

He smiled. "Touché."

She brought out an album. Some of the photos were in their slots, but most were loose. Her mother used to keep them organized. She handed him the album and sat down in the chair across from him. She didn't want to see the photos, especially the recent ones of Pony when Pony had no idea she had only eight months to live, or three weeks, whatever. It freaked her out too much. He looked quickly through the loose pictures and then went page by page through the older ones. He held up the album. "That's you, right?"

The picture had been taken at one of the summer slumber parties. She was about eleven. There were five or six girls. Their mother always made them use the sleeping porch for slumber parties, so she'd hear if somebody got up in the middle of the night with the bright idea to go swimming. Their mother was petrified of the water. She was always on high alert during those things. They'd arranged their sleeping bags all in a circle, like the spokes of a wheel, heads in the middle. They were going around from one to the next, telling which boys they liked, and then—Mira thought it was because Katherine Nicely's grandfather had shot himself in the head the winter before—Pony said they should go around the circle and tell how they thought they were going to die. Tinker got all bent out of shape over it. She kept saying, "Don't ever!" and what bad luck it was. She said they'd regret it one day, wanting to die a certain way, and didn't any of them know what a self-fulfilling prophecy was? Mira had told her that was the whole point, because everybody dies, so why not come up with a good end and then hope it actually *did* turn out to be a self-fulfilling prophecy. Like, duh! And Katherine Nicely, who was light-years ahead of them all even then, had said nobody was wishing to spend their last days in hospice care, in case Tinker hadn't noticed. "And anyway," she told Tinker in the kindest way, "it's not how you *want* to die, because nobody wants to die. It's how you *expect* to die. There's a difference. It has to do with the way you live." So it was about living, not dying. Katherine said her older sister had had to write her own obituary for an English class at Skidmore, that it was a very in thing to do in college courses. Tinker still wouldn't do it. She said they were all dooming themselves.

Mira remembered looking for the most flamboyant and shocking death she could conjure up. Finally she said she expected to die like Isadora Duncan, with her scarf caught around the wheel of a moving car, or shot by a jealous wife. And what had Pony said? Mira studied the picture in the album Keith was holding and tried to remember. Pony's hair bushed out around her face. Her smile was electric, huge. Pony was all life. What could she possibly have said?

Keith continued to look through the pictures. He was an evolved man, in some ways. Or trying to evolve. Like he knew it was important to be sensitive, but he didn't have it down yet. She found that endearing. He'd slip sometimes, like that question about her mother, and then realize he'd been out of line and do something to recant, even if it was clumsy. She got up and went to the bathroom. Looked at herself in the mirror. She looked great. Her skin was perfect, her eyes wide, her lips full. She could be beautiful sometimes. And right now she had it in spades. She went out to the porch and sat on the wicker sofa, her feet propped up on the rail, listening to the peepers and other far-off sounds that traveled over the water. After a time Keith came outside and sat beside her. "You're lucky," he said.

"How's that?" she asked.

"All this. A nice family. You're just lucky." He took her hand and brought it to his lips. She wanted to feel something. She was desperate to feel something, and yet she didn't. The numbness of grief, she supposed.

"Somebody's out there," he said. "Did you see?"

"Where?"

"Over there."

She could see someone in a white shirt near the edge of the woods, almost at the lawn. "It's probably one of the Bell kids. Those kids are up half the night. Don't worry about it."

"Where do you keep your flashlights?"

"In the front closet," she said.

Keith went inside and came right out again with the biggest light they had. He was down the steps of the porch and heading toward whoever it was. "Hey," he shouted, the beam seeking the person out. "You!"

Mira stood, astonished. Whoever it was ran off. She didn't know if it was one of the Bells or not, but she never would have done what Keith had done.

"You've been through too much, Mira," he said when he came back. "Your whole family has. You don't need somebody gawking at you in the dark. What if it was a Peeping Tom?"

She had to laugh.

"I'm serious."

"I really think it was just the kid from next door. What did you say to him?"

"He ran off. Let's get going."

Well, she thought, *maybe what he did was nice.* Maybe she did like the feeling of being taken care of, a feeling she wasn't exactly used to.

He took all the back roads too fast as they headed for the highway, skidding around corners and throwing up gravel. Mira said nothing. And once on the highway, Keith again opened it up. They were doing eighty-five, sometimes ninety. He was hunched over the wheel at first, and then he leaned back and drove with one hand, the other looped behind himself over the seat back. She thought it was possible he'd drive the car through a guardrail or off a bridge and they'd plunge hundreds of feet. But she didn't tell him to slow down. She considered the possibility of being dead. She thought of Pony as frozen in time. Pony was dead, the first of them to die. Crossed over, some people called that, and Mira knew what they meant. Not that Pony had stopped living but that she'd gone somewhere Mira couldn't follow.

Chapter 9

Tinker

Tinker arrived at Pony's apartment with a sense of purpose. She let herself in and stood in the gloom, looking around. She was ready to work, ready to do what she did best, bring order to this corner of the family's life, and in so doing, find relief for herself and for them. A fine veneer of dust had settled over everything in the month since Pony died. The last time Tinker had been here, she'd come to pick out something for Pony to wear.

She'd come while Isabel was in school, but she'd had to bring Andrew along. She'd intended to get in and out quickly. She'd set Andrew down and bolted across the living room, through the bedroom, and opened Pony's closet door. But then she'd dropped to her knees in the darkness of Pony's closet, overwhelmed by the scent of her youngest sister. When she had recovered, she'd sorted among the mishmash of shoes and purses and art supplies stored in shoe boxes stacked at the back of Pony's closet, looking at everything. Ten wide, the shoe boxes said, a detail Tinker hadn't known. Large feet for a woman. Larger than Tinker's own, which were narrow and only seven and a half. It had given her a rush of guilty delight to learn that in one area of femininity, she reigned. She'd tried on Pony's shoes and swam in them. She'd clopped around the place like a little girl playing dress-up. Pony and her big feet.

Tinker had slid the wire hangers across the rack one by one, seeing all of Pony's familiar clothes from years and years. Pony never threw anything out. There were men's shirts she used to paint in, old sundresses from when she was in high school, and, way at the back, a Mexican peasant blouse with the tag still attached. Tinker had held it up. It was beautiful and a good color for her, turquoise with bright embroidery. It was loose on her, too. She'd turned this way and that in the mirror, then took it off and stuffed it into her purse. At that very moment, the blouse was at the back of her closet at home. She liked thinking about it. Liked imagining the day she would wear it. She'd need to wait, of course.

Finally, she'd found an electric-green dress at the back of Pony's closet, still in its plastic dry cleaner's bag, which was what she'd dropped off at Becker's and then worried that it was too shiny, too dressy, too promlike.

It had been on her mind so much after that—waking her at night, even—so that before anyone arrived at Becker's, she had gone into the viewing area. She'd run her hands over the casket, over the shiny hardware, and then looked down. Pony was beautiful. Her color was high, her lips full. She was serene. To Tinker's relief, the dress had been a calmer green than she remembered, a fabric not so shiny as she'd thought. She'd tugged the neckline a bit and was surprised to find the dress wouldn't move, as if it had been glued to Pony's skin, an idea that made her shiver.

Now she stood again in Pony's living room and took in the place. On her way over, she had picked up a dozen boxes at U-Haul and some rolls of tape, which she dumped on the floor. She went about, opening shades to let in the light, opening windows, closet doors and kitchen cupboards, drawers of furniture. She took inventory.

The apartment was very small. The living room held only a brown couch, a coffee table, and a wooden chair. A small table and a high chair sat against the wall where Pony must have taken her meals. Pony had piled her belongings here and there so that it seemed everything she owned showed. A stack of books was in the corner. Portfolios of her sketches leaned against the wall next to a stack of shoe boxes holding the things most people kept in drawers—Scotch tape and pens, maps and receipts. In the bedroom, the bureau was empty, but on top of it were Pony's clothes, folded in stacks. Her thong panties, her brassieres, her T-shirts.

Tinker still felt numb to Pony's death. She was able to remember both the wake and the funeral in detail but without feeling grief. She knew it was peculiar, not something she could mention to anyone, especially not Mark. And what she certainly couldn't tell Mark was that her grief was really for her father. She felt his agony far worse than her own. Just last weekend she'd gone to his house and noticed the neglect. The grass was too long. The rosebushes were already lacy with Japanese beetles.

She'd gotten out of the car and gone around back. He was sitting on the stone bench in his bathrobe, in the middle of the afternoon. He'd looked so broken. She was struck by how thin his legs were, white as fish bones. Overnight he'd become an old man. It had been like opening a hotel room door on something you shouldn't see. Shameful in a way she couldn't explain. Tears had welled in her eyes at the sight of him, at the job ahead of her, getting him dressed, seeing to it that he ate something. But when he'd noticed her, oh, the transformation in him. The sudden taking over. Himself again, on his feet, striding toward her and the kids as if everything was normal. She wished he'd just give in and let her take care of him the way she wanted to.

She made her way to Pony's cramped bathroom. The toothbrush still lay on the sink, welded to the white enamel by a spill of once watery blue toothpaste. Pony's long dark red hairs were stuck to the sink. Her medicine cabinet was bare except for Band-Aids and Tampax, a roll of dental floss, some scrunchies, and a rectal thermometer for the baby. Pony apparently used no makeup, took no pills. A small bar of soap sat in a dish. Tinker held it to her nose and sniffed. Ivory. She threw back the shower curtain. The tub was full of colorful rubber toys. The word "unsanitary" crossed her mind. She would have to throw out the toys.

She turned back to the sink and looked at her reflection in the mirror. *That awful curtain of hair, dear*, her mother used to say to her. *It hides your beautiful eyes.* And so Tinker pulled it away and off her face and secured it with one of Pony's scrunchies, a great frizzed knot on top of her head. She turned slightly to the right, leaned in to see her eyes more closely. They were gray and large, and they sloped downward at the outside edges, like a puppy's. She undid her hair again, twisted it at the nape of her neck. Was that more flattering? She had no idea. She could try it both ways and not see the difference, and yet her mother used to say to her unexpectedly, *How nice you look today, dear*, and Tinker would never know what it was she had done. She still didn't know. Not that it mattered. The whole reason women made themselves attractive was for men, i.e., for sex, which was something she didn't need to worry about. She and Mark made love four or five mornings a week. Mark would reach for her, lifting her gown, and she was always pure compliance. She would take him in her hand and feel satisfaction at the size of him, the strength, and at her own power to do this. The act itself was automatic and satisfying not so much for the sex, since she rarely had orgasms, but for her wonder at being so needed, at her ability to satisfy her husband blindly, unconsciously, without coquetry or complication. Their mornings, she believed, were what bound them, not just her and Mark but the three of them, and now Andrew, too.

She thought with satisfaction about how she'd handled Donna, the secretary at Mark's office. Were they still called secretaries? Tinker didn't think so, but Donna was the person who often answered the phones in her cigarette voice, the voice of a much older woman even though she was only in her thirties, a single mother with a son to support. She was the source of speculation fairly often for the remarks she came out with. About a month earlier, apropos of what, Tinker didn't know, Donna had said, *I can get it up on a dead man. A showstopper,* Mark had told her, shaking his head and grinning in mock disbelief. While laughing and seeming to share her disapproval, Mark was also intrigued, Tinker knew. Donna was like an exotic foreign country.

She turned from the mirror and went back to the living room, where she set about assembling one of the larger boxes. She opened it, flattened down the flaps on the bottom, and taped it shut. The box stood fresh and square, ready to receive, evidence that life went on. The man at the U-Haul had told her to use the larger boxes for lighter-weight and bulky things like clothing and bedding and lamps, and the smaller boxes for books and records and dishes. Tinker liked the whole symmetry of that, the fact that somebody had already figured out an approach. He told her that people always left the kitchen for last. A big mistake. They'd think they were almost done, and then they'd start on the kitchen and it would take as long as the rest of the apartment put together. "So do the kitchen first," he told her. "Get that over with, and you'll sail through the rest of it, believe me."

She was emptying the kitchen shelves when Mira finally showed up. Mira appeared at the door in a black dress so thin it was more slip than dress. Her body was visible underneath, a child's body. Her hair, ungelled today, lay flat. Her face seemed larger, younger, and whiter.

"Oh God," Mira said, glancing about the kitchen. "I don't know if I can do this."

"Sure you can," Tinker said, trying for equilibrium in her voice, trying not to show her annoyance, because she might have predicted this. Mira the drama queen. "The thing is to begin." She explained about the boxes, but Mira didn't seem to be listening, she was walking around the small kitchen, trailing her fingers along the countertops. She disappeared into the living room. Tinker could hear her out there and went back to packing up the things in the kitchen. She was pulling canned goods out of the cupboards when Mira came back and sat down at the kitchen table.

"This food is all perfectly good," Tinker said. "We can divide it up."

"Ugh," Mira said.

"It's just soup," Tinker said. "Spaghetti sauce. You eat that, don't you?"

"I'm not taking Pony's food."

"I don't know why not," Tinker said. "It's just food." She held up a can of creamed corn.

"You can have it all," Mira said, and Tinker felt the slap in that remark. *Let the fat one have the food.*

"But you can—" Tinker began.

"I can what?"

"Never mind," Tinker said. *But you can pick up a guy at Pony's funeral,* she thought. Outrageous, inappropriate, for Mira to be on the prowl at a time like that, and what kind of a man hits on the bereaved sister at a funeral, anyway? "Are you still seeing that guy?" she asked. "The guy who spoke at Pony's funeral?"

Mira hopped up on the counter and swung her bare feet so they banged against the lower cabinet. She had a fresh pedicure. "He might come over later," she said.

"First Pony and now you." Tinker couldn't resist saying it.

"He's an old soul," Mira said. "It's not like that."

I'll bet, Tinker thought.

"I told him I'd be here. He's looking for an apartment, so I thought maybe—"

"First things first," Tinker said.

"Anything new about that guy at the lake that Denny Bell saw?"

"We'll probably never know," Tinker said, and pointedly went back to work.

"I'd like to rip his face off. He just left her there. It so sucks," Mira said.

"Maybe he had nothing to do with it," Tinker said quietly, and

138

thought that maybe Denny was just confused and the guy he'd seen was only William.

"He, like, came out of nowhere and went back to nowhere," Mira said.

"We can talk while we work," Tinker said.

Mira was looking through some of Pony's drawings. "She would have been so good," she said.

"See that roll of plastic bags? Those are for the trash. There's a Dumpster outside." Tinker was still thinking about Denny Bell. She wished he hadn't seen the guy at all. The news that somebody had been there had sent everybody into a tailspin and opened everything up all over again, just when they were starting to heal. "Daddy's calling everybody in her address book," Tinker said. "To find out if any of them were there that day or know anything. He's a wreck. I'm so worried about him."

"He'll be okay," Mira said.

"But what if he isn't? He's getting old," Tinker said. "We need to acknowledge that."

"Like he'll let us." Mira pulled one of the plastic bags from the roll, dropped to her knees at the refrigerator door, and started emptying the contents. She wasn't paying attention to what she was doing, just reaching in and grabbing. Tinker would have sorted through things, salvaged what she could. There were cans of beer and soda in there, full containers of juice, expensive jams still within the expiration date. *Keep your mouth shut,* she told herself.

Mira slammed the refrigerator door. "I can't do this. I can't touch her things like this. It feels like we're throwing her away."

It didn't feel that way at all to Tinker. It felt useful. It was the best way she knew to cope.

"It's like she's just vanished off the face of the earth," Mira continued. "And now we can't wait to get rid of everything she had."

She did *just vanish off the face of the earth,* Tinker thought. *That's what death is.* "Look at the dust in here already," she said.

"So what? It isn't right to do it so fast." Mira got to her feet and left the room.

"Daddy wanted us to," Tinker shouted behind her. That wasn't exactly true. On the same day she'd found him in the yard, she'd gone inside to make lunch. He'd come in and gone upstairs to dress, and when he didn't come down, she'd gone looking for him. She'd found him in Pony's old room, sitting on her narrow bed with the contents of a drawer spilled out. He was sorting through the things Pony had left behind years earlier. School supplies, her hastily written papers, poorly typed, C or D written across the top, her old sketchbooks and report cards, the dusty debris of an old desk, pencil shavings, and paper clips. He could die of sadness. "Daddy, you need your lunch," she'd said, urging him to come downstairs and eat the sandwich she had made.

"It shouldn't just sit there," he'd said angrily, and she'd thought he meant the sandwich at first, but then it became clear he was talking about Pony's apartment, saying it was still untended, and she had that awful sudden guilt that only he could cause, the feeling that, my God, she should have known, what was the matter with her anyway, not to have acted? It was like those dreams in which you were supposed to have been going to class for a whole semester but you forgot, and now there was a final exam. It was the same panicked horror. Her father said he knew of a service. Apparently, there was an agency that went in and boxed things up and delivered them to Goodwill and the soup kitchen and whatever and then cleaned the apartment, but Tinker, hot with guilt, had said absolutely not, she would take care of it, of course she would. She was desperate for his forgiveness.

And she would enlist Mira. She wasn't going to let Mira get away with not helping out this time. No, Mira needed to participate. She needed to get her hands dirty for once in her life. You couldn't just float along without ever really doing the tough stuff, and the sooner Mira understood that, the better.

"Can we keep things?" Mira asked.

"Like what?" Tinker said.

"Oh, wait. Answered my own question. Of course we can," Mira said. "You're keeping the food. So I can keep things, too." She left the kitchen.

Tinker stood up. She went into the living room, where Mira was picking things up, putting them down, looking for something. "It was right here," Mira said.

"What was?"

"A pillow I wanted." Mira made a small shape with her hands. "Yay big. Says 'Fuck housework.' "

"You've *been* here before?" Tinker asked.

"Sure," Mira said. "Lots of times."

It was like hearing about a party Tinker hadn't been invited to. Her first time in Pony's apartment had been with their father the day Pony's body was found in the lake. She'd assumed that, like her and Mark, the family lived independently of one another except for their times together at Steele Road or at Fond du Lac. "Maybe you could start bagging the newspapers." Tinker handed Mira the stack of brown bags.

"Look, Tinker, you do it the way you want, and I'll do it the way I want," Mira said. "Right now I'm looking for that pillow."

"We just need to keep at it," Tinker said. "If we keep stopping all the time, we'll never get it done."

Mira wasn't listening. She was still going around the room, picking up things and looking under them. "I'm *looking* for that little pillow."

"Let's just set aside things of value, and then later, we can—"

"The pillow has no value," Mira said. "Jesus, Tinker. You've got an answer for everything. And that wasn't even a question."

There was a knock at the door and a man's voice. "Hello?"

Mira's face lit up. "Keith!" she said. "Hey!"

He was dressed in black, as usual—black jeans and a black shirt and a belt with a very large silver buckle in the shape of a steer's head. He gave Mira a kiss, crossed the room to Tinker, and held out his hand to her. "We haven't officially met," he said. "Keith Brink. What can I do to help?"

Tinker had dismissed this guy as just another one of Mira's boyfriends, so it came as a shock when she felt immediately drawn to him. He had a large, rough hand, a firm handshake, and she found it difficult to take her eyes from his. He had a strong face and eyes of a lively beautiful blue, darkly rimmed.

"You're the organizer, I hear," he said, not letting go of her hand or breaking eye contact. "The mover and shaker. Every family needs one."

"Who told you *that*?" She felt confused and glanced quickly at Mira, who shook her head. Those were not Mira's words. Mira never would have described her in such a benign way. "Bitch" was more like it.

Keith walked around the room as if he belonged, so easy. So sure of himself. "Pony." He smiled at her question as if it was charming.

"She talked to you about me?" Tinker felt both wary and pleased.

"She talked about all of you. I was telling Mira about it." Keith looked at Mira. "You didn't tell her?"

Mira shook her head.

"What else did she say?" Tinker said.

"That it was hard raising a baby on her own."

"She brought it on herself," Tinker said.

"She said coming from a family like yours made it hard to be a single mother." He pointed at Tinker. "You, she was afraid she'd disappointed," he said. "I got the impression she was sorry about that."

"No way." Tinker pushed her hair back and tried to tuck it behind her ears. *Show your face*, her mother always said. *Don't hide those beautiful eyes.*

"She said you did everything by the book, that everywhere you went, you were followed by a little trail of order." He grinned, and she was taken in again by the blueness of his eyes, the steadiness of his gaze. She loved hearing this. She gathered her hair at the base of her neck, twisted it into a rope, and pulled it forward over one shoulder.

"You girls are busy," he said. "I shouldn't interrupt."

"We can take a break. What else did she say?" Tinker asked.

Keith sank down, his arms stretched out over the sofa back, his knees apart. "She said you girls had all the earmarks. You know, the oldest is the most responsible, and the youngest gets away with murder." He glanced at Mira with a smirk. "And the middle one is the most unhappy."

"I'm not unhappy." Mira batted him. "Anyway, Tinker and I are both middle children. William's the oldest."

"I know that now." Keith shook his head. "But from what Pony said, I thought Tinker would be the oldest."

"Pony must have meant Tinker is the oldest sister," Mira said.

"No." Keith shook his head again, thoughtfully. "I'm only reporting what she said. She talked about you two, and she hardly mentioned William, so I'm in the dark about him. I thought he'd be here. Helping out. This is heavy work."

"Well, he's not," Tinker said, letting the impression stand that William was shirking his duty when in fact she'd never asked him. Mira was the one she'd wanted here. The one she could boss around. "He hasn't really helped much at all through this whole thing. And when you consider that he was Pony's favorite—"

"Not what I heard," Keith said.

"What's *that* supposed to mean?" Tinker said, sitting up quickly.

"I don't want to cause trouble," Keith said. "Forget it."

"You can't just blurt that out and then not explain." Mira slapped him lightly.

"Okay. I got the impression she was afraid of him," Keith said.

"Afraid how?" Tinker couldn't contain her amazement. "How could Pony be afraid of William?"

Keith raised his shoulders, like *Don't look at me*. "You asked what she said. I'm just telling you. She said William had a short fuse sometimes. He was maybe a little quirky. She was a little wary of him, I thought. It was something that had happened recently. I thought you girls might know."

"He was up there that day." Tinker felt positively titillated by this new information.

"But he left," Mira said.

"Says who?" Tinker asked. "Says William. Daddy even asked him, remember?"

"Asked him what?" Keith asked.

"If he had anything to do with it."

"Whoa," Keith said.

"He didn't mean that, though," Mira said. "He wasn't accusing William, just finding out what happened. Anyway, Denny Bell saw that guy who was there after William."

"What guy?" Keith asked.

"I still think it's possible Denny saw William and was mixed up about the time." Tinker liked the discussion and wanted it to keep on going.

"Denny knows who William is," Mira said.

Tinker said, "Not that well. I mean, none of us really knows them. If you saw Denny Bell on the street—I mean, before all this—would you know him?"

"You never told me about this," Keith said to Mira.

"I just found out," she said. "Anyway, I don't want to keep laying this stuff on you."

"William wouldn't hurt Pony." Tinker looked doubtfully at Mira. "Would he?"

"Look, as long as you girls are going there," Keith said, "Pony said something about William. How can I put this—he was interested in her. Not like a brother should be."

"No way!" Mira said. "That's impossible. No fuckin' way."

"I don't know," Tinker said. "I don't know anything anymore. We better tell Daddy."

"Let's not rock the boat," Keith said. "I could be mistaken. Anyway, it was ruled an accident, right? By the cops. Let sleeping dogs lie."

"Daddy's going to hold a meeting," Tinker said.

"Maybe you should be there," Mira said to Keith.

Keith cleared his throat and stood. "I had no business getting you all dusted up. I'm sorry. Just forget what I said. You girls need some help. You can put me to work." Without waiting for direction, he picked up one of the boxes and started putting it together. When he was done, he took it into the bedroom and began filling it with Pony's clothing. Mira went in after him and sat on the bed, talking as he worked.

Tinker couldn't get over what Keith had said. Afraid? Pony was afraid of William? She went back to the kitchen, glad to be alone. Something nagged at her. She was remembering the night of her father's seventieth birthday the summer before. After the dishes were done, she'd gone outside to the porch, pulling one of the rattan chairs into the corner to the left of the living room window and sitting in the darkness, so tired. She'd put together the whole event again, as usual. Assigned food responsibilities and then done most of it herself. William brought chips, for God's sake. And some bags of Oreos. She'd cooked. She'd been on the phone for a couple of weeks, inviting the neighbors from around the lake. And the party took off. After dinner, the kitchen filled with dishes. *What can I do to help?* people always asked, but they never really meant it. You could tell by the desultory way they walked around, picking things up and putting them down. *I can manage*, she always said, because to think up the jobs and then supervise them on top of it was just a lot more work. It was easier to do it herself.

While she sat on the porch that night, a pale form ran across the lawn and down to the water from the side door. It was Pony, her bare skin a greenish gray in the moonlight. She looked so carefree, so lovely, Tinker thought. So pretty to watch as she dabbled her toe into the lake, swirled it in a circle, her arms out to the sides for balance. She made a smooth, splashless entry, *slick as a whistle*, their father like to say of an entry like that, something Tinker had achieved only a few times. Pony swam underwater to the float. Tinker had half a mind to go this time. For once.

Inside, the party had settled down to serious quieter drinking. Her father's friends were old men and women, all still elegant in a way Tinker never would be. The women wore their silver hair coiffed. They had the accent of the rich. Tinker rose and went quickly down the front steps, feeling the thrill of fear. She hadn't done this in forever. She kept to the left, where the bushes separated their property from the Cushmans.' She slipped off her shoes and unbuttoned her blouse, loving the sweet cool air on her bare skin. She'd just unfastened her bra when she heard the sound of footsteps on the gravel. William dashed across the grass to the lake, and she stood still. He was looking for Pony. And then right behind him came Mark. The two of them spoke. William slapped Mark on the shoulder in what she'd thought at the time was a friendly way.

William swam out to the raft quickly, almost as though trying to outswim Mark. Mark went in more slowly, and finally, he was out there, too. For a very long time Tinker didn't see any of them. They must have gone under the raft or beyond the raft, out in the lake where she couldn't see. Once in a while she heard a whisper, and then Pony's raised voice. Then there came a noisy disturbance in the water, and the next thing Tinker saw was Pony swimming like hell for shore, kicking for all she was worth. Then Mark right behind her.

Something had happened out there, she realized now. She hadn't thought much about it at the time, at least not that part, but thinking back and tying in what Keith had said, she remembered it had taken William forever to come in. Had William scared Pony? She could ask Mark, but that would mean admitting she'd been spying on him. She tried to remember more from that night, but the thing that had struck her most was seeing Pony. There had been a moon. Pony had gathered up her clothes and walked quickly, still naked, up the lawn to the house. Pony was more beautiful that night than Tinker would ever be in her life.

Chapter 10

William

The house in Glastonbury where Ruth was working was easy to spot; it was the biggest on the street, the one with Tyvek sheeting all over the sides. William pulled to a stop and got out. There were wheels of sod lined up on the driveway and ready to roll. Maybe a dozen trees, each with its root ball in burlap, stacks of flowers in flats. Instant yard.

Ruth didn't see him. She was out back with a tall, black-haired woman dressed all in white. The owner. The woman stabbed the air with a rolled magazine, pointing at something. Ruth followed, frowning, cocking her head. William watched. He mulled over, for the hundredth time, what Denny Bell had said and what Randy Martine had told him. William had been on the phone with Randy half a dozen times since they'd talked to Denny. Now Denny was changing his story a little bit. He didn't think he could identify the guy after all. Maybe the guy was older, shorter, maybe it wasn't a baseball cap but something else. What was going on? The kid was scared. Randy was checking all around the lake again to see who'd seen what. So far, nothing. Checking Pony's address book, but with Denny's description getting so slippery, it wasn't easy. William had the feeling they were missing something big. Something really obvious.

He knew from a message Tinker had left on his machine that his father was calling another meeting for the coming weekend up at the lake to talk about it. "Denny Bell *claims* he saw somebody—a guy, of course—up at the lake with Pony that day, around six. He *claims* the guy went in after her. I don't know what to think anymore. It's a whole new can of worms, if you ask me. Anyway, Daddy's holding a meeting on Saturday. We all need to be on the same page about it." From the message, it was clear that Tinker thought William knew nothing about what Denny Bell had said he saw, which was galling enough, but the business about being on the same page was depressing, as if the information would shrink instead of expand.

William was leery about going. Maybe it was better to talk to Randy and leave the others out of it. When he told Ruth, she'd said that if it was up to her, he'd go to that meeting, no question, and if he didn't, he should at least let them know he wasn't. She had a point, but it was only Wednesday, the meeting wasn't until Saturday, which meant there was time to decide. Right now what he wanted to do was make good on his promise to Ruth to go back to the Catskills and finish what they'd started. They'd do some peaks, fuck, be out in the mountain air.

Ruth and the owner of the house were looking in his direction now. The owner came mincing over in gold sandals. Ruth gave her the finger behind her back, and William smiled. He got out of the car. The woman extended a small tanned hand. "Mindy Mills," she said. "And you are . . . ?"

"William." Sometimes he said Carteret, but more often not. A lot of people who'd lived in the area a long time knew the name. "I came to pick up Ruth."

"I need to keep her a tad longer."

William checked his watch. It was almost five. "We've got a long drive ahead of us."

Mindy grinned, wrinkled her nose. "Just a minute or two. Actually, you can mediate something." She had a tinkly little laugh. She was younger than William, a few years out of college, he thought. Where did people that age get the money for a spread like this? She unrolled the magazine and flicked a polished nail against a photograph of a large abundant garden surrounded by acres of green lawn. At the center of the garden was a fountain spraying high from a bronze statue of the Three Graces. "This gorgeous fountain," she said, and pointed to her own yard. "Over there. What do you think?"

William didn't answer.

"Yes or no," Mindy said.

It would look pretentious as hell. "No," he said.

"Well, I still want it," she said, and became all business, pushing her sunglasses up onto her forehead. She turned to Ruth. "I know it means we have to undo things, but it's my nickel. I don't know what the problem is. It's more work for you, and that's a good thing, yes? More hours?"

"The point is, Mindy, that fountain won't look right."

Mindy winked at William. "She's stuck in a time warp."

"Look," Ruth said in a very calm voice. Mindy obviously had no idea how angry Ruth was. "You're paying for my ideas. You said that yourself on my first day. And I'm telling you the fountain is a mistake. Your yard isn't big enough."

"Nonsense. We're on almost an acre here. Anyway, I *love* your ideas," Mindy said with another irritating wink. "Don't be ridiculous."

Ruth indicated the magazine in Mindy's hand. "You love *Town and Country*'s ideas."

"Well," Mindy said. "They're a maga*zine*, after all."

"Hey, Mindy," William said.

"I beg your pardon?" Mindy said.

"That's insulting," William said. "Just because you have money to throw around doesn't mean you have good ideas. Listen to Ruth on this one, okay?"

"I'd like you out of here," Mindy said.

"Thanks," Ruth said later in the car, kicking off her shoes and putting her bare feet on the dash. "It just gets worse and worse." As they drove through Hartford, she told him that Mindy wasn't her only problem. Her landlord had come into her attic apartment the day before, some ruse about needing to check the storm windows, but then he'd sat himself down in her living room chair and said, "So tell me about Ruth Czapinski." Ruth grinned at William. "Oh, brother," she said. "What an idiot. I told him Ruth Czapinski knew the law well enough to know that the landlord wasn't allowed to make himself at home in the tenant's quarters. He reminded me there was no record of my being a tenant because I pay in cash and I'm there at his will. My days in the attic are numbered."

"So move in with me," he said.

"You feel sorry for me?" She smiled at him.

"Not at all. Yes," he said. Once, before Pony died, back when life was normal, back when he worked for days and nights on end and then took off for a week of hiking and hiked for fun. Back when his biggest problem was taking on too much work and wondering if he could get it done on time. Back then, once, Ruth had stayed over at his house. It was a Saturday night, and on Sunday morning he'd driven to the CVS on New Britain Avenue for a *New York Times*. When he drove back, the way he always did, up Trout Brook and over on Phelps, no big deal, nothing special, he pulled into his driveway and looked at his condo, and it just looked better because Ruth was in it. He knew then. He knew for sure. "Think about it, though, okay?" he said.

Their lodge in the Catskills was owned by an art dealer who specialized in portraits of women. There were portraits everywhere of prim, dour women sitting with hands clasped tightly in their laps, a few lush nudes thrown in. The art dealer's wife ran the inn with a man named Marcus whom, Ruth was sure, was the lover, although of husband or wife, neither she nor William was sure.

They climbed every day. They did Twin, Slide, Peekamoose, and Table. William thought only about the peaks. He dreamed only about the peaks. The climbs took all his concentration. He studied the maps, he planned their routes. They set out before daybreak. They came back to the lodge for dinner, they made love, they slept. William was given over completely to the needs of his body, to keeping it safe on the trail, then satisfied and rested at night. A person couldn't climb and be preoccupied by any other thought. Physical exertion obliterated everything, even grief.

They checked out after breakfast on their third morning. They planned to climb Sugarloaf and then drive back to Connecticut. Theirs was the only car in the parking lot that morning. They paused at the kiosk with its usual warnings about Lyme disease and timber rattlers and requests to pack it in, pack it out. Sugarloaf began with a fairly level path over traprock chinks that made a distinctive tinny sound underfoot. They passed through large soupy swamps and pine groves where the ground was spongy with needles. And then they came to the Wizard's Chair. William had read about this in the hike description but was unprepared for the reality of it.

The woods opened to a wide clearing, and he stopped to take it in. Before him lay a kaleidoscope of rock spread across a wide expanse, as though a giant hand had swept away the forest and spread these mean shards. Like an optical illusion, an Escher print, the Wizard's Chair came into focus. It had to be eight feet tall and seemed to William like a towering, angular gray man with his arms outstretched, his knees open. Ruth clambered across the rock to see it. "Look!" she shouted. "There are side chairs! Tables!"

William adjusted his eyes again and this time took in the rest. The Wizard's Chair was flanked by smaller chairs, two to each side, and tables and platforms, a great semicircle like King Arthur's court, he thought. He sat in one of the small ones.

"Huh," Ruth said before she made a beeline for the Wizard's Chair. She sat in the grand chair, looking tiny, her legs outstretched, the edge of the seat hitting her at the calf.

William settled back and looked across and up at the mountains into the sun, and as he did, he felt something give inside him, a sweet shift that caused him to become aware of the cool smooth stone beneath his legs, the clean air filling his lungs, the great beauty of what he was seeing. He could stay for a long time, breathing in the air, breathing it out, feeling connected to all the outdoors.

But they had a lot ahead of them. They left the Wizard's Chair and continued up to Pecoy Notch and then on to the Devil's Path, where the climb became serious. Ruth went first, finding the toeholds and handholds in the tree roots that made a kind of ladder against the sheer rock faces—not technical but steep. William inched up, flattened against the rock face, occasionally looking up at Ruth's little ass in shorts, her boots in their precarious toeholds.

She was getting too far ahead of him. Why wasn't he keeping up? He felt leaden. He tried to hurry, slipped, and had to steady himself. He looked up. Ruth was way ahead, nearing the top. He looked down. He was maybe twenty feet up, not that far, but below were rocks. He felt his bowels loosen. The hot sweat of panic broke out on his forehead. "Ruth," he said.

She must not have heard. He knew from the sound that she was continuing to climb. "Ruthie?" he said louder.

"What is it?" she said from above.

He didn't dare speak again, didn't dare risk the vibration that could loosen his hold on the rock. The slightest movement would send him plunging down. His hands felt weak; his fingers slipped.

"Did you say something?" Ruth asked him.

He couldn't answer.

"William?"

Urine trickled down his leg. He fought to hold it.

"William, what is it?"

He didn't dare look up. He heard her feet just above him, her boots inching back down. "Are you okay?" she said.

He shook his head.

"Okay," she said. "I'm coming."

He felt rather than saw Ruth come back down. He pressed his whole body, including the side of his face, against the stone, as if the more surface he could touch, the safer he would be. He knew this was wrong, even less secure, but he was obeying instinct, not reason. When he dared to open his eyes, she was there, to his right, talking. The sound alone was something to hold on to. He felt her hand on his. "I'm going to get you down."

"Can't," he rasped.

"Yes, you can," she said. "You have to. You're going to be fine. Just listen to what I say."

He didn't dare move.

"Baby," Ruth said. "You know what we have to do."

"I can't."

She tapped his hand. "It's a few inches to the right. You're going to move this hand."

He would do as she said. He released some of the tension in his hold, then held again. It felt as though his whole body was about to slip. "Oh, no."

"You're not going to fall," she said.

He let his hand relax, and she must have felt that. She slid it across the rock to the large bolus of a root. William grasped it and felt hope. The root was large and sturdy. It fit perfectly into his palm.

"Good," she said. "Now we're going to move your left foot. There's a shelf about six inches to the right. It'll hold you. Shift your weight to the right foot and move your left toe over. You'll have more support. I swear it will be better."

For a terrifying moment he had only three points of contact. His foot fumbled at the rock. He felt her hand guide his foot firmly to the spot. Yes. He felt the divot in the rock where it would go. He planted the toe of his boot, dared to shift a small amount of weight.

"Great," she said.

"I might shit," he said.

Ruth laughed. "Just rest there a minute. Get your breath. The worst is over. I'll keep moving down. I'll help you get where I am

153

now. There's really lots of handholds over here. We probably should have come up this way."

It took half an hour to move the fifteen feet down. She had to talk him through every single handhold and toehold. "I feel like a jerk," he said. "I don't know what happened."

When they reached level ground, she had him lie down. She helped him off with his pack, opened it, took out his space blanket, and spread it over him. The warmth told him how cold he had been in spite of the heat of the day. Ruth rolled his spare jacket and made a pillow for his neck.

"I am so messed up," he said.

She kissed his forehead lightly. "What did you expect? You think you can get off scot-free after Pony's death? Life isn't like that."

After a time she let him sit up. She helped him to a sitting position and propped both packs behind him for support. She mixed some Jell-O crystals with water and had him drink the sweet fluid. She broke off pieces of a sandwich, and he ate them. After about half an hour, she helped him to his feet. "Now let's get you out of here," she said.

Ruth went first, slowly, turning often to make sure he was okay. He felt shaken to the bone. He kept trying to snap out of it. He'd pause, tell himself not to be such a jerk. This wasn't even a steep trail. He could do better than this. He could run a trail like this. But when he tried to go faster, he stumbled. He hoped Ruth didn't hear his clumsy footfalls.

In the car going home, he relived the moment, torturing himself with it, beating himself up. It had come over him so abruptly. Fine one moment and paralyzed the next. He'd walked knife-edges in the White Mountains, where a slip of the foot meant dropping into a crevasse and almost certain death. He'd loved exposure, the steeper and more dangerous, the better. He'd craved the feeling of it. Not fear. Kin to fear but more an electric sixth sense that caused his pulse to quicken, his concentration to become sharp. He was alert as hell at those times, and it was what kept him safe.

154

But this? He'd had contempt for people who were afraid, people who backed away. Maybe he still did. A person could buck fear if he wanted. William sped up. He glanced over at Ruth and felt a weird mix of gratitude and annoyance. She'd seen it, been witness to it. He slid an Aretha Franklin CD into the slot. His hand was trembling. He willed it to stop. He fumbled with the knob to turn up the volume.

"You better pull over," Ruth said.

"What's the matter?"

"Please," she said.

The car bounced along the shoulder beside a field of early corn and came to a stop. His hands still trembled. He made fists so she wouldn't see. "I wasn't that high up," he said, as if that made it all okay. "It was nothing."

"It wasn't about being high." Ruth reached for his hand. "William. It's about shock. You're not the iceman. You've got to grieve, like everybody else."

He snatched his hand away.

"I'm not the enemy," she said.

He got out of the car and walked up the road a ways, taking deep breaths. He hated the feeling of weakness. He'd been that way as a kid. Always scared. Something he'd made up his mind to overcome, and he'd done it. It had been years since anything like that had happened. He went back to the car. Ruth had gotten out and was leaning against the hood. "William, grief just takes time. It has its own schedule. Give it time."

He had to walk away again. What was that supposed to mean? *Oh, it'll pass, you're just having a bad day. It'll blow over, and you'll be fine.* He wouldn't be fine. He was back where he'd started. He came back. He stood over her, towered over her, and put his face close to hers. "Here's what I want to know, Ruth. Since you seem to know so much. What the hell am I supposed to be doing while I give it time?"

She didn't flinch. She stood straight up and glared back at him.

Nose to nose now. "Go to that meeting your father called, for one thing."

He laughed, sounding loud to himself. Where was this coming from, and who was she to tell him how to deal with his family?

"You don't think they're suffering as much as you are?" she asked.

"Those meetings are a farce. It's my dad's show. My dad's chance to show he's in charge. That he's something and we're not. Believe me, I've been to plenty of those meetings. He'll keep us guessing. He won't say, 'Okay, let's meet at four this afternoon,' or ask when's good for everybody. He won't say anything like that, and nobody will ask."

"Why not?"

"We just don't," William said, like it was obvious. "It keeps everybody on a short leash. You stay close so you don't get caught out on the water or up hiking when he calls the meeting, because it'll be out of the blue, and you'll be late. He'll say, 'Why don't we all sit down and talk this thing over,' like the idea just occurred to him. And we'll sit down at the dining room table, and he'll engage in some small talk or ask what people did that day. We're the openers at these things. The warm-up act. Nobody will bring up the real subject. Pony. The guy on the beach. Because that's Dad's job. He'll tell us what I already know. What I found out, for Christ's sake. And no credit for it, either. I guar-an-fucking-tee that. I'm the one who got the information out of Denny Bell. I'm the one who took the initiative."

"So if that matters to you, say so."

"Oh, Ruthie Ruthie Ruthie." He put his hands on her shoulders and shook her gently. She wasn't getting it.

She looked up with those fierce brown eyes of hers. "Maybe he's got all of you on a short leash," she said. "But he doesn't have the world on one."

"You know nothing!"

She threw off his hands, stepped away, and turned her back on him. Deciding, he figured, between getting really pissed off or letting it go. She decided to let it go. Sort of. "Here's what I do know." She faced him. "I know your father is a human being like anybody else. He's just a guy."

William had to laugh. He shouldn't have, but he did. His father was a lot of things, but just a guy? Nope. And William wasn't the only one who knew so. He'd find plenty of support. His sisters, for sure. His father's old business cohorts. The neighbors on Steele Road. The families at Lake Aral. Nope. His old man was definitely not just a guy. His father had the world knocked. Not a man to be cowed. Except once, and that was a total anomaly. Man, William hadn't thought about that night in years. The night the cop had pulled his father over.

"Fine. Make a joke of it." Ruth pushed him in the chest hard enough that he had to step back.

"I'm not laughing because it's funny, Ruth. He's just not your average Joe. I'll never be what he is."

She frowned up at him. "What are you even talking about?"

"Huge company. Lot of money. Hundreds of employees. Everybody knows him. He's got a roomful of honors and accolades. I'll never be that. I'll never even be close."

"You're not serious."

"The man's bulletproof."

"Wow," she said. "Can you *hear* yourself?"

"Of course."

"Want to know what I think?" She didn't wait for an answer. "I think he's a guy who just sat back and let things come to him. I see a passive guy. He inherited everything you think is so great about him. Never had to lift a finger. The business, for one. He ran it down and sold it, if I understand things correctly. He inherited the house where he raised his family. Even the house on the lake. He's just a sad old man who's lost his wife. Now his daughter. He's a guy with no clue how to connect with people. I can't believe we're even having this discussion. It's so obvious." She took a deep breath and blew it out.

"And bulletproof?" She shoved him gently in the chest again with her palm. "*Bulletproof?*"

Cars whipped past them on the road. William felt equal parts thrill and shame at the pleasure he took in hearing that his father looked ordinary—maybe less than ordinary—to her. Oh yeah, he loved it. He didn't believe it, but he loved it. He walked down the bank toward the field, grinning to himself.

"I can't believe you'd miss this meeting, William," she called to him. "Maybe there's new information about the guy Denny Bell saw. It's important."

"I know as much as any of them know. More," he said. "I've been in touch with Randy all along. There's nothing."

She hopped up onto the hood, and damn, she looked cute. Big smile on her now, like she'd won a round. "Come on, go. For me. I for one would like to see this family in action."

She looked so great up there. Her turquoise halter top, shorts. That white hair and the great big smile. And hell, if she wanted him to go, it was the least he could do for what she'd just given him. If she grooved on his family, well, then, fine.

They got back into the car and turned east, heading for Vermont. William still felt great. Upbeat in a way that was new, as if life held promise now. They passed a cop lurking in some trees at the side of the road. William slowed down. And he got to thinking again about the time the cop had pulled them over. The one time his father had surprised him.

The family was all packed into the Volvo. It was a June night, and they were heading to Fond du Lac for the summer. Mira and Tinker were in their car seats. William was in the way back, and William's mother held Pony on her lap in the front seat. He must have been sleeping, because all of a sudden, he was startled awake by bright re-volving lights.

It was a cop car behind them. William had been excited by the commotion, the lights, the prospect of something about to happen. The cop had swaggered up to his father's window and shone his light into the car, letting it rest on each one of them in turn so they'd had to look away. "Nice family," the cop had said to William's father. "You trying to kill them?"

William had been floored. Didn't this cop know who his father *was*? His father was Jasper Carteret. He owned Carteret Ball Bearings in Hartford. You didn't talk to him that way.

The cop waited for an answer, but William's father said nothing. Nothing! He just stared into his lap.

"Know how fast you were going?" the cop said.

Silence.

"I clocked you at eighty," the cop said. William knew that couldn't be true. "Car hits a guardrail at eighty, these kids will be spread over the road like hamburger." The cop shone his light onto Pony. "Little one, too." The blinding beam of his flashlight whipped through the car again, landed again on his father's face. "You want that?"

Say something! William thought. *Jesus, Dad. Stick up for yourself.*

"I'm asking you a question," the cop said.

His father said nothing.

"Get out of the car, sir."

Now, William thought. *Now he'll let the cop have it.* But no. His father obeyed. He got out and placed his hands on the roof of the station wagon and let the cop pat him down. He let the cop take his driver's license out of his wallet. Let William's mother hand over the registration from the glove compartment.

The cop went back to his car to write up the summons, and William's father still didn't even move; he stood with his hands against the top of the car like a criminal. It took a long time. Finally, the cop came back and handed the ticket to William's father. "Maximum" was all the cop said.

After the cop walked back to his patrol car, William's father didn't make a move. The cop gave them a few bursts of light from behind, and William's father got into the car as if he'd needed permission. They drove off slowly, nobody saying a word. After a minute or two, the cop shot past them in his cruiser and disappeared into the night.

When William used to tell the story, and he had a few times in high school and college, he'd tell it as a lesson. *The best thing to do when a cop pulls you over is keep your mouth shut. Let him ream you out and give you the ticket. Don't give him the satisfaction.* But he didn't actually believe that. He'd been pulled over a few times, and he'd always answered the cop's questions respectfully.

He told the whole story to Ruth as they drove, and she wanted to know what his father should have done.

"I kept thinking my dad had something up his sleeve," William explained. "That he was laying a trap for the cop and he would come roaring back at the guy. But he didn't. He was meek."

"Hmm," Ruth said, exactly what she'd said when he hadn't sat in the Wizard's Chair, which caused him to wonder about that, too. He pictured the clearing, at least an acre, dominated by that chair somebody had made, somebody's labor of love. A gift for weary hikers. So why the hell not sit in the big one? What was the matter with him? And it hadn't even been a choice. He'd taken a look at the big one and gone right for the small one.

Chapter 11

William

By the time William and Ruth arrived at the lake, the others had already come, but the place had an empty feel to it. On a day like this, you were supposed to be outside. You were supposed to be engaged in something healthy and athletic. Mira appeared on the porch as they pulled their luggage from the trunk. She wobbled down the stairs in clunky high heels. She had done something to her hair. Gotten rid of those electric-blue tips. She still looked a little scary, if you asked William. A long black skirt hung from her thin hip bones, and a section of white midriff showed. Her eyes were very dark, lined in something heavy. "What are you *doing* here?" she said.

"Hi to you, too," William said.

"I just meant nobody expected you," she said. "We didn't know if you got the message."

"Well, here I am."

William wondered what it was with women and hugs. Ruth barely knew Mira, right? And there they were in a big hug, but it made Mira smile. She had a great smile when her guard was down. "I'm watching the kids," she said. "I think it's penance for bringing Keith to this thing. I didn't know we weren't supposed to. Why doesn't anybody say?"

"Who's Keith?"

"You know. He bought one of Pony's paintings. I met him at Daddy's."

The funeral *guy?* William wondered.

"Randy Martine is coming around suppertime, and that's when the meeting is. Just so you know. Do you think somebody murdered her?" Mira asked, her eyes wide.

William was about to answer, to say it was a very big possibility as far as he was concerned, when the screen door slammed and Isabel shot out. She hugged William hard. He picked her up and swung her around. She was so light, so small, for eight. She had this surprised little face. It was something in her upper lip. It peaked at the center, like an isosceles triangle. "We have Andrew," Isabel said.

"I know," William said. "Do you like having Andrew?"

Isabel nodded.

"He's around here somewhere," Mira said. "Jesus, where did he go now?"

"I can look," Ruth said, disappearing into the house.

"They move so fast," Mira said. "You put them down in one place, and the next thing you know —"

"I think you're supposed to watch them all the time," William said.

"I do that," Mira said.

"Like every minute," William said, and Mira stuck out her tongue at him.

Ruth came back outside carrying Andrew. "He was in the kitchen," she said. She gave William a private look that said, *Yikes.* William loved Ruth's restraint. He knew what she was thinking—a baby alone in the bloody *kitchen*? She handed Andrew over. Right away, he remembered the heft of Andrew from that day at the lake. Why had he not liked Andrew then? He didn't know now.

"You should hold him like this, Uncle William," Isabel said, crossing her hands over her heart. William swung the baby around the way Isabel had said. "That's right," she said. "Doesn't that feel good? It's because his heart is right next to yours. Mom said."

"Yeah?" William was impressed. "Your mom told you that?"

Isabel nodded. "She said it soothes them because they start out in the womb listening to the mother's heartbeat, and it's the nicest sound they know."

William had to smile. What a cool thing! He loved it that Isabel could use a word like "womb," that Tinker had told her that. And yes, he thought he could feel Andrew's small heart through the fabric of his T-shirt. William adjusted the baby, raising him up a little. Andrew twisted around to get a better look at who had him.

"He needs his diaper changed," Mira said.

William tried to hand the child back to her.

"You're the guardian," she said.

"I can show you." Isabel led the way to Pony's old room on the second floor, William and Ruth following. "Put him on the table," Isabel said. She walked William through everything. He removed the baby's shirt and shorts, taking the pins out of the diaper. "Oh, good," she said. "He didn't poop. It's worse when he poops. Aunt Mira won't change him then."

God, he was beautiful. William ran his hands over the child's small shoulders and marveled at the perfection of them. The skin was so pure, and the whites of his eyes were so clean, the irises a spectacular hazel-brown. Even his eyelashes looked fresh. William slid his hand over Andrew's silky blond hair, smoothing it back from his face. The small skull fit perfectly into William's palm. William held his hand still a few moments, loving the slight pulse. "You think he remembers?" William asked Ruth.

"Of course," she said. "At some level."

William looked into the baby's delighted face. Didn't you need language to remember? An understanding of cause and effect? Unless what babies stored wasn't the event itself but the feeling of it. William touched the baby's cheek and knew Ruth was right. There would be moments in Andrew's life, triggered by something connected to what happened—whitecaps on the water, maybe, wet grass, certain sounds or smells—that would set off a primitive terror the way, for William, the glittering blue water of a swimming pool in the hot sun could blindside him with sadness.

"Andrew takes a nap now." Isabel wound up a mobile over the baby's crib. Was it playing what William thought it was playing? "Off We Go, into the Wild Blue Yonder."

Downstairs, Mark and Tinker were just coming in from somewhere. Maybe canoeing. She had on khakis, a white polo shirt, and deck shoes, the Lake Aral uniform that made them all so sexless. Tinker used to have a body; William was sure she'd once been a good twenty pounds thinner. That summer she was going out with Randy Martine.

"Oh," she said, seeing William and Ruth. "You came. Oh. Well, good." She smiled at Ruth. "This changes things."

Mark clapped William on the shoulder, one of those smooth corporate moves he'd picked up. He kissed Ruth.

"We can put Mira and Ruth together in Pony's old room," Tinker said to William. "You and Keith share yours."

He let it go. You had to let her think she was running the show and then just do what you planned to do in the first place. She had circles under her eyes, and she was nervous, picking at a cuticle. She had a stain front and center on her shirt. Mira came in just then, followed by Keith, who carried a red cooler on his shoulder, his neck craned to one side. He swung it around and let it down just inside the kitchen door. "Help yourselves," he said.

He slung a hand out. "You're William." He was a muscular guy. *Football*, William thought. *End.* "Keith Brink." He had a big grin on his puss, and he stood close. "I'm here with Mira."

He was eyeball to eyeball with William, one of those guys who pulled you toward him when shaking hands. William pulled away, but Keith hung on, grinning. "What?" William asked. "Is something funny?"

164

Keith released him, still grinning. "Sorry, man. It's just a bad habit of mine, being an only child. I met your sisters. I was checking out the resemblance between you and them."

"Knock yourself out," William said.

"William can be a jerk sometimes. Don't pay any attention," Mira said.

He almost called her on that one but decided against it. He went into the kitchen to find Tinker. "Where's Dad?" he asked her.

Tinker seemed to deflate. She made a worried face. "Taking a nap, I think. He went to his room after lunch." She hove herself up and pushed her hair back over her shoulder. "I worry about him."

"Why?"

"He's so tired," she said. "This whole thing."

The other thing about Tinker. You didn't let her get going on the subject of their father. "Mira said Randy's coming around dinner-time? So that'll be the meeting?"

Tinker tucked in her shirt, glanced at her reflection in the window. She sighed like it was all too much. She was about to start in. He knew the signs. "So we have a couple of hours, then," he said.

She nodded.

He escaped from Tinker and found Ruth outside on the porch with Isabel. "Let's go for a swim," he said. They changed and went down to the water, already in shade. He watched Ruth plunge right in, the way Pony used to. The water today was warm. He swam ahead of her to the raft. They hung on to the ladder. She wrapped her legs around him, and there, unseen, he pulled the crotch of her swimsuit aside and backed her against the ladder, held to the ladder's sides, and entered her, slow at first, just resting where they were and he could look into her eyes and be lost until Ruth started to breathe faster, to pull at him, begging him to move inside her, and he did. Afterward they went up the ladder and lay in the last of the sun, watching clouds. "So far, so good?" Ruth asked him.

"So far, outstanding," he said.

After some time, they swam back to shore. The beach, the house, and the lawn were in shade now. William caught sight of someone on the porch, alone, rocking. His father was watching them. William felt a stab of dread that he and Ruth had been seen. He tried to remember which way the ladder had faced when they were making love against it. "Hey, Dad." He shook his father's hand, Ruth leaned over to give him a kiss. His father beamed at her. And then he said to William, "You decided to join us after all," which William took as sarcasm and which was what he told Ruth later in their room. She frowned, thinking it over, and then said, "I don't think so. I didn't hear it that way at all. It's just, you weren't coming, and then you came."

While they were out on the raft, Mira must have been putting out pictures of Pony all over the living room. There were dozens of them, leaning against the walls and along the floor, on all the tables and chairs. Mostly snapshots, curled with age, ancient Polaroids. Keith was behind her, looking at each picture carefully.

"We found some of these in Pony's apartment," Mira said.

" 'We'?" William asked.

"Keith and me," she said.

"You *went* there?" he asked Keith.

"Man, I live there," Keith said. "Didn't anybody tell you?"

"Mira, what's he talking about?" William asked.

Mira raised her shoulders as if to say, *What can you do?* "He's been there three weeks." She looked at Keith. "Two?"

"That's very strange," William said. "How could you do that?" He couldn't believe it. What was happening to them all?

"If you'd pick up the phone once in a while, you'd know this." Tinker's voice rang out from the kitchen. She came into the room, wiping her hands on a dish towel. "Pony owed back rent. Keith needed a place and was willing to make up the difference. Voilà. Somebody has to live in it, might as well be family."

"He's not family," William said.

"Sorry, man," Keith said. "I can move out if it's going to start a war."

"I'd like that." William glared at him. "Sooner the better."

"Then *you* pay her back rent, William. If you're going to be like that," Tinker snapped.

"Oh. This is about money. Of course," William said.

"It's about moving on." Tinker came right up to him, nose to nose. "It's about you never being where anybody can find you when big decisions are made and then coming in at the eleventh hour like this and trying to tell us what to do." Her face was red.

"What the hell is that supposed to mean? What big decisions? I'm just asking how he ends up living in Pony's apartment all of a sudden." He pointed at Keith.

"*He* helped us clean it out, for one thing."

"I would have helped. I didn't know you were doing it."

"You never answer your phone, William."

"Oh, brother." William threw up his hands.

"Well, it's true. I mean, finally, what's the point in even trying? You're always off somewhere."

"Off somewhere," he said. "That's right. Like up here getting that information out of Denny Bell about some guy tormenting Pony on the beach."

"Denny told Randy that."

"Tinker, Katherine and I talked to him. *Then* he told Randy."

"The point is that we have the information."

"You're sounding more and more like Dad."

"I'd like to know how much credibility we should give what Denny said. What if he made it up?"

William never saw that one coming. "You're not serious."

"Why did he wait so long to come forward? It's been over a month, and he just now remembers it? It sounds fishy to me. Maybe he wants to be the center of attention. And now he's backpedaling."

"He's scared. The guy saw him. Threatened him."

"He shouldn't be scared," Tinker said. "And if he's so scared, he should just go back to Worcester. Nobody's making him stay up here."

She lives in her own world, William thought. *With all its tidy shoulds and shouldn'ts.*

"And it's possible it was you he saw. You were up here," she went on.

"Denny Bell knows who I am."

"We shouldn't be talking about all this before the meeting," Tinker said. "Side talking is counterproductive."

Oh, for God's sake, William thought. *Who brought it all up in the first place?* But he let it go. He turned to Keith, who'd been standing by, listening to all this. "Can't you find something better to do?" William said, and stormed off.

"Did you hear that?" he asked Ruth upstairs in the bedroom. She was sitting naked on the bed, her small form tight, knees clasped, head down.

"Of course I did." She widened her eyes. "Everybody did."

"We're going back to Connecticut."

"You can't bolt when things get uncomfortable."

"Randy has nothing new. I already know that."

"You don't know that. Anyway, that's not why you're here," Ruth said.

"Sure it is."

"You're here to be with your family while everybody is hurting so bad. Don't you get it? You have to participate. You have to be present." She hesitated. "And not just with your family but with me, too."

What the hell was that supposed to mean? "I think I was pretty present out there in the water."

"You have a way of cutting out, William. There's always an emotional back door for you. Sometimes you just have to stick around and feel the discomfort."

"What I feel about Pony, for your information? One hell of a lot more than discomfort, and a hell of a lot more than they do," he said.

"Oh, really?" Ruth's gaze was cool and steady.

"Yes."

"They need you here," she said. "And you need them." She looked at her watch. "Anyway, it's too late to drive back. Tinker's been working on dinner. I promised to help her. And I'm a guest. I can't just cut out."

"You're with me," he said.

"I am not *just* with you, William Carteret. I have a presence here, too." She stood up and faced him. "You asked me to move in with you, remember? This is the reason I won't."

He was a hair away from saying something he would regret. The words were swimming to the surface. The ones that would end this thing flat. *You thought I meant that?* But he didn't. He kept his mouth shut. He went for the next level. "You want your guy to sit in the Wizard's Chair. Is that it? It all goes back to that?"

"Damn straight," she said.

He changed without saying another word and went downstairs. He wanted a drink. "William!" Tinker shouted from the kitchen. "Where's that little girlfriend of yours?"

Both sisters were in the kitchen. Tinker had changed into a big scary shirt of shiny red material and black tights—presumably, he figured, to look thinner. Her hair was pulled up in a bushy ponytail at the top of her head that didn't look half bad, but her skin was white and uniform and her eyes were dark, as if Mira had done the makeup. Maybe Tinker was three sheets to the wind. One or two, anyway, but the way she was going at it, number three was coming. She filled her glass to the top with red wine. Mira lifted a glass to him, smiled, and took a big sip. "Cheers," she said.

"Randy's coming for dinner." Tinker tightened her ponytail. She turned to Mira. "How do I look?"

"Never better," Mira said, crossing her eyes at William out of Tinker's view and mouthing the question, *How do I look?*

He wondered where Keith was but decided not to ask. He was glad the guy wasn't around.

"Put me to work," Ruth said, squeezing past William. She grabbed an apron and tied it behind her, the whole time ignoring

169

William. He poured his wine and went outside. Screw it. His sisters would know there was trouble in paradise. They had radar for that stuff. Ruth could be explaining the whole argument to them right then. No. She wouldn't do that. They'd want to know, but she wouldn't tell.

His father was down at the water, pulling the boats higher up the beach for the night. "Hey, Dad," he called, and bolted down the lawn to the water. He took the bow end of a canoe from his father, hauled it up onto the grass, and turned it upside down. The fight with Ruth had given him energy. Fights always did. A fight to him was like a look at the open road. He could call it quits, leave the whole thing behind. He pulled the rowboat up, lifted the side, and turned that over, too. He stashed the oars underneath. He kept working, feeling that his father must be watching, careful to do everything right or the old man would correct him. But when he looked up, his father was sitting awkwardly on the sand, staring out at the lake. He was in the exact spot where William had taken over, as if he'd fallen. "Dad?" William said.

His father made a *Carry on* gesture.

"You okay?"

"Of course," his father said, but his eyes glistened with tears, and William had an urge to do something. Sit beside him, put an arm around his shoulders. Instead, he cleared his throat and hoisted another canoe. He was afraid of what his father would do if he made an effort toward him—shrug him off, show annoyance. Comfort was not something they held out to one another in the Carteret family.

Randy arrived at about six, and they all sat on the porch at two tables pushed together and covered with an oilcloth, the slick part rubbed away in spots, its beige weave showing through a pattern of faded green and white plaid with cherry clusters. Tinker, Mira, and Ruth brought out the food. Tinker's color was high, her voice loud. She had a voice that carried anyway, but it was louder tonight; it spelled trouble. She made a big fuss over Randy, insisting that he sit beside her at the table, making sure he got enough to eat. William tried to catch Mark's eye, but Mark looked away.

William's father sat at the head with his back to the railing. He bowed his head, said grace, and they all passed the platters of food without saying much. The dishes were chipped, handed down over the years. Tinker refilled her glass of wine to the top. It was surreal to see Keith Brink sitting where Pony was supposed to be. William felt his anger—was it anger? Whatever, it was loose, rolling around like a steady river looking for an outlet. Keith was an easy target, but it wasn't the guy's fault. He was just trying to get along.

William had caught sight of Ruth a few times in the kitchen with Mira and Tinker as they got dinner ready. Ruth had been laughing with them, leaning in while Tinker stirred something on the stove. It was as if she'd crossed over into their camp. He'd felt monumentally alone. They'd had an uncomfortable half hour in the bedroom after that, avoiding each other as they changed clothes. But now, sitting beside her, he reached out for her hand under the table. She squeezed it. His lifeline.

After the food was cleared, his father tapped his glass with a knife. He gave the old Chamber of Commerce introduction for Randy. A little background, his years on the force, for Christ's sake, his promotions, as if they hadn't all known Randy Martine since he was a kid. As if they didn't know Randy was the one who'd sailed a rock through the library window that time. "Officer Martine," William's father said, "has been kind enough to come and tell us what he's learned."

And it was nothing. Randy ran through the time line, if you could even call it that, starting with William's departure between five and five-thirty. Dennis Junior saw Pony immediately after that. She was swimming, watching the child. A man arrived on the property at some point between six and seven, Dennis thought. Death was between six-thirty and nine. They couldn't pinpoint it any closer, unfortunately, because of the water temperature. "Angela was swimming in the nude," Randy said, consulting his notes. "The man apparently taunted her. He picked up the child. It seems she did what she had to do. She revealed her body to the man, presumably to lure him away from the child. The man followed her to the raft. Dennis did not see her after this. It's possible she drowned then. Or she could have drowned after he left. It's possible the man went into the house. Dennis wasn't sure, but according to Mr. Carteret, nothing was missing."

"Except that picture," William said. "Not to beat a dead horse, but Pony did show me a picture of Mom and a boyfriend or something when she was young. And I never did find it."

"Boyfriend?" Mira asked.

"I know of no such picture." His father shook his head dismissively. "I would have seen such a picture."

"I saw it that day, Dad," William said.

"What did the boy look like?" Mira asked.

"I don't know, Mira," William said. "Just a kid. A guy. Why?"

"Just wondered." Mira got up and started clearing the plates. Ruth got up to help. Randy waited for them to come back before he continued. The police had virtually nothing. There were no tire tracks, no unaccounted-for footprints. From Denny's account, the man was somebody Pony knew but not well. It was possible he was a stranger. Someone who'd come down their road. It wasn't altogether clear if the man had been aggressive toward Pony or not. Randy went down the list of people he'd contacted. Old boyfriends, friends. None of them was of interest to the police.

"Are you saying you think somebody killed her? That it was a murder?" Mira said.

"We know she drowned because her hair caught. Why she was down there in the first place is, as all of you know, at issue. Had someone pursued her? We don't have that answer."

His father cleared his throat. "And until we do, anything we might come up with is speculation. Am I correct?"

"Denny Bell is scared of something," William said.

"Officer Martine?" his father said. "Is that correct? We can be sure of what we know and delay speculation until we have something more concrete?"

"Dad, somebody might have done this to her," William said.

"Why would anyone ever want to hurt Pony, though?" Mira asked. "Everybody loved her."

"That's one way to look at it, Mr. Carteret," Randy said.

His father nodded and folded his hands on the table. "We can certainly keep an open mind. But until there's something more concrete, unless someone can add to what Officer Martine has said, we have to believe Pony's death was an accident."

"What if the guy was Andrew's father?" Mira said.

"Mira, please," his father said.

"Whoever he was, the guy just *left* her there—" Mira said.

His father shut his eyes and said nothing.

"We don't *know* that," Tinker said. "Right, Randy? Right, Daddy? We don't know the guy had anything to do with it. For all we know, he was a tourist who took a wrong turn. It was eight before Anita heard Andrew, so it sounds like Pony was still alive after the guy left. Think about it. If Pony died at six-thirty or seven, Andrew wasn't going to wait until eight to start screaming."

"Unless Anita didn't hear him till then," William said with another quick glance in his father's direction. They were doing exactly what he'd told them not to do.

"I'd like to play devil's advocate here," Keith said.

"I'd like you not to." William was offended at how much this guy butted in.

"He can talk if he wants," Mira said.

"Tell William what you told us," Tinker said.

Keith raised his hands and shook his head. "I spoke out of turn. I was mistaken."

"I think Pony was trying to unlatch the anchor chain," Mira said. "Not checking it but actually trying to undo it."

"She couldn't possibly," Tinker snapped.

"I didn't say she *could*. I said she was trying. If there was a scary guy there. Unhook it, let the guy drift out, and swim underwater back to shore."

"If there really *was* a guy there, and that's a big if, she had other options," Tinker said.

"Like?"

"Like screaming bloody murder, for one thing." Tinker's ponytail sagged off to one side. Her eyes glistened dangerously.

Mira turned to William. "I wish you could remember what the guy looked like in that picture Pony had."

"I'm not finished." Tinker raised herself up. "Nobody else is going to say it, so I will. What was she doing swimming naked like that in the first place, okay? With Andrew right there on the shore? In broad daylight. And drinking again. I hate to say this, but—"

"Then don't," William said.

"Mira opened the door, William. One theory is as good as another if it fits. I'm just stepping inside. It was a chain of events; it was a *continuum*, and dammit, Pony set it in motion. I mean, God, all this discussion makes her sound like she was this complete helpless little victim when—"

"When she was asking for it?" William asked.

"Yes." Tinker made the same come-hither gesture Pony had made, her great body swaying obscenely in her red shirt. "I mean, come on!" She looked around the table. "She was *always* asking for trouble. Right, Mark?"

Mark opened his hands. "Leave me out of this."

"I can't believe it. Why am I the only one who thinks this?"

"Because you were always jealous," Mira said quietly.

William checked his father again, expecting the old man to put an end to it. He was surprised to see his father not paying attention; he sat staring at the middle distance on the table, his hands folded carefully in front of him.

"Jealous?" Tinker exploded. "Her mess of a life? With a bastard child? My God! How could anybody be jealous of that?"

"While you're still ahead, shut up," William said.

"Pony the goddess, Pony the great. Even now. Now, when we're supposedly trying to understand what happened to her, everybody goes tiptoeing around what we know is true. Daddy, you, too."

William wanted to belt her one. Mark tried to get her to sit down, but she shoved him off.

Randy got to his feet and edged between the chairs.

"You're not leaving!" Tinker said. "You can't leave."

"Mr. Carteret, sir." Randy leaned over and extended a hand. William's father took it. Randy couldn't wait to get away. Tinker followed him down the steps all the way to his patrol car and then leaned way in the window like she was trying to kiss him. Mark had his back to the action.

A wailing started overhead, and Ruth excused herself to escape. She came back inside with Andrew just as Tinker was headed across the lawn. Andrew was fresh from sleep and looking from one face to the next, full of delight. When Andrew saw Tinker, he lifted his hands to her. "Mama," he said.

"What?" Tinker wailed. "Why did you have to get him up, Ruth?"

"He was crying," Ruth said. "I thought—"

"So kids cry, you let them cry." Tinker pulled out her chair and sank into it. "Not that you'd know."

"Lay off her," William said. The whole scene was falling apart, had been since it started, and all because his father was being so passive. It was almost as if Tinker was pushing and pushing, like she had no limits unless Daddy told her where they were. She was unstoppable. She was still on the subject of Andrew, crabbing about how it all fell to her and how she wished Ruth hadn't gotten him up.

"You're the one who woke him up, Tinker," William said.

"And you're the guardian," Tinker exploded.

"He's the guardian?" Keith asked.

"Stay out of this." William really didn't like the guy. Didn't understand what in the name of God Mira saw in him or why he was here.

Tinker was on a tear about Pony and the baby out of wedlock. Ruth took Andrew out of the room so he wouldn't hear. Tinker kept appealing to their father. "Right, Daddy?" she kept saying. Their father was watching without seeing, as he'd been that afternoon sitting on the grass, oblivious to William's presence. Tinker wasn't letting up about the unfairness of it all and how irresponsible Pony had been and how William should be taking Andrew but wasn't, and then she just sat down, *slid* down was more like it, into her seat and started sobbing that none of this ever would have happened if their mother were alive, Pony never would have dared have Andrew out of wedlock, and she, Tinker, had tried to hold the family together, but what was the point when they were all so hell-bent on falling apart?

When she stopped her rant, there was a harrowing silence during which they could hear the distant chirp of crickets. William stole a glance at his father, not knowing what to make of the old man's silence. This was supposed to be his meeting, and now it was no-body's.

Finally, Mira spoke in a very quiet voice. "Mom would have been okay with Pony having Andrew."

"Oh, please," Tinker said. "What planet are you on?"

"She would have welcomed him with open arms." Mira appealed to William. Her eyes glistened. "Can I tell her?" she asked him.

William had no idea what she was talking about. "Tell her whatever you want," he said. He hoped it would be good. He hoped Mira could even the score with Tinker.

"Mom had *William* out of wedlock," Mira said. "Right, William? Right, Daddy?"

Silence ate the porch.

"She *what*?" William said.

Mira's color drained. "You didn't know?"

"Dad?" William said.

His father looked at each of them in turn, then rose to his feet, pushing the table and knocking back his chair. The table screeched, tipping glasses, sending the silver rattling to the floor. He stood un-steadily. He was a giant of a man. He supported his weight with those monster hands spread on the oilcloth. William had never seen him like this. His face was red, his chin trembled. William didn't even breathe. He hadn't done anything wrong, but still he felt that ancient fear, the shame of misbehavior, waiting for the wrath of God to descend on them all. Watching. Waiting. The old man opened his mouth to speak. His eyes were slits. And then, as if in slow motion, his body pitched forward, his hands splayed to either side of the table, and he dropped to the floor like a stone.

Chapter 12

Mira

He was standing one second. Down the next. Dishes and glasses crashed to the floor. He landed hard, his face creased and pushed where he came to rest, as if it were made of rubber. He left a smear of bright red blood down the oilcloth. Tinker screamed that he'd had a stroke and pushed her way around the table to get at him, tipping more stuff over. Mira couldn't move.

William shouted out orders. He shook Tinker. He told her to give Dad some room and to stop screaming. He said they didn't know it was a stroke. It could be anything. He told Keith to call 911 and do it now. He barked at Mira to help Mark pull the table away and give them more space. They needed to move their father to the couch. Tinker tried to block the way. She kept saying, "No. You never move the person." William told Tinker to shut up. She didn't know what she was talking about. Their father didn't have a spinal-cord injury. Tinker crouched over him as if nobody else had better touch Daddy; he was hers, all hers. Ruth kept trying to ease her away. Their father could be dead, for all anybody knew by the sight of him. He was white as a ghost.

They got him to the couch in the living room. Tinker kept saying they should wait for the EMTs. The EMTs would know what to do. Ruth told her really it was okay, that William had the same training as EMTs, more, even, which was news to Mira but didn't impress Tinker. William tilted their father's head back, put an ear to his mouth, announced that the old man was breathing okay, that he hadn't choked on anything. Mira hadn't thought about that, but of course it was a possibility. William opened their father's shirt and felt along the neck, said his pulse was good. Mira's world went from black and white to color when William said that. Their father was alive.

And then there came the candy-apple-red lights flashing in the driveway, a gorgeous color, and these three big guys came up to the porch. Really big. Like sumo wrestlers, and so tender with her father. They treated him as though he was almost delicate, and he looked completely peaceful as they ministered to him in that brief window before he was crawling with tubes and all the other equipment of life. One of the EMTs, a kid younger than Mira was, with a very big face, sat the family down and asked questions. *Has Mr. Carteret complained of pain?* They all looked at one another and shook their heads. *What was his medical history?* Not even Tinker knew that. They were private about medical problems in their family. What medications was he on? Tinker ran to the bathroom and came back with her hands full of prescription bottles. The EMT wrote down the name of each one.

It was all Mira's fault. *Mom had William out of wedlock.* She had said out loud what she'd promised never to tell.

The men strapped her father onto a gurney, and he was just starting to wake up as they loaded him into the ambulance. The EMTs gave the family no warning that they were about to leave. They were there one minute, and then the ambulance was heading out the drive with those beautiful lights going, and the siren firing up, and the family left standing dumbly in the yard.

The Bells were watching from their part of the woods, with flashlights. Anita came forward in her bathrobe. "What happened? What can we do?" she said.

"Everything's fine," Tinker said. "Daddy just had a little fall."

A little fall? What was the matter with her?

They were ready to leave, but where was Keith? Mira had to go back to the house to find him. He was upstairs getting his hat, he said. He wondered if he could borrow a jacket; it was cold out there. It wasn't. It was still warm, but whatever, she thought. They had to go. People were waiting. She found one of her father's coats in the downstairs closet and gave it to Keith. He put it on, turning up the collar as if headed out in a storm. What was his problem? Mark said he would stay back at the house with the kids, and maybe that was a good idea for a lot of reasons. Something was up with him and Tinker. William's car was blocked, so they went in Keith's. Mira was in the middle of the backseat between Ruth and Tinker. Keith stepped on it down the dirt road. He tore out of the driveway when they hit the pavement after the ambulance, which they could see way in the distance. He leaned on the horn a couple of times. He caught up with the ambulance and then ran an intersection to keep on its tail.

William told him to slow down or they'd all be killed.

They had to wait in the emergency room. It was an old country hospital with yellow linoleum floors worn in paths. It was hot in the waiting room, and the air conditioner was loud. Tinker sat apart from everyone else, one side of her face pressed against the wall. Ruth went to the cafeteria and came back with paper cups of coffee for everybody. Mira kept glancing at William. He was staring at the floor and wouldn't meet her eyes.

She'd always thought he knew. How could he not? That was the thing. She thought it was one of those secrets people knew but didn't talk about. It had never been a matter of informing William, just of not talking about it. A big difference, she saw now. But the look on his face when he said *She what?* Worse than seeing her father down was what she had seen in William's face. Like a scared child. *She what?* But William had said Pony showed him a picture of their mother and a guy when she was young. So maybe Pony knew, too. The secret was leaking out in other ways. Like water, a secret sought its own level.

The doctor came out and told them they could go in to see their father. He would be kept overnight, but he was stable. Suffering from exhaustion. His EKG was normal. His brain function fine. Still, they wanted to observe him. He needed rest and calm. Tinker said she'd stay at the hospital with him. "Somebody has to," she said, and normally Mira would roll her eyes, but not tonight.

The porch light was on when they got home, and one of the lamps in the living room. Mark had cleared the table, done the dishes, and moved the tables back into the house. The porch looked like nothing had happened there. They went in. Someone turned on another lamp. Mira had a heightened sense of William's whereabouts at every moment, as though he were a magnet and she the metal shavings. When he passed her on his way to the kitchen, the hairs stood up on her arms and the back of her neck. Why wasn't he asking her about what she'd said? His silence was making her scared. The longer he went without asking, the guiltier she felt. She went upstairs to the safety of her bedroom. Keith came in a few minutes later. "You disappeared," he said.

She used a wet wipe to take off her makeup. She didn't dare use the bathroom in case she met William in the hall. She looked in the mirror and dragged the little square across her forehead.

"What was all that about?" Keith was sitting on her bed. "Right before your father fell?"

"Nothing," she said. He was the last person she wanted to discuss it with.

She heard William or Ruth going up the hall to the bathroom. She got into bed. The light went out in the hall; the slit under her door darkened. She lay rigid in the bed. This might have been the night they made love for the first time. But she was unresponsive when Keith tried to touch her. "No," she said. She lay awake for hours, it seemed. *What I've told you was for your ears only, Mira,* her mother had said. And Mira had promised. How could she have spoken those words aloud?

A knock came at her door. A very light rap. William stood in the darkened hallway. Mira put on a robe and followed him downstairs.

He was sitting at the table in the kitchen, waiting for her. He still had on the same T-shirt he'd worn earlier, streaked with their father's blood. He indicated the other chair. He looked exhausted. "What did you mean tonight?" he asked her.

"You didn't know? They never *told* you?"

His face. Oh. "Solemn" didn't begin to describe it. Blank except for his eyes, so black she couldn't see where the pupil ended and the iris began. "Told me what?" he said.

"That you . . ." She couldn't believe he hadn't known this at all. "That you had a different father. Before Mom married Dad."

A spasm ran through him, a tiny visible shiver. "I don't believe you," he said.

She felt frightened all of a sudden. "Mom told me once," she said.

He just stared at her.

"Lawrence. His name was Lawrence?" she said as if the name would jar a memory.

His face seemed to collapse. "What?" He shook his head. "What?" he said again.

She couldn't stop now. She wished she'd never started. "Your, you know, your father."

"Mom told you *what*?"

"That she had you before she married Dad. That you had a different father."

"Mira." He looked around the room.

"I'm only telling you what Mom told me," she said. "I'm sorry. God, William. I just thought you knew."

"Well, I didn't," he said. "Nobody happened to mention it."

"I'm sorry," she said again. It was all she could think to say.

"Why you?" He said it like *You, of all people.*

In all the years since it had happened, she had never told anyone about the abortion. Not even when she went to see her gynecologist. *Have you ever been pregnant?* "No," she always said. She knew they'd disapprove. But William deserved the whole thing. "I had an abortion in Canada when I was fourteen. Daddy didn't even know. Mom wanted to make sure I was okay with the abortion because if I wanted to have the baby, I guess she would have helped me. But I didn't want it at all. So she said she'd had you, you know, out of wedlock, and the guy's name was Lawrence, and Daddy adopted you. You were born someplace out west. She said he was mercurial."

"This is fucked." William pushed back his chair and got up. He went to the sink to splash water on his face, then out to the front porch. She followed as far as the living room. He came back inside. "Mercurial," he said.

"It means—"

"I know what it means." He paced back and forth in front of the door. "Why didn't anybody tell me?"

Mira felt the tears coming. How could she say "I'm sorry" one more time? How could she say she hadn't known again? *I'm sorry I'm sorry I'm sorry.* She made a small shape with her hands, as if packing a snowball. "All I know is what I said." She opened her cupped hands. "I only know this much." She held her hands out to him. "That little bit. That's it. I've told it all. That's all I know. What I just told you. I never talked about it to anybody else."

"What about Tinker and Pony?"

"I don't know."

"You don't know." He sat. He got up. He looked out the window on the lakeside. And then he left. Out the screen door again. Bang. Across the porch. She followed him to the door and watched the glow of his headlights disappear into the night. She sat back down on the couch in the living room. The only sound there was the ticking of the clock. What had she done? She could feel the rhythmic pressure of her heart in her ears. She rocked back and forth. She'd broken the promise to her mother. William hadn't known. She couldn't imagine the shock of that. The damage was out there. It was done, and it was only beginning.

She heard a sound. Her heart stopped. She sat still and listened. Someone was in the room with her. Yes. Whoever it was took a single careful breath. The sound came from the corner by the window behind the drapery panels they used in cold weather. "I hear you," she whispered. Nothing stirred. The house had always frightened her. She hated being alone. She heard every creak and moan. But this was real. Someone was there. If only William hadn't left. She should get up and look. Maybe call for Ruth or Keith or Mark. But what if it was nothing? She'd look ridiculous. She got to her feet. "Please?" she whispered.

The curtain moved, and Keith stepped out.

"You?" she said. She couldn't put it together. Why he'd be hiding.

"I heard a car leave," he said. "I came down to check who it was."

Did he think she was stupid? "You were listening in."

"Nonsense," he said.

It ripped her. Nonsense. She peered out the window. "You couldn't even see the driveway from that window," she said. "It looks over the lake. You were listening in."

He came toward her, and she backed away. He was weirding her out big-time.

"Why don't you just admit it? I'd understand."

He opened his hands, the gesture of the wrongly accused. "Jesus. You can be a real wack job sometimes."

"Look, Keith, I've been right here the whole time, except when I was in the kitchen with William."

"So who are you now, Jack McCoy?" He came toward her again, and she stepped away.

She considered calling for Mark. "I think you need to leave."

"Okay, Mira, have it your way." He gave her the big smile she'd once liked. "If you want me to say I was listening, I'll say I was. There. Does that do it for you?"

"I want you to leave."

"You're making a mistake," he said.

She sat on the couch while he went upstairs loudly enough to wake the whole house. He came down, put his suitcase by the front door, then went into the kitchen for his cooler. He came back into the living room lugging the cooler. He put it down on the dining table. "You'll regret this," he said.

She waved him away. She listened for the sound of his car leaving. She half expected him to come back, and she sat on the porch in case he did. After a while she was sure he was gone. What had it been about him in the first place? That he'd known Pony, she supposed. That had been powerful at the time. They hadn't even made it. Everyone thought they were, but they weren't. And he'd stuck around anyway, which had been strange. She shuddered. *Good riddance,* she thought.

She wrapped herself up in the same blankets they'd used for her father. She turned out the lights and lay down on the couch. She'd wait for William. William was her responsibility now. She'd set these events in motion, and now she'd stay on the couch and wait until he got home safely. But she fell asleep. She woke up early. She tried to remember why she was there. And then it came to her. The whole evening before. Her father's fall, the hospital, and then, oh God, what she'd said. William. She tore upstairs to make sure he'd come home.

The door to William and Ruth's room was wide open. The bed was neatly made. The closet was empty. William and Ruth were gone.

Chapter 13

William

The culvert crossed over one of the wider feeders to the lake, opposite Fond du Lac, and ended in a small turnout on its other side. William pulled over, got out of the car, and made his way down to the water's edge to a small crescent of sandy beach.

The truth of what Mira had told him was a weight, a plumb that had sunk right down to the core of him. The rightness of what she'd said was mixed with the memory of her blank face, her plain strange face, her eyes pale and small without the makeup. Who was he now? He felt the question all through himself. He raked the sand with his fingers. His mind was alive with memories, glimpses, bits of conversation. The whispers of adults when he was a child and all those lessons in high school biology about blue- and brown-eye dominance. He'd studied that section hard in school without knowing why. What he'd learned? Dark-eyed parents can have children with any eye color. But light-eyed parents didn't usually have dark-eyed children. His eyes were much darker than those of his parents. "Possible but unusual," his textbook had said. *How come you didn't get the red hair?* People asked that all the time.

Nobody had ever called him Will or Bill or Billy. He was William Carteret and only William Carteret. Friends of his had asked about that, too. Why did his sisters have those with-it names when he didn't? He'd said his parents had needed a boy to carry on the Carteret name, and lucky for them, the boy child, the official heir who would carry on the name, was born first, and with that out of the way, they could have some fun. They could have all the girls they wanted and give them playful nicknames, playful lives.

He said this tongue in cheek, but he believed it. He was the only boy in the Carteret family line. He was being groomed to take over the business, as all his predecessors had, as his own father had. They'd begin in the summers during college and then, upon graduation, work full-time in sales or production, then move up the ladder until the patriarch stepped down. It was history. It was a given.

In the family library was a book titled *A History of the Carteret Ball Bearing Company of Hartford, Connecticut*, put out on the occasion of the company's fiftieth anniversary. It was full of black-and-whites of the old factory buildings, groups of laborers standing around cold heading machines, grinding and lapping machines. Pictures of the men shaking hands with other men, sealing deals. A photograph of a roomful of women in high-collared white blouses and slender waists all sitting at typewriters and smiling. There were old advertisements for Carteret ball bearings and the great things they could do. The invention of the ball bearing was second only to the making of iron.

William had asked his mother about his name once. Why he was William and not Jasper? She'd just smiled and said that Jasper was such an old-fashioned name, didn't he think? And William was just, well, more up-to-date. He hadn't been convinced. Something in her tone, and being a brooder, made him wonder if his parents had noticed some quality about him that immediately said *This isn't a Jasper*. Now he could almost laugh at that. Not because he wasn't a Jasper but because he wasn't a Carteret.

And that business about his birth certificate. *My God. The lost original.* When he needed it for a passport application and asked his mother, she said it was lost but that she would write away for a copy. What came back was a small square of paper, embossed with the seal of California, that gave his name and date of birth but nothing else. It all made sense now. The original was elsewhere or destroyed. The original would have given his real father's name. And the lost photographs. There were drawers full of photographs of the girls as babies, but none of him. Again, the explanation was always vague. Something about a flood in the basement years earlier, a robbery. Never one clear answer. The explanation in his own mind had always been that he was born when his parents' life together was new and chaotic, that he was unplanned, that they were poor and had no money and no time for the frivolity of baby pictures. The girls were born in more stable times, when their parents were organized enough to file birth certificates and put photographs into albums. And the dearth of pictures of his mother. It was what had made the picture Pony showed him so unusual. They had dozens of photographs of his father as a boy, and of generations of Carterets, but none of his mother as a child. The boy in the picture he'd seen, he realized with a start, must have been his biological father.

As if a light had been shined onto the past, he had answers to so many questions that had gone unanswered. There would be more, hundreds more, he knew. It hadn't been chaos at all. It had been secrecy. But why? Why hadn't they said anything? Was his father a criminal? Mentally ill? What was so awful that it could not be spoken aloud? Except to Mira. The deepest cut of all. *Mira!* William was a fool. The one who didn't know. That was the worst of it. And Pony must have known. It couldn't be a coincidence. The picture of his mother and that boy? The boy *was* his father.

He looked up. The early sun struck the top peaks of the mountains. Below, barely distinguishable from its surroundings, Fond du Lac looked benign, like any summer house in which a family would get up, have their coffee, and take out the canoes.

William drove to the general store. The newspaper delivery trucks were there, unloading bales of *The New York Times* and *The Boston Globe*. William used the outside pay phone to call Minerva. It was very early, and he woke her. "It's William," he said. "Is it true I'm not my father's son?"

A long pause at the other end, and then she said, "Oh, Jasper finally told you."

"Mira told me."

"Not Jasper?"

"He's in the hospital. Exhaustion, they think."

"I see," she said. "This is a great deal for you, William."

"You bet," he said.

"I wasn't aware that Mira knew."

"Maybe they thought it was none of my business."

Minerva didn't respond.

"Mira said his name was—is—Lawrence. Did you know him?"

"Not well, but yes," Minerva said.

"I'm coming down there," he said.

He slipped quietly back into the house. Mira was on the couch, looking worried even in her sleep. He awakened Ruth and told her they had to leave. And Ruth—God, he loved her—took one look at him and just did it, packed her stuff, no questions asked until they were in the car and he told her what Mira had said. She told him to pull over and say it again. She asked if he'd like her to drive.

"After we pay Jasper a visit," he said. "Then you can drive."

The hospital room was small and very white. The windows were open, and there was a fresh smell to the place. Jasper lay in the far bed, propped up, an oxygen tube coming from his nose, machines at his bedside blinking and recording things. His eyes were shut. Tinker was asleep in the near bed, still in her red shirt and tights, barefoot.

"Jasper?" William said.

Tinker startled awake and swung her legs over the side of the bed. She reminded William of a child, her face puffy and confused.

William raised a hand to quiet her. "I won't be long."

"What do you want?" Her eyes were huge.

Jasper opened his eyes and blinked. William leaned over him, so close he could smell the old man's medicine breath. "Is it true I'm not your son?"

Jasper glanced toward the window.

William jabbed the old man's shoulder lightly. "Yes or no?"

"I'm calling a nurse," Tinker said.

Jasper's lidded eyes met William's. "Yes," he said.

William had expected this, but even so, he sagged under the weight of it and fell into the chair drawn up beside his father's bed. Beside *Jasper's* bed. He opened his hands. He didn't know where to start.

"Leave him alone," Tinker said.

William didn't take his eyes off Jasper. "And you never mentioned this because . . . ?"

Tinker moved protectively to her father's bed.

"Because your mother wouldn't allow it," Jasper said. Or that was what William thought he heard him say.

"Mom's been dead a while," he said. "Not a good excuse."

Tinker fumbled for the buzzer again and pressed it hard.

"Your mother wanted the matter put behind her," Jasper said.

"The matter," William said. "The *matter?*"

"You're my son." Jasper's voice was stronger now. "You've always been my son."

"Not your son, Jasper. I'm Lawrence something's son. What's his last name?"

Tinker's buzzer was going nonstop. William knew he didn't have much time before they kicked him out.

His father shook his head. "I campaigned for telling you the truth, believe me. But your mother was adamant. It was her information to reveal, William. Not mine. Don't forget that."

"And what about me?" William said.

A nurse appeared in the door. "Is there a problem?" she asked.

"I took you in, William," Jasper said, his old growling self coming back in spades. "I made you my son. I made you a Carteret."

"I'm not a Carteret," William spat out.

"What more do you want?"

What more? He wanted everything. He wanted everything back, a life re-lived in the light of truth.

"Sir, I have to ask you to leave," the nurse said.

"I drove her to San Diego." Jasper smiled at the memory of it. "I helped find a place for the two of you. I loved her. Larry never found her. He never came after her. She didn't want to tell you because if you'd known, you'd have wanted to find him, and he'd have found her. She was afraid of him."

"She could have told me that," William said, the words bursting from him. "I would have understood."

"No, you wouldn't." Jasper sounded disgusted.

"It's why you want Andrew with Tinker instead of me. Right? Raised by your own flesh and blood, right, Jasper?"

"Stop calling him Jasper," Tinker said.

Two more nurses—a man and a woman—came into the room. The man took William by the elbow. "Come away, sir," he said.

But William had one more shot: "And it's why you sold the business, right? There wasn't a real Carteret to take over." He never got the answer.

"You saw that," he said to Ruth in the car. "The son of a bitch."

Ruth said nothing until they reached Springfield. "You're still the person you were, William. In the important ways. You'll always be who you are."

But who had he been? He felt parts of himself falling off, like the calving of a glacier. What would be left? His life was a lie. Everything about it. So many people had known. The realization that he was no one came in waves, worse than grief. Why had his mother told Mira and not him? His mother, Jasper, Mira had watched him grow up thinking he was Jasper's son, and all the time they'd known he wasn't. Had they laughed? It was as if the ground had opened up and he was free-falling. Who was he? And why had the people he thought loved him lied to him all this time?

He dropped Ruth at the house in Glastonbury where she was working. Mindy was in the garage when they drove up. She came to the car. "Well, well, well," she said. She seemed ready to argue with him again. The old William would have done it, but not this William. No matter what Ruth said, he wasn't the same guy he'd been before, so what the hell? He spun out of the driveway, drove to New Haven, where he left the car in a high-rise parking garage, and took Metro-North into Grand Central, then the subway uptown.

Chapter 14

William

At the Seventy-seventh Street subway station, William emerged onto the street, walked back along Lexington Avenue to Seventy-fifth, then over to Minerva's building, just off Park. He gave his name to the doorman, then took the elevator to the seventh floor. She met him in the hall. She had on a black cardigan sweater over a yellow shirt, a long brown skirt, and under the brown skirt a pair of red slacks. She squeezed his cheeks. "My dear William," she said. "Yes, yes."

The apartment had a small foyer crowded with cupboards, coats hanging from a long wooden rod, and stacks of old magazines and newspapers. The foyer gave onto an equally crammed living room, stuffed with furniture and filled with light.

He knew there would be no rushing her. She led him by the hand to the spare bedroom at the back, explaining as they walked that she'd started dozens of seedlings in small pots under gro-lights in the winter, and now she had early tomatoes, peppers, and zinnias. In the bedroom he inspected her city garden under its humming fluorescent lights against the wall. She was having an ongoing fight with the building's board of directors for not letting her keep pots on the roof. "Honestly, William. These people have no imagination," she said. "So unreasonable."

He recognized, as they made their way back to the living room—stopping in the hallway so Minerva could point out a photograph or two—that she did exactly what Jasper did. If there was something important to discuss, there was a delay, a stage set, as she was doing now. He never minded it in Minerva, though.

She pushed back her jet-black hair, a gesture of vanity held over from her youth. She'd fixed the roots since Pony's funeral. In the photographs she pointed to, she was at first a tailored, chic, and beautiful young woman, becoming exotic and then eccentric as time and the photos wore on. She came to the end. "Here," she said, taking a small framed photograph from the wall and handing it to him. "This is your mother and me. It was taken in 1957. I was twenty-two, and Olivia, your mother, was about ten or eleven. Papa had died the year before. We were terribly sad."

He looked closely. Minerva stood with an arm around his mother's shoulders, wearing a pale dress with a full skirt and a belt tightly cinching her small waist. His mother, even though she was so much younger, was almost the same size as Minerva but robust. She had on a sleeveless blouse, jeans with the cuffs rolled up, and bright white socks, and it must have been a breezy day, because her blond hair was blown across her neck. She scowled into the camera. "You do know the story of Papa's accident?" Minerva asked.

William shook his head.

"Well, for heaven's sake, he worked for the railroad. A piece of heavy machinery broke loose, crashed down through the ceiling of the warehouse where Papa was working, and sheared the top of his head off. He died immediately. Mother had to go to work to keep us fed. I was old enough to work, too. Poor Olivia was left alone so much after that. Larry Anholt wooed her, and poof, she was gone."

Minerva led the way back to the living room and indicated an armchair, tucked in between more trays of plants, where he was to sit. Glasses of red iced tea and a plate of cookies were on the table beside the chair. Minerva passed the cookies to him and slid a glass of iced tea across the table. She took a sip of her own.

"It was Mira who told you?" She frowned. "Curious."

"She's known for years. She said Mom told her when she had an abortion."

Minerva raised her eyebrows. "Oh my."

"Did you know that?"

Minerva shook her head. "This is a great deal for you so soon after Pony's death. But it should have been done years ago. After Olivia's death, I urged Jasper to tell you. And at the wake for Pony, I made clear to him I would tell you if he did not. I was not aware that Mira knew. How very curious. I apparently felt an unnecessary urgency. You see, I was afraid that if Jasper did not tell you and I went to my grave with this information, you would never know. I'm an old lady, William. Death awaits."

"Oh, come on," William said automatically, then felt embarrassed. It was what you said to flatter women. What Minerva had said was true.

She threaded her fingers together and shut her eyes. "Your parents believed they could triumph over the past," she began. "I'm speaking of your mother and Jasper."

"What about the other guy?" William said.

"Bear with me, dear." She smiled. "Your mother and Jasper thought they could ignore an unhappy past and create a dazzling new future for themselves. Today people are more apt to indulge the past. Am I correct? To dig up secrets and so on."

"People like to know what happened. Bad or good."

"And you?"

William shrugged.

Minerva sipped her tea, smoothed her skirts, checked her image in the mirror. "I appall Tinker, don't I?" She laughed. "She has very little curiosity, that one. Why, children come right up to me in the subway and ask if I'm poor or crazy. But the family? Never. We're a family of silence, William. And things that cannot be spoken become powerful."

She fingered the cuff of her sweater. "Your mother gave me this for Christmas once. The trousers belonged to a man with whom I traveled in Asia. A lovely man. I had them taken in, of course. For me, memory is attached to my clothing. And you? Where do you keep the stories of your life?"

"Never thought about it." William tapped his head. "Here, I guess."

Minerva pressed a hand to his heart. "Perhaps here?"

"I'm not following, Minerva."

"What do you remember of your early life?"

"The usual. Growing up. Vacations. Christmases. I remember when the girls were born."

"Your earliest memory. The very first."

"California," he said without hesitating.

"Aha. Tell me."

"There was a green tree in the backyard. The bark was green and smooth, like a lizard."

She nodded. "A paloverde. What else?"

"I went swimming in this pool. I didn't want to go in, and I tried to get away, but the teacher pulled me away from the fence and held me under."

"A frightening memory. What does it mean to you?"

"I knew I'd better do what he told me to do. I learned to swim."

"Do you find it odd that your mother and Jasper lived in California?"

"Didn't used to," William said. "Now everything is odd."

"What explanation did they give you?"

"They met out there. That's all I really know. They weren't big on reminiscing." William hadn't been told any of this specifically, but what he'd pieced together over the years was this: that Jasper had left the family business and gone west to try his hand at other endeavors, and there he'd met William's mother. William had never probed because underneath that story was something darker. He was afraid to find out that his own unplanned birth and the responsibility of having a child had driven his father back home to Hartford, back to the family business he'd tried to escape. If it hadn't been for William, his father might have pursued a dream.

The heat in Minerva's apartment was stifling. All the windows were wide open, and the smell of pavement and exhaust, not exactly unpleasant, floated through the apartment on the occasional hot breeze. Minerva put a gold cushion on the coffee table and raised her bare feet. "Jasper adopted you here in Connecticut. You are the child of my sister, Olivia, and Lawrence Anholt. People called him Larry."

"Anholt," William said.

"A-N-H-O-L-T." Minerva placed her hands over his and leaned into him, her eyes glistening. "Shall I tell you again?"

He nodded. Tears filled his eyes, and he tried to squeeze them dry.

"Your biological father was named Larry Anholt. Your mother had you in California. Jasper Carteret met your mother there, and by then she was desperate to leave Larry. Jasper helped her to do that. He adopted you when you came to Connecticut."

William needed to move around. He went to the open window. The air was as thick there as inside, and hotter. He went down the hall to the bathroom. He shut the door, sat on the edge of the tub, and pressed his face against the cool white tile on the wall. He couldn't think. His mind raced. When he could breathe again, he stood at the mirror and splashed water on his face. He stared at his ashen reflection. How in hell could he not have known this? Why hadn't Minerva told him? Like a life spent with spinach between your front teeth and no one saying a thing. Up until yesterday he would have said you were what you believed. People became who they wanted to become. Belief and behavior trumped biology. Now he knew that was a crock. Biology was everything. He did not have Jasper Carteret's blood in him. He had Larry Anholt's. But who was that?

Minerva knocked at the door. "William. Dear. Are you all right?"

"Out in a minute." He splashed once more and dried his face on a hand towel. When he returned to the living room, Minerva was back on the sofa. She patted it with one hand, and he sank down beside her. In her other hand, she held a black-and-white photograph. It showed two people standing beside a car. Beyond them lay an expanse of desert, as if they'd stopped at a scenic overlook out west. "Olivia and Larry," Minerva said.

William held it close, tilting it for better light. His mother and father were the same height. His father was lean, like William. He looked hard into the man's face as if it could tell him something. "That's him?"

"He was very handsome," Minerva said. "I'll give him that much." She handed William a magnifying glass. Under the glass, his father's face was dark, perhaps sunburned. He squinted so hard it was difficult to see what the man really looked like. His arm was tightly around Olivia. The fingers dug into her sleeve. Could this be the guy in the picture Pony had shown him? He hadn't looked closely.

"Where are they in this?"

"Puma Springs, California. It's a small town close to the Mexican border. In the Sonoran Desert." Minerva shook her head. "I'm so sorry, William. I wish I didn't have to do this."

"Better you than Dad," he said. "Than Jasper." William felt a rush at using the name. "Why the big mystery?" He wanted it to sound light, almost funny. It was the most terrifying question.

"Jasper had better answer that," she said.

"But what do you think?"

"People believed they could control their futures. I can't exactly say it was their fault, William. Belief governs with an iron hand."

"What was Larry like?"

"I met him only twice. The first time was in Puma Springs. Larry was working there. An agricultural job of some sort. The pool you remember is most likely the pool at the motel in town.

The only pool. He made clear that he was not happy to have me there, that he wanted Olivia to himself. We walked in the desert. I think they liked to do that. It was recreation for them. He was very much the outdoorsman, like you. I didn't have the proper shoes, and I turned my ankle. Larry stopped and watched your mother tend to my foot. I remember distinctly that he made no move to help. I thought it might even please him that I was injured. He insisted upon continuing the walk, but of course I was unable. So the two of them went on while I waited in a bit of shade. It was an hour before they returned. My ankle had swollen by then, and it took us a long time to walk back the little distance I had come. At the time, I felt distinctly that I was at fault for slowing them down so. But in retrospect, well, it was irresponsible of them to leave me there such a long time in the baking sun. I knew your mother thought it was wrong, but she did as Larry said. She was besotted with him."

"You didn't like him, did you?"

"He was too strong for your mother," she said.

"And the other time?"

"Years later. I was living in Los Angeles." Minerva pronounced it the old way, "Los Angle-ese." "Larry didn't knock. He just came inside my house. A woman was with him, and he wanted me to know he had married her, as if that would encourage me to tell him where Olivia was. She was a very plain woman with watery blue eyes and mousy hair, but aggressive, too. She sat herself down at my dining room table as though she owned the house. You can tell so much from the way a woman sits. She looked around, sizing things up. I had many lovely items, and not one of them escaped her notice. I told them I didn't know where Olivia was. As much as his wife was an offensive person, I was glad for her presence, because Larry had a temper. I thought he wouldn't lose it with her there."

"So he was a son of a bitch."

"But you are not, my sweet. If that's what you're thinking. You inherited your mother's temperament, not his. I've been watching, and I can assure you of that."

It was exactly what he'd been thinking. "It feels like half of me is up for grabs," he said.

"Everyone deserves to know his biological past." Minerva's cheeks colored with indignation. "It belongs to *you*. It is your birthright. I've held my silence. I knew that as you grew older, you'd pay attention to Jasper's health for information about your own. We all do that, start looking to our parents for clues about what might go wrong. Or right. It was critical for you to know that Jasper's health does not apply to you."

"That was the argument at the wake, right?"

Minerva nodded.

"Am I a bastard?"

Minerva burst out laughing. "I believe you are."

"So where is Larry Anholt?"

Minerva clasped her hands. "I don't know," she said. "Perhaps this will be a start." She handed him the envelope he'd seen earlier on the table. It contained a small, aged newspaper notice from *The Puma Sun* newspaper, a poor photograph of five men standing in a row. Lawrence Anholt was identified as second from the left, and he stood, as did the others, with his arms folded across his chest and his head back. The text explained that the five were foremen at DiRisio Farms and that Lawrence Anholt was formerly of Stanley, Idaho. William stared at the tiny, grainy face of his father.

"Stanley, Idaho," William said. "Puma Springs, California. All this time I thought I was so eastern. I guess I can't claim Jasper's *Mayflower* ancestry anymore." He grinned. "I'm the son of a foreman on a farm."

Neither of them spoke for several moments. Then Minerva said, "Come."

He followed her to the small Pullman kitchen and stood at the door while she took out a platter of sandwiches and two cans of beer, which they drank from the cans, sitting at the dining room table.

"I understand you're to be Andrew's father," Minerva said.

"Guardian," William said.

Minerva smiled at him. "And what do you perceive as the difference between the two?"

"I have to wait until I'm better set up. Tinker has him for now," he said.

"Don't let that go on too long," Minerva said. "Promise me."

After lunch she suggested a walk. "You must keep your body moving in the coming days. But I don't need to tell you that." They went outside into the bright summer light. They walked slowly up Park Avenue. At each cross street, William took Minerva's elbow for the curb down and then the curb up. They walked along Seventy-seventh Street toward the park. They crossed Fifth Avenue to the cobbled sidewalk and sat on a bench. William was remembering the only fight his parents ever had, one that had started at a picnic when Mr. Pereen and his mother were leaping over the campfire together, holding hands. It had been innocent, just silly fun, but his father had snatched his mother away and they'd gone home, riding in an ominous silence. That night his parents had argued long into the night. Minerva had been visiting at the lake at the time, and he asked if she remembered the incident.

"Jasper never forgave Olivia for having loved anybody else. He was fiercely jealous."

"But he knew when he met her," William said. "He knew she'd had a child. *And* he held it against her? What a prick."

"Love is irrational, William. Don't be too hard on Jasper."

"I keep thinking I need to tell Pony all this, and then—"

"Take a deep breath, sweetheart," Minerva told him. "Don't forget to breathe!"

On their way back to the apartment, they walked arm in arm, in step. "Besotted, eh?" William said.

"Drunk on love," Minerva said.

"You didn't like him, did you?" he asked again.

"I didn't know him. He kept her from us, from Mother and me. I certainly didn't like that."

"I like knowing they were in love," William said.

"I have a box for you," Minerva said when they reached her building. "It's Olivia's clothing, a few personal effects, I suppose. She left it with me when she moved to Connecticut with Jasper. It's been in my storage unit all these years. You're the one to have it. Do whatever you like with it. Save it, throw it away. It's up to you." She led the way down the back stairs of her building to a long row of fenced-in stalls. Minerva's was crowded high, everything thrown in over the years. She disappeared into it and emerged with a yellow Seagram's 7 box, taped shut. She handed it to him. "What will you do now?" she asked, looking up at him.

"Try to find him," William said.

Minerva nodded. "Just be careful," she said.

On the train back to New Haven, William lifted the box to his lap, sliced through the tape with a key, and lifted the flaps. The smell was musty, the clothes neatly folded. There was a crocheted vest, purple and pink. A short flowery dress, several blouses all printed with flowers, too. He held it to his face, breathed in his mother's scent, and wept quietly.

At the bottom was a baby blanket. The blanket was thick, folded, and tied with a blue ribbon, flattened from all its years at the bottom of the box. There was something hard inside the blanket. He undid the ribbon. Inside was a flat white canister bound by a thick rubber band. He pulled off the rubber band and opened the canister. It contained a reel of film.

Chapter 15

William

William picked Ruth up at her job site in Glastonbury. Mindy was going ahead with the fountain. She announced this, leaning into his side of the car, her skinny cleavage at eye level. "Go for it," he said. He could scarcely remember having had a point of view about a fountain. That was light-years ago.

He and Ruth drove to the Steele Road house, and he let himself in using the key that Jasper kept on a hook by the back door. Ruth didn't want to go inside, so she pulled a lawn chair from the garage and sat there while he went inside; she didn't like the way he was doing this, going to the house to roust out the projector without asking. Ruth didn't have a sneaky bone in her body.

The house was steamy from having the windows shut tight for several days in brutal humidity. He remembered the smell and the feel of it from his childhood, his parents' low voices always in another room. And it was dark. The shades on all the windows were drawn, shades so old and brittle that over the years people's fingers had punctured them, and they were now dotted with points of light. William opened some windows to let in the air.

He had a vague idea where the projector was—in one of the closets upstairs, possibly the attic. But once he was inside, he liked having the house to himself. He walked soundlessly through, pausing in doorways, listening for sounds. He felt comfortable, being alone like this. What was it about the smells of a house that brought back so much? His sisters' birthday parties. All the little girls squealing in the corridors, running up and down the stairs. All the games of hide-and-go-seek.

He sat at the desk in Jasper's den, a desk that had been handed down through generations of Carteret men. It was a massive piece of furniture, with deep drawers and a leather top. As a boy, William used to sit at it and wonder about the men in his family who had used it before Jasper, and the day when it would become his, when he'd be a man, when Jasper Carteret would be dead. Now it was only a desk, and an ugly one at that, overly ornate, too heavy and too big. Now he didn't come from these people but from farm laborers. He felt a well of pride at that. He opened the top drawer, which was divided into wooden compartments. Jasper's pens sat side by side in one. Pencils in another, paper clips in a third. Jasper had two silver letter openers, a pair of scissors, several rolls of tape. The desk was as neat as the man himself, nothing out of place.

William thumbed through the bills, copies of legal documents, insurance policies. The files were all labeled, and each contained what it said. No surprises. All his life, William had seen his parents' lives as an open book. He thought he could look through any drawer, any closet, and not come upon anything incriminating. Until yesterday, theirs was the life without secrets, whereas his boyhood had seemed to be nothing but secrets—his stash of *Playboy* magazines hidden under his mattress, the occasional joint tucked into a shoe in his closet, the intercepted report card burned in his trash can.

When the girls were born, one right after the other, the house had smelled of baby food and baby powder and spit-up and diapers. One of them was always crying. That was when his secret life began. He did what he wanted. He and his friends went to Elizabeth Park and played tennis and sometimes hoops if the basketball court was free. They ran through backyards. A few times they skipped school. And fairly often, he and his friends had sneaked out of their houses late at night and climbed up the fire escapes of the buildings on South Main Street, where you could see the whole of West Hartford on one side and on the other, beyond, the Hartford skyline glittering in the distance.

But maybe, he thought now—and why was it that the truth took so long to announce itself?—maybe his life hadn't been so much secret as neglected. Maybe nobody had been paying attention to where he was or what he was doing. Maybe nobody had cared unless it involved one of the girls. Like that time with Tinker.

He was thirteen and Tinker was about seven, already an overweight, officious, bossy little girl in her baggy sweatshirts and her hair in two fat, frizzy braids. It was a Sunday afternoon, and William had been in his room listening to Metallica when his father knocked. He didn't wait for an answer before he barged right in and stood looking at William, at his disaster of a room, listening to the music, and without a word was able to pass judgment on all of it, on everything William was, everything William liked, and then he said, shaking his head as though William was some kind of a freak, "It's too nice a day to be inside." The least that William could do, Jasper said, was go with Tinker to the Walgreens at the corner of Farmington Avenue and Prospect Street, so she could spend her allowance. Just to make sure she got there and back okay.

And so William led the way, riding his bike as fast as he could down Steele, waiting at the corner until she almost caught up and then taking a left up Fern Street, a quick right to cut through an alley, going fast on purpose to lose her, pausing at the corner of Farmington until the second he saw her and then taking off again.

"Wait up, William," she was screaming at him furiously, pumping the pedals as fast as she could, her squat little figure almost comical behind him. Near Walgreens, he again turned back and watched her approach. At the cross street, she stopped, got off her bike like the little dweeb she was, and checked both ways before walking her bike across. He didn't know why he had to go with her if she was going to be this careful. Tinker was an old lady.

He was coming to Walgreens, a huge drugstore, part of a chain, set back from the street, a parking lot in front. He turned again to check on Tinker, who was just about to cross South Highland. He rode toward the parking lot, no hands, his arms folded across his chest. It was spring, the lousiest time of the year. The trees were still without leaves, the air was damp and cool, and there were puddles on the ground and, here and there, small lumps of snow. As William entered the parking lot, he noticed three kids who were a year ahead of him in school.

Chuck Gallo, Andy Mahan, and a Russian kid, new this year, whom people called Mafia. There were Russians everywhere in West Hartford. Even the Walgreens had a sign out front that said APTEKA.

The three kids had on black T-shirts airbrushed with graffiti, and their bare arms were blotchy from the cold. They wore bandanas low over their eyes. They noticed him at the same moment he noticed them, and William knew by some sort of innate triangulation that he would reach the door to Walgreens and the three of them at the same moment that Tinker, who was gaining on him from behind, would reach him. There was nothing he could do to change that. There would be trouble.

"I'm telling Daddy," Tinker wheezed out as she slammed on her brakes, squeaking to a halt.

"She's gonna tell Daddy," Andy Mahan said, and Tinker, who hadn't even noticed the three kids, got this stricken look. Sometimes you really did have to feel sorry for her, but she was also about to make everything five thousand times worse.

"You have fat sister," the Russian kid said.

"Go ahead in, Tink," William said to her. "Go in the store."

"You *know* them?" she said, her eyes wide.

"Just go ahead and get what you came for," William said.

Tinker pushed down the kickstand on her bike.

"I'll wait out here," William said. No way he was going to leave their two bikes out in front with those three particular kids.

"Tink," Chuck said. "What kind of freaking name is that?"

"You wanted to get something," William said to Tinker. "So go inside and get it."

Tinker, head down, disappeared through the automatic doors.

"You not go, too?" Mafia said. "You worry about bike?"

"Yeah," William said. "I worry about bike."

"We watch bike," Mafia said.

Andy Mahan kicked up the stand on Tinker's bike and pushed it in a circle.

"Hey," William said. "Come on, Mahan."

"Come on what?" Mahan said. He slung a leg over the bike and rode it, wobbling, his long scissors legs rising over the handlebars. He bumped over the curb and into the street.

"You go get," Mafia said, a big smile on his face.

All of William's options were clear and none of them was any good. Go after Mahan on foot and leave his bike to Mafia and Chuck? Ride after Mahan? And then what? Tinker comes out and has to deal with those two. And just then Tinker did come back outside, her cheeks bulging with the huge gumballs she'd spent her allowance on, the empty package in her fist. "That's my bike!" she yelled. "Make him give me back my bike, William." She actually drooled, her mouth was so full of that junk. And then a man, a total stranger, must have figured out what was going on and went after Mahan: "Hey you, kid, give the little girl her bike." He was a big, formidable-looking guy. Mahan dropped Tinker's bike and took off, the other two behind him, down Farmington Avenue.

Tinker went running to the street. Her shorts were all hitched up and caught in her crotch. William couldn't even look at her. He muttered "Thanks" to the man and took off, this time heading a different way. Not the way Mahan and Chuck and Mafia had gone.

"We're not allowed to go that way," Tinker called out when she saw the direction he was taking.

"Screw allowed," he said to himself. He rode down Prospect and took a left onto Fern, which was one of the busier streets. He stayed in the street and not on the sidewalk, like he was supposed to. He let the cars slow behind him and then shoot past in annoyance when there was no oncoming traffic. He didn't care. He didn't even look back to see where she was. He knew. She'd be off her bike, pushing it along the sidewalk, because they were on about a one-degree hill.

When he reached the crest, right before Fern plunged steeply down, he looked back. Man, she was out of shape. Even at that distance, he could see she was talking to herself. Marsha Motormouth. Probably practicing what she'd tell their father when they got home. About him. Jeez. When she was almost caught up, maybe fifty feet away, he took off before she had a chance to say anything. He leaned into the wind, pedaling hard. A car came up behind him, and he raced it. The guy pulled ahead, gave him the finger.

The pothole came out of nowhere, huge and deep, rushing him. He crunched on the hand brakes, swerved left, skidded a full 180, and stopped. Shit. Cool. He looked up to see where Tinker was. Jeez, she was still up on top, still looking behind herself, letting one car pass her and then another.

She finally got up the nerve. Her bike was an old Schwinn with foot brakes. She stood on the pedals for more brake heft and came slowly down, still chewing that wad of gum, scared out of her fat little wits. Pony wouldn't have done that. Pony would have raced him down the hill, and she was two years younger than Tinker.

William watched her on the hill in a kind of fascination. She was picking up speed in spite of herself. Her mouth was wide open. In exactly the way he'd realized that he would get to Walgreens at exactly the same moment Tinker did, he knew she was dead-on for that pothole. He should have called out to warn her, but he didn't.

It happened in slow motion. The bike tipped forward, and Tinker was lifted into the air like an acrobat. Her body arced gracefully. *She should put out her arms,* William thought. *She should let go of the bike.*

But she held on. She and the bike skidded across the strip of grass that divided the sidewalk from the street. She lay still for a few seconds, and he thought she was dead. Then she opened her mouth and screamed bloody murder.

He rushed to where she lay. The right side of her face went from a nasty pink to red as tiny droplets of blood surged through where the skin was scraped away. She wiped at her face, which made it worse. A car pulled over, and somebody got out to help, and then there was a cop car, and William thought, *Somebody saw what I did.*

But no one had actually seen it happen. The cops brought Tinker home. William followed along with both their bikes, riding his, guiding her mangled one. He went right to his room, back to his Metallica tapes, where he had wanted to be all along. He waited for the boom to fall.

Soon William heard his father's footsteps on the stairs. Jasper swung open the door to his room so it banged against the wall and bounced almost closed again. His father stood framed in the doorway, his arms folded on his chest. His face was flushed. "What do you have to say for yourself?"

William said nothing.

"Well?" Jasper said.

William had never seen his father so angry. If William said anything about Mahan, Gallo, and Mafia, his father would say that was no excuse.

"She could have been killed," his father said.

"But she wasn't," William said in close to a whisper.

"What was that?" his father demanded.

"Tinker's fine," William said.

"She is not fine!" His father's voice exploded into the room. He took a step forward. "There are very good goddamn good reasons for all the rules in this household, William. Your mother and I do not make these things up out of thin air." His father was shaking with rage, but all William could think was *They're not Mom's rules.* "How many times must you be told?" his father raged at him. "She could have been killed."

"But she wasn't," William repeated.

The blow came so suddenly that William didn't have the time to raise his hands for protection. It sent him against the wall. He fell to the floor and was holding his face in one hand when Jasper said to him with a hatred more shocking than the blow, "You're no son of mine."

William was grounded two days for taking Tinker down that hill, plus a day for general insolence. He was required to tell Jasper, Tinker, and his mother that he was sorry. What they didn't know? He'd seen the pothole. He'd known it was there and didn't call out to warn Tinker. So his punishment was not only for the wrong reason but for a far lesser sin. He felt that lousy mix of relief and guilt. But the thing he'd never be able to explain—or if he did, they'd never believe him—was that he had not wanted Tinker to get hurt. He had not watched her head for that pothole, hoping she'd go ass over elbows. He'd wanted Tinker to sail down Fern Street the way Pony would have. He'd wanted her to see the pothole in time, jack her bike at the last minute, do a full 360, and come to a tearing, screeching halt. He'd wanted to see her sit there for a couple of seconds while she figured out she was still alive and that she'd done it herself. He'd wanted to see the look on her face.

William got up from the desk and went upstairs. He found the projector and the screen right away in the guest-room closet. It had been years since anyone had used them. He plugged in the projector and turned it on to see if it worked. The bulb lit up, and it began to make that familiar whir. He went to the window and called down to Ruth, "We could see it in five minutes and be out of here."

She rose from her lawn chair, walked to the house, and stood just below the window, looking up at him. She said in a barely audible voice, "If you want me to see it with you, we go to your place."

Well, fine. He shut the window and went back to the projector. He'd left it running, and already it had that familiar smell of heated dust, metal, and age. He could watch the movie in five minutes by himself. And wasn't he numero uno here when it came to need? You betcha. He opened the white plastic canister and removed the reel. A piece of paper was folded tightly and taped to the bottom of the canister. He cut the tape with his thumbnail and unfolded the paper. It was written in his mother's handwriting, both sides of the page, in turquoise ink. *In case anything happens to me—here's what's on the movie we made. As best I can remember. It was 1970. Spring?*

He put the projector back into its case and carried it with the screen downstairs to his car, then went back inside the house to shut the windows and pull the blinds.

"A letter?" Ruth asked when they were in the car.

"From my mother."

Ruth whistled.

Chapter 16

William

William lived in a condo in the Elmwood section of West Hartford, an area of mostly small Cape Cod–style houses in pastel colors, set close together. It suited him better than where he'd grown up. The people in Elmwood were friendlier than in the rest of West Hartford. It was a real neighborhood. The prices were lower, too. His condo was putty-colored, attached on both sides, with a brick patio in the back. He hadn't done much with it. He had a blue leather sectional (Ruth said the color was teal) that he'd bought at a tag sale. He used one of the bedrooms upstairs as an office.

His message light was blinking when he got in and he listened impatiently for the messages to run. The first was from Denny Bell, left that morning. "Please call me," the kid said, and gave the number. William dialed right away, but no one was home. He'd try again later. Right now he needed to see what was on the tape. Right now that was what mattered.

He set up the projector in the living room and fed the filmstrip onto the spool while the other message played: Tinker's voice. "Are you okay?" she wanted to know. "Of course I'm okay," he said, and winked at Ruth. It wasn't as though he'd broken a leg or had a heart attack or been in a car wreck. Hell, he was fine. He just wasn't her whole brother anymore. Everybody wanted to know, Tinker said in that drama-queen voice she could drum up. They were so *worried*. Daddy and Mark and Mira. And Isabel; that slowed him down a second. He really didn't like it that Isabel was worrying about him. Ruth was eying him oddly. Was she worried, too? Didn't *she* get it? What a *gift* all this was? He'd just been released from the one person in this world he could never please, from Jasper Carteret himself, who could never again make him feel worthless.

"Which first?" Ruth asked. "The letter or the film?"

"Film."

Ruth hit the light, and the film began. The camera panned over bleached-out landscape, stopped, backtracked, and moved forward again. A small house made of concrete appeared. It had a cement walk that led to a faded red door, and a driveway to the left with a carport. The sun beat down hard. The front door opened, and a woman walked toward the camera. She had on jeans and a tight-fitting white shirt. Her hair was long and very blond. She was smiling.

"That's my mother," William said.

"Oh," Ruth said. "She's so beautiful."

He rewound the film. His mother backed into the house in fast motion like a Keystone Kop, shut the door, opened it again slowly, and reemerged. She was very slender. The camera panned up and down her body, zooming in on her breasts. She made a motion to the filmer to stop that right now, to cut it out. The film went black, then bright again. Another day? It panned over a vast rock labyrinth. Then it swung to a sandy knoll with sparse bits of brush. A man in a cowboy hat and aviator sunglasses walked up a rise and faced the camera, his arms open wide. He waved with both arms and grinned. His face was shaded by the hat, his eyes hidden behind the glasses. William tried to sharpen the focus, but the face remained a shadow, smiling at the camera with white teeth. A small boy ran up the hill to join him. The boy was perhaps two or three, wearing green shorts and a striped T-shirt. The man picked up the child and held him facing the camera. He took the boy's hand and waved it at the camera. The child squinted into the sun.

William could barely breathe. He rewound the film and replayed it over and over, in slow motion, so he could relish every detail. The child floated up, was lifted into his father's arms, put down, and floated back down the hill. William zoomed in on the child's solemn little face, on Larry Anholt's grinning one. The big hand that guided the tiny wrist.

A new scene: Larry Anholt was seated on a large brown horse. He was in a corral of some sort. Larry sat tall in the saddle. He was lean and straight. He kept making the horse do figure eights. The horse balked, sidestepped, threw its head, but Larry persevered. He looked at the camera as if to say, *I don't stop until I make this animal do exactly what I want!*

William felt excited, a joy he'd never felt. Here was his own father, young and strong, a cowboy, the polar opposite of old Jasper Carteret with his buttoned-down life, his rules for the way people did everything. His real father was an elemental person, at home with life's basics. He felt a powerful nostalgia.

"Are you okay?" Ruth asked him.

"I've got to find him." On the screen Larry walked toward the camera, carrying a saddle over one shoulder, relaxed as hell.

"Look. Swimming lessons," Ruth said.

The screen had switched from Larry Anholt on horseback to a small swimming pool, glistening turquoise in the desert sun. Larry stood up to his chest in the water, grinning at the camera, his black hair slicked back. His face was sharply in focus this time. William paused the projector, the better to see the rectangular shape and jutting jaw. And an underbite. More pronounced than William's, but that was where it came from. No question. A naked baby lay prone on the water beside him, supported from underneath by Larry Anholt's large hand. The baby seemed very small. Almost a newborn. William hit forward, and the film continued.

Larry grinned and let go of the baby. The baby sank.

"Yikes!" Ruth said.

The picture went black and then came on again to the same scene, but this time, as Larry let go of the baby, he kept his other hand palm out to the camera angrily, obviously telling Olivia to stay where she was.

"She doesn't want him to drop you again," Ruth said.

The camera was unsteady but continued to roll. The baby descended a few inches into the blue water of the pool. While he was under, Larry alternately looked at the camera and into the water, speaking constantly. The baby bobbed to the surface, and Larry held him aloft like a trophy. The baby was screaming.

"I'll read the letter," Ruth said.

In case anything happens to me—here's what's on the movie we made. As best I can remember. It was 1970. Spring? We borrowed the movie camera from Mr. DiRisio, Larry's boss, but now Larry's quit (or been fired?) and we can't very well ask to borrow his projector. Here's what I remember from when we took it:

I know it opens with our house on Coyote Street. The Badlands out at Liars' Point may be next, I think. Maybe not. Larry on Blaze at some point, teaching her a thing or two. William "learning" to swim. I dropped Mr. DiRisio's camera when Larry let go of William in the pool and he sank. Larry says infants know how to swim when they're born because their first nine months are spent in water. I suppose it worked. William isn't afraid of the water. Larry tried to teach me the same way (not in the movie). The sink-or-swim method. I was floating in a tube in the deep end and he toppled me. I thought the bottom of the pool was the top. I kept scratching at the pool floor trying to get air and he had to come down and get me. I don't dare go on the float anymore if Larry is anywhere near. He learned in the River Idaho. The cur-

rent once caught him and took him down the river and he had to get himself out. Necessity is the mother of invention—Larry's philosophy about everything. The best way to learn anything is when you have no choice.

William rewound the film and zoomed in on the face of the baby in the water. "If that's me," he said—he rewound the film and found the dark-haired child—"then who's that?" He and Ruth stared at the screen. The child was unsmiling, somber. William turned off the projector and flicked on the light. He swung around and dialed the number for Fond du Lac. Tinker picked up. "Oh God, I'm so glad you called," she said, and started in on something, but he cut her off. "Put him on," he said. "It's important."

"Don't talk to me like that."

"I need to talk to Dad. To Jasper."

"Not if you're going to upset him with that tone," she said.

"Put him on, Tinker," he said.

"He's supposed to stay quiet."

He wanted to kill her. "Ask him if Mom had another kid besides me."

"Of course she didn't."

"Ask him!"

"I'm not going to dignify—"

He slammed down the receiver and called Minerva. She would know for sure.

"It's William," he said. "There was a reel of film in the box you gave me. I need to know something. Was there another child besides me?"

"Oh, no," she said.

"And you'd know, right?"

"Certainly," she said. "She had only you."

William set up his laptop on the kitchen counter. He Googled Larry Anholt. Not a single hit. He went to the Social Security Administration website and found *Anholt, Lawrence b September 1, 1935 d July 27, 1995 Stanley Idaho.*

William took a beer from the refrigerator, popped the top, and took a long drink. "He's dead," he said. "The motherfucker should have told me. Now I'll never know."

"And which motherfucker would that be?" Ruth asked quietly from the sliding door.

"Jasper," he said. "Who else?" He drank more of the beer and then flung the can. It spun over the lawn, pinwheeling beer.

"Seems a lot of motherfuckers knew, William. To use your terminology. Larry Anholt knew. Minerva knew. Your mother, of course. Your mother knew everything. Mira. Why is it all Jasper's fault?"

Pony would have understood. And the thought of Pony was a stone on his heart. He swung at the wall with his fist. The pain seared all the way up to his elbow. He sat down at the laptop again. For $14.95 on his credit card, he got access to a database of out-of-date telephone directories. And there it was in Stanley, Idaho. Anholt, Lawrence.

"All right!" William shouted, slapping the counter. The number was there, but no address. He wrote the number down on a piece of paper. "Ruth!" he shouted, but she was still outside on the patio. "Ruthie, I've got the telephone number." He was so psyched. "A number in Stanley fucking Idaho."

She came inside. He waved the piece of paper at her. He dialed the number from the kitchen telephone, grinning. A woman picked up. She had a throaty voice. A smoker. "I'm looking for Larry Anholt," he said. "Please."

"Oh, honey," she said with a mocking laugh. "Larry's dead. Who is this?"

William's heart sped. He was one up on her. He knew the guy was dead. He was ready for this. "Oh, ma'am, I'm sorry. I wonder, though. I'd like to ask you about him." *Tell me everything.*

"Who is this?"

"Are you his—"

"Maybe," she said. "You tell me who you are, and I'll tell you who I am."

"Did he have kids?"

"It's not the way I do things."

"You won't even tell me if he had any kids?" There was a pause of several seconds, and then the woman hung up on him.

He popped another beer and dialed the number again. She picked up the phone and put it down without a word.

"She hung up on me again," he told Ruth.

"Maybe you should take a minute and think this through," she said.

"Forget that." He sat back down at the laptop and went to the Stanley Chamber of Commerce Web page. "Come here and look at this." The town looked almost medieval, wooden buildings huddled together at the center of a grand valley, wide and green, flanked by snowy mountains. It was something out of a kid's picture book. William clicked to the next screen and the next. There were vivid blue lakes, meadows alive with wildflowers, raging rivers. But most of all, there were mountains. William skipped to the shots that took in the range of the Sawtooth Mountains. He thought he'd never seen anything so beautiful as those peaks, so jagged they resembled black shards. A sight that made his blood thicken. This was the place his father was from. His roots. He felt alive. He picked up the phone and hit the speed dial. The urge to tell Pony was automatic. The phone rang twice and then an automated message, saying, "The number you have called is no longer in service, please check—"

"You little shit," he said, and slammed the receiver down. Ruth was staring at him. "What?" he said.

"Oh, nothing."

"I'm going out there," he said. "I might have brothers and sisters I don't even know about. Man. It could be a whole other family out there, and I'm as much a part of them as I am of the Carterets. But I need to get to that woman fast. Before she—"

"Before she what, William?"

"I want to surprise her."

Chapter 17

William

Boise International Airport was small and hot. Most of the people in the waiting area wore spanking-new microfiber clothing. Khaki zip-off pants, fleece in purples and oranges. Several were talking on cell phones, shouting the way people used to shout on long-distance calls. Listening to the conversations while he waited for his bag, William knew they were wrapping up business before heading off on their white-water-rafting trips or their backpacking extravaganzas. The gear sat in heaps around the room. Big duffels, backpacks, life jackets, and camera equipment. He'd done his homework on Stanley. It was a mecca for river running on the Salmon at this time of year. The population was a hundred in the winter, tens of thousands in the summer.

Outside, it was blistering hot. Over a hundred at midday. William picked up his rental car, a compact, loaded his suitcase into the back, and took to the road. He had to jack up the air just to breathe. Once he was in the mountains, he could turn it down, open the windows.

He'd maxed out his credit cards to buy a ticket to Idaho at the last minute and rent a car in Boise at the height of the season. He didn't care. He'd blow through his 401(k) if he had to. So what? But hell, his father was dead; he'd waited too long already. He wanted to talk to that woman, his father's widow, and go from there.

He hadn't called her back. He wanted to let her think he'd given up, so she wouldn't expect him. He'd ask around town first. With only a hundred people living there full-time, somebody would know where she lived. Then he'd just go over there. Ambush her.

As he drove, the landscape went from city to rural to mountains, with vast pastures of grazing elk. His ancestors had been from Idaho. Maybe they'd driven this road fifty years earlier. His aunts and uncles. Grandparents. Sure they had. It was the only route. Where had they come from? Anholt was German. Or Swedish, depending on what you read.

Larry Anholt.

Big-sky country.

Be careful, Minerva had said.

Stanley was small, and once William got off the main drag, the roads were gravel. Ramshackle houses sat next to fancy cappuccino places, and it seemed to him that everything was made of raw redwood except for roofs, which were slick green metal. In the distance were the Sawtooth Mountains. He'd never even known about them, and they were something else. He'd bring Ruth here. She'd love it.

He pulled into the Stanley Mercantile. The Merc. The parking lot was a mess, with people in cars and trucks crisscrossing to get to the gas pumps, to get water, to get into the store. There were pickups with dogs in the beds. He counted seven or eight in one, plus more in the cab, hanging out the window in pairs, panting from the heat. There were bearded guys with leathery women. A sign at the CITGO said they'd fix a flat for fifteen dollars a pop. Another sign, for a sockeye fish hatchery, featured pictures of lurid red salmon and explained that this was what happened during spawning seasons to males and females alike. William took a postcard down from the rack and wrote it right there before even paying for it: *I love this place. The sky never quits. I love you.*

When he paid at the register for the card, the stamp, and a sandwich for dinner, he asked the clerk where he could camp. "Anywhere you want, so long as you don't get caught," the kid said. He told William about some places down at the river and gave him directions. William drove the two miles out Route 21, hung a right onto a dirt two-track, and stopped the car in a clearing. He carried his gear down to the river, walked around for a while searching for a good site, and found one at a bend in the river, a distance from the only other tent there. He pitched his tent and changed into trunks. A path cut alongside the river, and he followed it, looking for slower water where he could safely go in. He swam against the current for a time, then let it carry him downstream for a hundred feet or so, and found a rock shelf to sit on, held there by the current. His father had learned to swim in this river. It was a nice feeling to be held in place by cool fresh water on a broiling late afternoon. His father's river.

The next morning he woke to the sounds of people. They weren't being careful about how loud they were. At first he wondered where he was and then remembered. He smiled. He opened the tent flap and peered out. The grass and the leaves were covered in a thin frost, and steam rose from the river. He threw on his trunks, crawled out of his tent, and headed toward the voices. At the bend, he stopped short. Seven or eight people were hurriedly taking off their clothes on the bank. One by one they plunged into the icy water, shrieked, and fled to the shore, where they dressed without even drying off.

"They've come every morning all week," a voice behind him said, startling him half out of his skin. "Ed," the man said, extending a hand. He was thin and small, with dark blond dreadlocks.

"William," William said.

The swimmers were white as clams, except for their tanned faces and hands. They were laughing and shouting. After dressing, they ran back to a van idling near William's rental car and sped off.

"I saw you come in yesterday," Ed said. "I'm camped up the river a bit, but you're welcome to stay where you are."

"I won't be here long," William said.

"Hiking?" Ed asked.

"Sure. These are some mountains."

Ed grinned, showing a mouthful of perfect teeth.

"What about you?" William asked.

"This and that," Ed said.

"You spend a lot of time here?"

"Born here. Winters, I work down at Ketchum, running a snowcat. Summers, I'm right here."

"I'm looking for somebody," William said.

"Who's that?"

"Larry Anholt," William said.

"He's dead." Ed studied William's face.

William affected surprise. "I'll look in on the family, then," he said.

"That would be Mim," Ed said. "Anholt's wife."

"Kids?" William asked.

"Couple of girls in Ketchum. A son."

"What's the son's name?"

Ed shrugged and laughed. "You think I'm the Census Bureau or something? Go ask Mim for yourself. The house is on Ace of Diamonds Street in town. The name is out front."

The house was made of the same redwood as the other houses in town. It was small, with a porch on the front. William slowed when he drove past it the first time, around the block and then around the block again, preparing himself. When he got out of his car and started up the path, the front door opened, and a woman came out onto the front porch. She was heavyset, with short gray hair and a ruddy complexion. She wore plaid shorts, a dark sweatshirt, and she was barefoot.

"You Mrs. Anholt?"

She took a drag from her cigarette and nodded. "That's right," she said. She tipped her head and blew a flute of smoke straight up.

"I'm William Carteret," he said, extending his hand.

No sign of recognition crossed her face. "And?" She took his hand in a surprisingly weak grip.

"Larry Anholt was your husband, right?" He'd prepared what he wanted to say, how he'd say it. He wanted to be straightforward, to put her at ease, too. Even down to what he'd learned selling magazines one summer: Always stand on the bottom step so you'll be shorter and less threatening to the lady of the house.

"That's right," she said.

"I don't want to be a problem." He hadn't meant to say this, but he was trying to talk to her and take in the house at the same time, and it was the truth.

"What makes you say a thing like that?"

"I just don't intend any trouble." He was blowing it. He could tell by the way she cocked her head.

"Don't, then."

"I just recently learned—" he began again, back to script. "A couple of weeks ago, I learned from my aunt that my mother, Olivia Murphy, was married before she married Jasper Carteret, that I'm her son from that marriage. I'd never known that. The name of my biological father was Larry Anholt." He was breathing hard, watching her face. She was hard to read, squinting at him into the sun and pulling on that cigarette.

"He never married her," she said in a *so there* tone. He'd pictured sitting down with her, letting her get to know him slowly. But now he had the feeling that she could go inside and slam the door on him at any moment. He had to push on, play all his cards.

"Okay, look. There was a movie, a home movie that my mother kept. She's dead. I didn't tell you that. I was a baby in the movie, and it's possible that Lawrence Anholt had another child who would be a couple of years older than me, and if that's the case, he'd be my half brother. And I'm interested in finding him."

"Full," she said.

"Excuse me?"

"He'd be your full brother."

"No. My aunt said—"

"Your mother was his mother, too." She stubbed out her cigarette in a dish on the rail and looked down at him. She was smirking a little, enjoying this. "You didn't know about that?"

He felt a loathing for her. She was making it up. She was vindictive as hell.

"She kept it a secret, did she?" Mim's voice rose as if she were about to burst into laughter. "Son of a gun—" She made a face, her mouth drawn down like the tragedy mask, ugly as sin. William remembered what Minerva had said about a woman who had come to the house with Larry years earlier. This was the woman. It had to be.

"Do you think I could have a glass of water?" he asked.

She considered the question for a few beats, then motioned to him to follow her inside and led the way through a mudroom with its mess of coats and boots and into a small, cramped living room where someone had tacked dollar bills to the ceiling so they fluttered on the current caused by the opening and shutting door. "Larry did that." Mim stood looking up at the ceiling and grinning. William could only think about what she'd said. A brother. A full brother. Mim kept talking. "For a rainy day. He left everything to me. It's all in my name in the town hall, and you can go and check on that yourself. I'm the legal heir."

"I don't want anything," he said. "I'm just trying to find out about my real father, and now you say I have a brother."

She ran a glass of water for him at the kitchen sink. "There's no jewelry. No money," she called to him.

William accepted the water from her. He kept looking around at things, at the details of his father's house. It smelled of cigarette smoke. Years of it. There was a dark purple couch and a couple of wooden chairs. There were river paddles in makeshift racks on the walls. Several pairs of snowshoes hanging from a long peg. A calendar with a praying Jesus and then, the more closely he looked, pictures of Jesus here and there. Tiny framed ones and some larger, and a sagging tapestry of the Last Supper.

"Was he Catholic?" William asked.

"That's right," she said. "We are."

He checked out the rest of the room. A chain saw hung by its safety bar at the edge of the fireplace. Some books were stacked in the corner. His father had lived here. His brother. He still couldn't believe that. This was exactly what he'd wanted to see—his interest was benign—and yet he had to be careful. All he was to her was a threat. He didn't know how to make him trust her. He didn't know why she should.

"Do you have any pictures?" he asked. "Of my father or—"

"We don't go in for that. His name is Patrick. Your brother."

Patrick. "He was raised here? You're his stepmother?"

"He was raised here," she said.

"Where is he?" William asked. When she didn't respond, he took a chance. He reached for his wallet and checked inside. "I can give you a hundred dollars."

"I heard you people were well off," she said. "Owned some big company, is what I heard."

"Not that big," William said, then felt stupid. Big compared to this.

She took the money and stuck it in the pocket of her shorts. "That man stuck out like a sore thumb. With his car and his clothes."

"What man?" he said.

"The man Patrick's mother ran off with."

"And?"

"All this time you thought he was your real father. Hah," she said.

"Do you know why—"

"Sure I know. She didn't want Patrick, that's why," Mim said. She was moving toward the front door. Any second she was going to open it and tell him to leave, and he'd have to do it. "She didn't want Patrick."

"How can I find him?"

"When I see him, I'll tell him you were looking for him." She had a hand on the knob.

"When will you see him?"

"I'm done talking to you," she said. "You had your water, now go."

"But I paid you a hundred dollars," William said.

"And you got your money's worth," she said.

"Tell him I'm down at the river camping, It's a half mile out on Route 21, go right down a dirt road."

"I know where it is."

He bought a burrito and a bottle of lemonade at the Merc. He was starved. He sat on a bench eating, staring at people walking by, and wondering which ones knew Larry Anholt. Patrick. It was easy to spot the year-rounders. He looked for people in their thirties who might have gone to school with Patrick, and he felt again the bottomless sense of being a jerk. He threw the last of the burrito in a bin. The phone in the kiosk was available now, and he hadn't caught up with Denny Bell yet. One thing at a time. Again nobody answered. He tried the lake house. The girls might be there, but no one answered. He tried Ruth last, and she didn't answer either. He left a message: "Can you please call Denny Bell and find out what he wanted? Tell him I'm out of town."

He drove back down to the river for his gear. Ed was nowhere around, so William went in for another swim. He found the same ledge from the day before and sat, feeling the weight of the water. The current pinned him to the rock. How could his mother have left a child behind? She'd lived for her children. It was the main thing about her. *She's so beautiful,* Ruth had said when she saw the film, and it was true. Beautiful but also slightly inept, not especially good at things. She'd had that very weird way of swimming, stiff as a board and her strokes very shaky. And all those years, watching her children at the water and not really knowing how to swim herself.

She had depended on William. *The girls want to go in* was all she'd have to say, and he'd be there with them, down at the water, supervising, counting heads over and over. He was their guardian when he was eleven, twelve, whatever. His mother never made a direct request. He must have been her other, more capable self. He taught the girls everything they knew about the water, because she couldn't. All because Larry Anholt had once dumped her in the deep end of a pool in the California desert, and she'd been terrified. She had been determined not to pass that terror on to her children.

A lot was coming back to him. Nice things. Sometimes he'd catch her staring at him, and he'd ask if something was the matter, and she'd smile and say, *Oh, nothing.*

He'd been at the lake the weekend his mother died. Just him and his sisters. He was still working the nine-to-five at Aetna back then, dating his old girlfriend Virginia, the one he'd met in his senior year at Trinity. He'd been in the water with Isabel. He was teaching her to swim, and what a little pistol she was in the water. Not even three at the time, and he'd been sidestroking alongside her as she dog-paddled to the raft, her delighted little face just breaking the water, straining with effort but happy as ever. It would have been just about then that, alone in her room, his mother had died.

The ganglia at the base of his mother's brain were malformed, a rare and silent condition she'd apparently had since birth, undetected. The ganglia ruptured while she was drying her hair, sitting on the edge of the tub and leaning over so her hair hung almost to the floor. William had seen her do it many times, her hair like liquid silver, swirling under the hot air of the blow dryer.

They should have sold the Steele Road house. The day it happened, they should have put it on the market, taken whatever they got for it, and cleared out. But old Jasper said that was out of the question. You didn't run from pain. Oh no? Then what did Jasper call running off in the middle of the night with his mother and him? If they'd sold the house, Pony would still be alive today.

He had a brother. Patrick Anholt. He should have called Ruth right away. She could have Googled him. He didn't need Mim to find him. He was hungry again, and cold. He should have saved the last of that burrito. He'd go into town and find a place to eat. He'd call Ruth from one of the pay phones in the parking lot in front of the Merc. He'd ask her to Google Patrick Anholt in case there was something. He'd ask her to look him up in the White Pages. But darkness fell quickly under a sky like that, and he swam back across the river and scrambled up the bank to the path. He hadn't brought a flashlight and had to feel his way through the underbrush along the path, back to the spot where he thought he'd pitched his tent. Normally, in a strange place, he would have made mental notes about the path, but he hadn't done that today. It had never even occurred to him to do it because he hadn't expected to be gone any time at all, and now he'd spent a couple of hours. He finally found his campsite. The night was so dark he had to make sure he was in the right place by feeling for the smooth-knobbed hiking stick he'd left propped up against the front flap. He'd lost interest in going into town, in getting dressed at all. He put off his hunger and crawled into his sleeping bag instead. He was exhausted from the trip, from the day. He had purposely not put on the fly, so he could lie on his back looking straight up at the sky, which was dense with stars, millions of layers thick and millions of miles away. It helped to make him feel the proportion of things, the enormity of the sky and the insignificance of everything on earth, and did it matter where one person had come from at all?

He woke to the shouts of the swimmers again. He crawled from his tent, wrapped a towel around himself, and went down the path. The swimmers were hopping out of their clothes on the shore. One of them told him to come on in, and William waded into the river with them. They were older than he'd thought at first, in their fifties and sixties. Seventies, even. They were doing something Jasper Carteret would never do. Having fun.

After they left, he swam some more, then wrapped the towel around himself and headed back to his tent, paying attention to the path and to the turns it took. When he came upon his campsite, he saw that a man was squatting a few feet from his tent, his elbows resting on his knees, a Padres cap shading his eyes. William stopped walking. The man made no move to stand. He stayed beside the tent as though it were William and not he who was the intruder. William recognized a familiar grin from under the brim of his baseball cap. The man reached up to the bill of his cap and cocked it back to reveal his face.

William was looking into the eyes of Keith Brink.

Chapter 18

William

William did a double take at Keith's familiar black shirt, his black Levi's, his bola. What went through his mind first, at the speed of light, was that Jasper had died and Keith was the messenger. But he killed that thought fast, because no one knew where William was. Ruth knew he was in Stanley, but not about his campsite by the river. Only Ed knew that. And Mim.

"You were looking for me?" Keith bounced on his haunches, grinning.

It was all some big practical joke. William looked wildly around, half expecting his family to come out shouting.

"I'm Patrick Anholt."

William might as well have been in a total whiteout for the sense he could make of where he was and what was happening. The disbelief. The belief. He could not connect what he saw with what was being said, with what he knew. Patrick Anholt. Mim had said, "His name is Patrick."

"I'm your brother."

"You're Keith Brink."

"Right, and I'm the brother."

Don't open your mouth, William told himself; it was the only strategy he knew. Call it lockdown. Call it anything. The point was to give himself time to get his head around any of it. *Do what's real first.* He'd left his clothes in the tent, and he went inside to get them; he was on autopilot. To get dressed, he went around the back, where he didn't have to look at Keith Brink. His mind raced. He had to concentrate on putting on his shirt, doing everything slowly, not saying a thing, stepping into his pants, pulling on his socks and a sweatshirt.

"You can call me Keith if it would be easier," Keith yelled to him.

William came back to the front of the tent, shook out his towel, and laid it across the bush to dry. He brushed his teeth using the water in his Nalgene bottle. *Not calling you anything,* he thought. He spat into the grass. Everything in him, every synapse, firing in an attempt to understand. Failing. A week ago William was Jasper Carteret's son. Now he was nobody. Now Keith Brink was his brother.

"You came looking for *me,* man," Keith said with the petulance of a whining kid, as though what this was about was who had come looking for whom. "You came to my house. You talked to Mim."

William screwed the lid back on his water bottle and replaced it inside the flap to his tent. He felt the red strike of anger and pushed it away. He told himself to count to ten. And then count again. He took a few steps toward Keith for a better look. He found in Keith's face the same slight underbite. The same angular chin. Why hadn't he seen that before? He stepped away, held open his hands.

"I wanted to know my mother's people. Is that so wrong?" Keith said.

His mother, William thought. *His mother was my mother.* "Are you for real? There are better ways to do that than lying your way in."

"Bad timing, man. What can I say? I got to Hartford right around the time Pony died."

231

"But you said you knew her. You spoke at her funeral." He was standing over Keith now, looking down.

Keith evaded William's eyes. He poked in the ground with his finger. He looked up. "I always thought you didn't come looking for us because you didn't give a shit. Why would you come looking for people like us when you had the good life?"

"Why use a different name?" William asked. "Why lie about everything?"

"I never meant to, I swear. It just happened. Keith Brink is the name of a kid I knew in Little League. I always liked the name. Brink. You know, brinksmanship and all that. Getting to the edge. Keeping your nerve. You can understand that."

"Don't tell me what I can understand."

"You're my brother. That counts for something."

"Sure as hell counts for Mira."

"We can go up to the Merc right now and call her long-distance," Keith said. "Ask her yourself. I never touched her."

"Why did you lie about it all?" William threw his head back and looked up at the sky. The big sky. The everywhere sky.

"Look. You're not going to take a swing at me, are you?"

William pulled a folding chair from in front of the tent and dropped it a distance from Keith Brink. He sat down. "Start talking."

"You have another chair?"

"No," William said.

"Okay, okay."

While Keith settled himself against a tree, William took the guy's measure. They had the same body type, but Keith was heavier. Running to fat, from the tug at his shirt. Not muscle. So he'd be slower in a fight. William had the agility.

"I was six when I found out," Keith said. "It was January, cold as hell. My dad was shoveling the walk up to the house. I had a snow fort down at the street that I made from what they plowed up, six, eight feet of the stuff. I wasn't supposed to do that, so I hid while my dad was out there. He didn't know I was in it. He kept saying,

'Livvy.' I saw him dig in, pitch the snow, and say it again. 'Oh, Livvy.' "

"He called her Livvy?" William said, remembering the photograph and *Livvy 1968* written on the back.

"I made the mistake of asking Mim what 'Livvy' meant. Big mistake. When Mim found out my dad was saying her name, she said, 'Livvy is the name of that whore of a mother of yours.' From then on, whenever Mim got pissed off, which was often, and she wanted to let my dad or me have it, it was all about that. Always about Olivia. Mim said Olivia had run off, taken her dying baby, and left me behind. That dying baby would have been you, I guess. Mim said Olivia was a gold digger and ran off with a rich guy from back east. But I always had the memory of my dad out there, mowing the lawn and saying her name. And he wasn't saying it out of hatred, I knew that, and I thought Olivia couldn't be that bad, right? Although he never talked about her. Not ever.

"I started looking through their stuff after that. Their drawers and closets, and there wasn't much. Mim raised me, mostly. My dad cooked in the summers for river trips, and in the winters he took farming jobs in the Sonora. He'd be gone for long periods. She's crazy, Mim is. I'm glad I don't have her blood running in my veins. I'm glad I come from better stock."

"What did he die of?" William asked. "Your dad."

"Cancer."

"Of the what?"

"Prostate. He let it go. Knew he had it and let it go. He wasn't a guy to listen to doctors."

"Anything else the matter with him?" William asked.

"The usual. He had ulcers. High blood pressure."

William nodded. "He ever say anything about me?"

"Like I said, he thought you were dead. We all did."

William could hear the river in the distance. The man had never bothered to find out one way or the other.

"I went east some years back," Keith said. "I drove by that house of yours. I couldn't believe it. I parked around the corner and walked by. I walked all around those blocks. Yards like golf courses, kids playing. I stood in front of your house and thought, *Score one for Mim.* She was right about one thing. Olivia hit pay dirt. I lost my nerve. I wanted to ring the doorbell, but I lost my nerve. I called her on the telephone instead, said I wanted to meet her."

"And?"

"And nothing. She said she didn't know what I was talking about. Which figures. She didn't want to upset the apple cart. I can understand that. I really can. Don't get me wrong. I was disappointed. But I understood where she was coming from. You hear about that all the time. It's not uncommon for birth parents to deny a child's existence."

"That was it?"

"That was it. I came back here. Bear in mind, I didn't know about you. I believed Mim, that you were dead. I thought I had half brothers and sisters, maybe. But never a real brother." Keith wiped his lower lip with his thumb. "My dad had a cabin. Well, your dad, too. This will take getting used to, won't it? Our father. Our mother. Anyway, cabin's not much, three sides and a roof, more of a lean-to. Mim doesn't know about it. My dad and I used to go there all the time. Maybe that's something you'd like to see. I think if you saw his cabin, you'd understand a lot more about him."

"Like?"

"You're a climber, right? Hiker or whatever."

"So?"

"So you do that because it's where you want to be. Simple. The cabin is where our dad wanted to be. Would have lived in it if he could have."

"He was a hiker?" William asked.

"Fishing. White-water. I take after him," Keith said. "Done a fair amount of river swamping myself."

Some Cub Scouts were pitching a tent twenty feet away. They had pretty foul mouths. A whistle blew somewhere nearby.

"It's a hell of a lot quieter up at the cabin," Keith said. "Only sound is the great Salmon River. Makes this look like a trickle."

William wasn't sure. Maybe they could go into town, find a bar, and talk. And yet there was a cabin. Secret, in the mountains. His father's cabin, the place his father loved. The pull was irresistible, Keith or no Keith. "How far is it?" he asked.

Keith helped him strike camp. He said they'd need to take both vehicles—William's car and Keith's truck. Keith explained that the cabin was on the Salmon River, and there was no more beautiful place in the world. "It's half yours, you know. Mim won't part with anything of his, but I will. And like I said, she doesn't even know about the cabin." He was eager as they packed William's gear into the trunk of his car, excited about showing this place to William, about the times he and his old man had gone up there together and how in any other family, that would have included William, and wasn't that something?

William followed Keith out of Stanley and along some secondary roads. The drive took longer than he'd expected; the roads were narrow and pitted. It was also quite a distance. William's thoughts couldn't keep up with the speed of what was happening. Here he was, driving behind his brother in the middle of Idaho, but his thoughts were way behind. Did he buy what Keith had said? Maybe it added up and maybe not. On the one hand, if Keith did just happen to arrive in West Hartford around the time Pony died, William could understand his reluctance to come forward in light of her death. He could also understand Keith's curiosity about the family and why he'd attend the funeral. And he obviously hadn't bought any painting from Pony. That part was all a lie. He'd never even met Pony, if William was to believe him now. So why did he speak at Pony's funeral? Why lie about knowing her in front of everybody that day, especially in front of the family he wanted to know? And why take up with Mira? By now Keith had had a couple of months to come forward, but he hadn't. What did he want?

Ahead, Keith swerved onto a dirt road, and William followed until the road ended at the river. He parked his rental car in some brush, hidden against thieves, and got into the cab of the truck. Keith explained that the best way to get to the cabin was on the river, using his inflatable kayak.

"The best way or the only way?" William asked.

Keith grinned. "Okay, the only way. We could ferry over, but we'd get moved too far downstream, and then we'd have to walk back up, which you can't do. It's too dense. This way we can relax, put in a few miles above the cabin, and take out a mile or so below. Trust me."

They doubled back along the roads they'd come on for a time and then along a better two-lane road. Keith said there wouldn't be any rapids to speak of, nothing over a category two at this time of year. And even if there were, it was no problem. He could read water easier than he could read a book. William was in good hands. Keith was loud, talking over the roar of the motor, gesturing large with his free hand, mostly about Stanley and the town and what it had been like growing up there, and about the lodgepole pine infestation that was browning out the hills, and he'd slow to point out one area or another where all the evergreens were the color of rust. "It's the topic out here," he said. "One of these days, it's all going to catch fire, and all those million-dollar homes hidden away up there will go up in smoke."

He swung off the main road onto a dirt two-track, and they bumped fast down it for a couple of miles. William heard the river before he saw it; he knew about its pitch, that it dropped seven thousand feet from the headwaters to its confluence with the Snake. He got out of the truck and went to the river's edge. The Salmon was like frothing blue steel. And looking downriver, you could almost see its downward cant.

As they readied the kayak, a good-size two-person inflatable, William studied Keith again surreptitiously. Keith, he thought, wasted energy; he used too much effort on small tasks.

"Technically, we're not supposed to be doing this," Keith said over the roar of the water. "These days everybody needs a permit, which is bullshit, if you ask me. But we'll only be on the water for a couple of miles, and I haven't been caught yet. Those river trips come by five or six a day sometimes. Every one of those guides is ready to turn in somebody for outlawin.'" He grinned at William. "Easterners like you, mostly. Liberals. Kids. Think it's their job to police our river. 'Take only photographs, leave only footprints.' Give me a break."

"So your dad worked on the river," William said.

"He did a lot of stuff. No one thing. Your dad, too, by the way. You've got to get used to saying that."

They worked smoothly together, loading the kayak, strapping down the gear. They set off, William in front and Keith behind. The water pulled them quickly away from shore, and they shot out into the middle part of the river, where the current was swift. William felt a sudden rush. God, it was spectacular. And fast. They rocketed along, digging in their paddles to keep a straight line. Keith shouted out commands: *Left turn, right turn, left back, right back.* During a period of flat water, William raised his paddle and laid it across the bow of the kayak. He realized with a start that no one knew where he was, and now his rental car was miles downstream, with no indication he was so far upstream from it. No one else knew that Keith Brink was Patrick Anholt.

"River left!" Keith thundered from behind. "Paddle like hell!" William dug in, impressed at how sure of himself Keith was on the river. Mercurial.

They eddied out into a backwater at the shore. "Big strainer downriver," Keith said. "I'll point it out later." They pulled the kayak up the bank and behind some trees, in case a river trip floated by. William followed Keith a few hundred feet up from the river by a path through dense growth.

The cabin sat on a ledge overlooking the river. It had three sides and a thatched roof and was built crudely of rough-hewn logs. The front was a makeshift wall of stone piled shoulder-high, with an opening to walk through. "Go on in and look around," Keith said.

William stepped inside, letting his eyes adjust to the darkness. It smelled damply of wood smoke, and it was cold. Something seemed to slide sideways inside him at seeing it all. His father had built this place with his own hands. He had breathed this air. There was a rotted tarpaulin on the floor, a small woodstove, and a pile of split wood beside it. A large pot hung from a hook overhead. William took it down and ran his hands over it, fingering the dents, the burned underside. He replaced it carefully. Two metal plates and two forks lay on the floor. He crouched and ran his hand over those as well, trying to picture the man who had used them. His father's fishing gear hung on the back wall. A small sheet of paper caught his eye. It was pinned to a beam. He read it in the dim light. TO DO was printed across the top in big letters. *Stove cold. Set kindling. Matches.* William touched the writing, which had been done with force in pencil, the letters deep in the paper.

It felt both foreign and familiar, being in this place where the ghost of his father hung everywhere, a man who liked to live in the woods. A man who could build things. A stranger but very like himself. He wished his father might have known about him, that he'd become strong, a climber, and that he was most at peace in the mountains. Would his father have loved him, knowing that?

"So what do you think?" Keith's bulk filled the door.

"Nice," William said.

"It's yours whenever you want to use it. This is all wilderness. Frank Church River of No Return Wilderness. It gets no better than this. Come on. I want to show you something while there's sun."

Keith led the way out behind the lean-to to a steep, densely overgrown switchback that zigzagged up an incline. As they went, William could hear that Keith's breathing was labored. The rise was steep, no question, maybe a two-hundred-vertical-foot gain in a quarter of a mile. Keith was full of contrasts. Powerful on the water, weak on the climb. When they got to the top, it was fantastic: a rock outcropping with a view for miles in three directions. Below them, the Salmon glittered in the late sun like a silver ribbon twisting through the mountains. "What do you think?" Keith asked him. "Is this great or what?"

"It's great," William said. And for a few moments he felt at peace with everything, here in his father's place.

"I knew you'd like it." Keith had his back to William and was rocking on the balls of his feet, his fists planted into his sides.

"So what do you want?" William asked.

Keith swung around. "What do you mean?"

"From us, from my family, from me."

"Nothing."

"Come on. You come all the way east two times, and you don't want anything?"

"You came all the way west," Keith said.

"Different," William said.

"Don't give me that. It was you who called Mim awhile back and wouldn't say who you were. She's not stupid, you know."

"She wouldn't have told me," William said.

"That's right." Keith made a show of checking his watch. He took the lead again going down, and William followed, keeping a wide berth between Keith and himself so he wouldn't be right on the guy's heels. Keith was slow and jerky in the way of people who didn't trust the terrain. He hung on to tree limbs, and in a steep place, he knelt on a rock instead of staying on his feet, the way he should. William enjoyed finding fault with Keith. The knee thing was key; a knee could slip.

Back in the lean-to, Keith put a few pieces of wood into the fire circle out front and lit it. He offered William some Scotch he kept hidden in a well under the tarpaulin. He opened a can of nuts. "I'm going to show you something I never showed anybody." He dug into the hard dirt floor at the door of the cabin, using a large trowel. He unearthed a small metal box that contained an envelope, which he gave to William. "He kept it here," he said. "Mim never saw it."

July 4, 1972

Dear Larry,

By the time you read this, I'll be far away.

I've felt frightened for a long time now. I'm worried for William's safety, and for mine. Patrick is the one you love.

I made up my mind last week. You won't even remember it and yet it was the deciding moment for me. You and Patrick were in the kitchen eating your dinner. William was with me as always. Patrick won't eat in my presence as you know. William went in to join you. I must have been mad to let him. You looked up. "Look. It's the troll," you said. Patrick laughed. Why did that matter so much? You've done far worse. But I knew in that moment I had to leave.

Patrick worships the ground you walk on. He says terrible things to me, imitating what you say. And do. He's struck me, but then you know all about that. He's my own flesh and blood and yet I have no choice. This is a terrible decision, but I have no other choice. William will be damaged if we stay.

You've caused the divide, Larry. How many times have I told you that William's development is within normal bounds for a premature baby. The doctor says he'll catch up at two or in adolescence. You've made clear you don't care about William. Like a weak calf, you said. Sometimes it's better to get it over with. You're pitiful. You're worse than pitiful.

You decide what to tell Patrick. I'll never tell William. I'll see to it that he never finds you and never suffers at your hands again.

I loved you once, Larry.

Olivia

William reread the parts about himself. Premature? He walked to the edge of the clearing and looked down through the trees to the river. *Catch up at two or in adolescence.* As a kid, he'd been so small. In grammar school, he'd been the smallest and thinnest, always made to sit in the front row in school. This in a family of giants. The girls came along smart as whips. William had had to try so hard. And the physical stuff. God, how he'd worked, lifting weights in his room late into the night. Pushing himself. Testing himself. Whittling his body. And he'd succeeded. He despised weakness both in himself and in others. And all because he'd been premature.

Keith squatted on his haunches and shook his head. "You were pretty sickly," he said.

William tensed and flexed his hands, reminding himself of his strength. "You never answered my question, Keith. What do you want?"

"You walk like him, you know. I was watching you. I noticed that at the funeral. You're probably like him. He could be a son of a bitch. I'll bet you can be, too. I'm more like my mom. I love saying that. My real mom. She knew what she wanted, the big house, the rich husband, and she went after it. I admire her for that. I'm able to do that."

"She wasn't like that," William said. "Not at all."

"I want in," Keith said. "To answer your question."

"In what?"

"The family," Keith said. "It's my family, too."

It was laughable, actually. It was nuts. "You could have told us that." William crossed the clearing to the point where the path led back down to the river. He could see water through the trees. *More water,* he thought. He could hear the uneasy sound of the river. On the other side of the river was his car, his safety. "He ever pull you off a fence at a swimming pool?"

"Sure did." Keith laughed. "Held me under if I didn't get it right. But that's another story for another time. The way I read that letter is that if it hadn't been for you, she would have stayed."

"It wasn't me. It was him," William said. His mother had done the only thing she could. She'd taken William to save him. She'd loved him because he was weak and he needed protection. Not the greatest thing to find out about yourself. But it explained things, like how he always expected the other guy to have the advantage.

"There would have been no Mim." Keith's voice was like a front coming in, a change in the weather that signaled danger. The guy was unstable. He was standing, arms outstretched, a cunning smile. "I was the better brother," he said. "I was the good brother. The strong one."

"What do you say we get going before the sun goes down?" It had been a mistake to come up here. "We can talk as we go. Talk when we get back."

"You scared of me?" Keith asked.

"It's going to get dark fast."

"You didn't answer the question."

"No," William said. A lie. "I'll get us some water for the fire."

"Suit yourself," Keith said.

William looked in the lean-to and found an empty bleach bottle. He made his way down the embankment, weighing his risks without knowing for sure what they were. The exposure here was the river, the miles ahead of them. William was a strong swimmer, but strength didn't matter. You couldn't buck a current with strength. You had to ride it out. As he made his way down the path, he reviewed what he knew. If he ended up in the water, he needed to go feet first. *Don't fight it. Ease over to the shore.* The unknown was Keith.

They'd stowed the kayak behind some trees, and William pulled it out to look it over in what was left of the light. He checked for the paddles, but they were gone.

"Looking for these?" Keith asked from behind him.

William swung around. Keith was holding both paddles.

"You weren't thinking about leaving without me, were you?"

"Why would I do that?" William said.

"I got the fire," Keith said. "Buried it with dirt. We can push off. I want you in the front again."

They shoved off. Now the river was a hungry black, and the mountains rising to either side cast giant shadows. The water was loud. William dug in his paddle blindly, straining to see ahead for obstacles, dangers. Keith was quiet, unlike when they'd come. No orders. No running off at the mouth about growing up in Idaho. Nothing. They coasted awhile. The water was swift but not dangerous. And it was cold against William's skin through the thin plastic of the kayak floor. In the shoals, rocks close to the surface knocked against his shins.

He heard the sound of the rapid before he saw it. A faint sound, lower and deeper than the regular rush of the river.

"It's nothing," Keith shouted forward.

"Let's stop and take a look," William shouted back.

"Hell, no," Keith shouted back. "I've done it hundreds of times, man."

"I haven't," William said. "We're pulling over." He paddled hard and alone, pulling the kayak out of the current and into quieter water without any help from Keith. He jumped out and landed knee-deep in the cold water.

"You're being a candy ass here," Keith said. "I know where all the holes are. We run a course right down the middle, between them. I'll tell you what to do."

"I'm not going down that blind."

"You're no brother of mine," Keith said.

William made his way up a steep incline and walked to a point beyond the bend in the river where he could see the rapids on the other side. They showed up as frothing grayish water against the dark river. They were big. "I thought you said nothing more than a category two," he said.

"That's a cat two," Keith said, scrambling up the path behind him.

"I don't think so," William said.

"You don't know much about moving water," Keith said. He was behind William, standing too close. William stepped back from the edge instinctively. Keith pointed to the left, to the point just after the bend. William knew the rapid Keith pointed to was higher than a two. "We'll come in up there. We'll keep right for a bit. Then ferry left. That wave you see"—Keith pointed downstream about twenty feet—"is a hole. We want to miss the hole."

Looking down at the water, William felt his bowels loosen, as they had that day on Peekamoose. His stomach churned. Keith continued, "As soon as we're around it, we need to head right again, and fast, so we can go down the middle. It's against the current there, but if we stay left, you see, we run into a pulse against the canyon wall." William studied the scene. He did the thing he knew how to do. Use his head. He repeated to himself what Keith had said, making a mental diagram. A zigzag shape. Start right, move left, drop around, below the hole, then move right again and shoot down the middle.

"You don't believe in life jackets?" William asked as they made their way back to the kayak.

"This is Idaho," Keith said.

William had no choice but to get in the kayak again. The water ran slow around the bend toward the rapids, like a big easy pool. Then it seemed to rise, as if gathering strength for what lay ahead. Small eddies swirled about the kayak. "Paddle up," Keith said. "Let it take us for now. It'll pull us right." William lifted his paddle from the water and waited, his heart racing. The sound of the rapids grew louder as they rounded the bend. Ahead, the water frothed and roiled. It looked nothing like it had looked from above. His stomach heaved. He was trying to see where the hole was that had been so clear from above, like a big smile. At this level, the water just churned wildly. But they were being pulled slowly to the right, as Keith had said.

Suddenly, as though hooked from beneath and thrust forward, the kayak picked up speed. "Left turn," Keith shouted behind him, and William dug in his paddle on the right side of the kayak, using all his strength. The water fought back hard, pushing them downriver, toward the rush of water that was the hole. "Harder," Keith screamed. William felt a sharp, stabbing pain at the center of his back, between his shoulder blades. The kayak spun. He was looking upriver. It came again, the stab in his back. He felt himself lifted as if in slow motion, airborne from the kayak. And then, smooth as a knife, he was underwater in a rush of gray bubbles, sucked down.

He shot to the surface, too stunned to take in air, and was pulled under immediately, down where everything was black, and then the quick wash of gray at the surface, and this time, yes, the gasp for breath, but right down under again. The next time he saw the kayak nearby in calm water. Keith was watching. Doing nothing. William was pulled under again and knew. Keith wasn't going to help. The stab in his back had been Keith's paddle. Keith had done it on purpose, and now William was in a hole. They called them Maytags for a reason. He let himself be pulled under again, was shot to the surface. It had a rhythm, like a washing machine. You had to let it take you and not fight it. Like a riptide. Like everything. *Don't panic. Think.* He remembered a diagram he'd seen of a hole. A stick-figure swimmer was angled downward, toward the river bottom, not the top. William let himself be taken up and shot down a few more times. He caught brief glimpses of Keith, arms folded, grinning. William took a breath and, at the bottom of the cycle, using all the strength he had, stroked downward toward the river bottom. Immediately, he was in calmer water. He tucked and turned feetfirst downriver. He wanted to scream, to whoop at how he had outsmarted Keith, but he kept his mouth shut. He sculled left until he could feel the riverbed under his feet. Once secure, he crept toward shore. He was psyched. He was alive. He was on dry land. And he was going to get that son of a bitch if it was the last thing he did. He understood now what Keith must have meant. For Keith Brink to be "in," William would have to be out, because only William knew who Keith really was. It was possible that not even Mim knew he'd gone under the name of Keith Brink or that he'd been back east.

Upriver, he saw light on the water. A beam swept the far side and the near, tracing the river's banks. The water was calm through that stretch, allowing Keith to pull over on one side and then the other, flashing his light about. It was a powerful beam, one of those big-battery halogen jobs. Keith was taking his sweet time looking for William. Looking for William's body. Keith knelt in the bow of the kayak, leaned forward, shone his light into eddies and inlets.

William crouched in the water, not daring to move. He didn't trust himself to win a fight with Keith. His only way out was to hope Keith would pass by him. The light approached as Keith let the kayak slip downriver, closer and closer. William crouched lower in the icy water as Keith swung into an eddy, just a few feet away. He found William with his light. "Damn," Keith said.

William tore from the water and up the bank, counting on his speed and on the time it would take Keith to get out of the kayak. When he was far enough up the bank, hidden behind some trees, he risked a quick look back. Keith was still taking his sweet time, tying the kayak to a tree. William felt along the rising slope. He scrambled up on his hands and knees. He counted on Keith's lousy cardio to slow him down. Keith called out his name, and William turned to see how close he was. All he saw was the light.

The ground underfoot was soft with pine needles, and William scrambled while Keith's light panned from behind; it found him just as he reached a place where he could go no farther. A rock face rose straight up. He tried to head back down toward the river, but Keith was below him now, moving up and across, ever closer. The light approached, blinding him. William covered his face. Keith dropped the beam but kept coming. William had only one option: He bolted. He scrambled down the slope but fell and rolled, and the next thing he knew, he'd come to a stop, and Keith's foot was pressed hard into his neck. William grabbed Keith's leg to throw him off, but Keith was too heavy. A rock dug into William's shoulder blade, causing breathtaking pain. Keith flicked off the light. "You keep asking me what I want. First off." His foot pressed more deeply, causing William to gag and cough. Keith let up a bit. "I'm the kid's father. Andrew's father."

"Aw, come on, man." William tried to twist away. "No way."

"You want to hear this or not?" Keith's foot bore down hard again. William thought his jaw would break. "I went back there a few times, and two years ago I hooked up with Pony at a bar. She was drunk. What can I say? I came back this year, and damn if she doesn't have a kid." Keith leaned into William's face. "And damn if the kid isn't mine." William tried to twist away, but Keith's sneaker pressed his face sideways and into the dirt. It was true about Pony's drinking. Pieces of information began to click into place. Her e-mails to Katherine. The timing. "It was you up at the lake that day," William said.

"Of course it was me. You people are slow on the draw. I go with our sister's theory about Pony, by the way. The fat sister. She had it right."

"Her name's Tinker," William said.

"What's that?" Keith blinded William with the light, laughed, and turned it off again. "Pony could have done a lot to help herself. She could have seen it my way. I gave her a chance. Call me old-fashioned, but when people have a baby, they get married, right? But hey, I'm getting ahead of myself.

"May twentieth this year I went back east to see you people again. I parked out front of Pony's place in Manchester. I was just checking things out. I liked her. But she saw me parked out there and came slamming out the door with that baby on one hip and said, 'What the bloody hell are you looking at?' She threatened to call the cops on me. She didn't know who I was. You believe that? She had no memory of me. I was pissed. I mean, how would you like it if that girlfriend of yours forgot your face? Bad. So I told her who I was, the guy from two years ago? And she got this look on her face. Oh, man. She went white—and I knew right then it was about the kid. That it might be mine and she knew it. I knew I had her. I had leverage." Keith's foot relaxed a little. William pulled in a breath quietly. "Here's the thing, William. I thought all I wanted when I went back east that first time was a look at you people, maybe get to know you. But now it's different. Now I have a son. I want to be part of it all. Hell, I deserve to be part of it. That Fond du Lac place. I love it there. I deserve that. Not as just a friend of the family but as one of the heirs."

It felt to William as though Keith had let his weight sag against something, a tree maybe, because of another change in pressure. "I can understand that," William managed to say.

"Yeah? You can? I thought you would. Pony didn't." Keith's foot slipped again, enough that William could take one deeper breath. Keith explained to William, his voice more thoughtful now, that he had given Pony proof of who he was. He had shown her the same letter he'd shown William, and his birth certificate, which listed Olivia Murphy as his mother. He'd shown her the picture. He laughed. "She had a very big problem all of a sudden. She'd fucked her half brother. She had to throw up. I know she did. She swallowed it. She wouldn't leave me alone in the room with the kid. She kept saying, 'What am I going to do?' like it was all up to her, and I said, 'Excuse me, but I think you mean 'we.' "

"Your baby, too," William said.

"Fucking A, William. People get married. I was in. It was easy."

William thought he might be sick himself. "How did Pony react to that?"

"She said fine."

"Doesn't sound like her, Keith."

"Okay, she needed time to think it over. A few days later, I called. She was on top of her game. Everything was cool. She said I should go up to Fond du Lac." Keith's foot slipped lower on William's neck. "I go all the way up there, William, and what does she do? She freaks out. She won't get out of the water because she's naked. She wants her clothes. What kind of a reception is that? Long story short, I picked up the kid. My kid. And she stands right up in the water and says come on in."

"Was that you who called her?"

"You bet. I thought I was going to be late, but then I wasn't. But anyway, like I said, she stood up in the water, and I said, 'That's more like it.' "

William understood now. If Pony had known there was danger, and she must have, she had no chance with Keith on land; her advantage was in the water. If he was going to threaten Andrew, she'd done the only thing she could.

"So I swim out to the raft after her. I don't know where the hell she is. There one minute, gone the next. I go up on the raft, and then I hear her under it. She starts going back and forth. Under the raft and then out. I mean, what the fuck? She's explaining to me how it's going to go down whether I liked it or not. She wasn't going to lie about anything. She's going to tell the whole thing about what happened and about who I am. The whole nine yards. She's going to start with you and then tell Daddy and the fat sister and Mira. I couldn't let her do that. I'd be crucified."

"What did you do?"

"She's just treading water out there, calm as a cucumber, saying that crazy shit. What else could I do? I went in after her."

"How?"

"How do you think? I jumped her from the raft."

"And she got away." William knew exactly what Pony had done. She'd wanted him to go for her. She had tucked her chin before Keith had her in a hold. She was out of his grasp before he even knew it.

"She didn't get away. I let her go," Keith said.

Bullshit, William thought. Just as she'd done with William, she would have approached Keith underwater. She'd had the upper hand. She'd had all the cards right then. It was the drowning game in spades, the martial arts of swimming. But something had gone wrong. She should have won.

"Bitch grabs my feet," Keith said. "She's trying to drown me. I'm going down like a stone."

"She wouldn't have hurt you," William said.

Keith jabbed William's neck with his boot. "You weren't there, William. She was trying to hurt me, all right. She was trying to drown me, but God was with me that day. I think I'm going to die, and then I feel that chain and I reach out for it and latch onto it and I don't really know how it happened. I was trying to shake her loose, and all of a sudden she lets go. I'm free. I got up on the raft so I could see down. I could see her. She was caught on that chain, all right."

"You killed her," William said.

Keith flicked on the light and into William's eyes. The glare was inches away. William had to turn his head. Keith turned off the light. William concentrated on exactly where it had been. "Whatever," Keith said.

The flashlight came on again, exploding in William's eyes, but this time he was ready. He rolled away, jumped to his feet, swung with his left hand, and knocked the light from Keith's hands. It bounced and spun down the slope toward the river. William groped for Keith in the darkness, found him, and pulled him to his feet. Keith swung and cocked William's shoulder. William felt his fist connect with Keith's soft belly, a satisfying hit. He did it again. He felt Keith's body fall away. He waited, breathing hard. He heard Keith retch. Then he felt himself being tackled. He was thrown down, and he rolled toward the river and to the light where it had come to rest, its beam illuminating grasses along the bank.

William scrambled, crawling as fast as he could on all fours to reach the light before Keith did. He grabbed it in both hands, turned, shone it in Keith's face. Keith's shirt was ripped, and he was staggering toward William but had to shield his eyes against the assault of the light. William had the advantage now. Oh yes. He had the light. He kept it trained on Keith, who dropped to his knees, groped for a stone, and flung it. The stone hit the light but missed William. William turned off the light. Everything went black. The only sounds were the rush of the river and Keith's harsh breathing.

William worked his way up the riverbank, then turned on the light again. Keith turned, stupidly openmouthed. William was almost enjoying this. With the light out again, he climbed partway up the slope, flashed the light again, and again took Keith by surprise. He had to get to the kayak before Keith did. He needed to get out of there, cross the river, and find his car. He spotted the kayak maybe twenty feet downriver. He climbed higher and flashed the light on and off to draw Keith toward him. Then he moved through the darkness, heading down, letting gravity take him at an angle back to the water. He didn't shine the light again. Now he didn't want Keith knowing where he was.

But he wasn't quick enough. Keith had found the kayak, pulled it from its mooring, and was already out on the river. William trained the light on it. Something wasn't right. The kayak was going in a loose circle. Keith had no paddles. That was it. He was lying across the bow and stroking with his hands, but something else was wrong. The thing looked deflated. When they'd shoved off earlier in the day, it had been gorged on air. Now it sagged. Keith's weight at the front tipped the rear up. It looked like a child's toy spinning along as the river built speed.

William expected to feel satisfaction but felt none. He scrambled up the bank. A trail ran along the Salmon, little used but good enough. He ran alongside the river, keeping his light now on the path ahead, now on the kayak, which angled and spun from one side of the river to the other. It stalled in eddies, caught on rocks, and shot out. All the time, Keith lay across the bow, frantically trying to guide it, aiming one way and then another. The thing kept losing air. William could hear the roar of another rapid coming up. He waded into the river as far as he dared, to the edge of a swifter current, and waited until Keith was closer. "Throw the line," he yelled to Keith, shining his light. "Over here." But Keith lurched and tipped as the kayak spun quickly downriver and farther away. William was trained to help people, not to kill them, not to let them die. Keith Brink. His enemy. His brother. He couldn't let it happen.

Staying close to shore, William ran, stumbling, through the water, keeping his light trained on the kayak. He needed to get downriver of it. Keith's arms were no match for the current. The kayak was lower in the water, Keith's body mostly submerged.

Around a bend, a huge evergreen had come down. It must have fallen years earlier from much farther up, slid down the hill, and landed halfway across the river, bringing down other trees and brush, forming a massive barrier across the trail and a good half of the river. It was a godsend, a last chance for Keith before he hit the rapid.

Holding the light, William climbed the trunk and tried to make his way through the dense tangle of branches out to where it lay in the water. He cast the light upriver and panned the water. He spotted the blue and yellow of the kayak, barely afloat and moving along like a leaf on a current. He panned once more for Keith and found the pale terrified oval of Keith's face moving toward him with the current. William waved the light, meaning for Keith to come that way. But Keith was frantic, panicked, as he tried to swim wide of the tree. In an instant he was shot forward into the dense suck of branches. William shoved the light down his shirt and used both hands to claw his way farther out the length of the tree, shouting, screaming, over the roar of the river that he was coming. He'd be there in a second. He would help. But he made no progress. It was like fighting through a solid wall. He pulled out the light, shone it ahead, hoping to catch sight of Keith pulling himself out. Instead, Keith lay on his side, entwined in the snarl of branches. The water roiled and frothed over him. His arm was raised up by the current and let down again. William lay on his stomach and reached out to grasp Keith's hand, but it was hopeless. Keith was being sucked back down and held under by thousands of tons of water.

Chapter 19

Mira

Mira's father, too weak to return home, had been sent to an occupational rehab facility to gather his strength. The doctors said he'd stopped eating enough after Pony died, but no one knew it. He was malnourished, weak, and exhausted by grief. Now he was being taught how to live. There were model rooms at the rehab place, a cool setup, Mira thought. They had a kitchen, a bathroom, and a bedroom. Whenever Mira went to see him, his first question was always about William. Had he been heard from?

And until now the answer was always no. But early that morning, while she was feeding Andrew in the kitchen, William had telephoned and, in a calm voice, told her he was in Idaho and he'd found his father's widow. He'd also found a brother. Would she please help him with something? He needed her to call a family meeting for Labor Day weekend. Everybody else would hear what he had to say at the same time. But there was something she needed to know first. He asked if Mira had her laptop with her, and when she said yes, he told her to go online to the *Challis Messenger* website

253

and do a search for a story titled "Man Dies in River Accident." Would she please see to it that everyone read it. Dad, Tinker, Mark, Isabel, and Minerva. Once Mira read the article, would she please call him back right away.

A brother, she'd thought as she set up the laptop, googled the *Challis Messenger,* then found the story. Well, as her mother used to say, wonders never cease.

Man Dies in River Accident

A 36-year-old man was killed Saturday as he kayaked a dangerous section of the Salmon River.

Patrick Anholt, a lifelong resident of Stanley, is the first boater to die on the Salmon this year, Salmon Recreation Area officials said.

Anholt was boating with his brother, William Carteret, of West Hartford, Connecticut, on Saturday afternoon in a section of the river called Rebar, a portion of white-water rapids rated IV to V, meaning extremely difficult.

Carteret told Chaffee County sheriff's deputies that he had fallen from the kayak in Rebar. He said Anholt was swept from his kayak below Rebar and was pinned under a logjam. Unable to retrieve his brother's body because of the current, Carteret found shelter onshore and waited out the night. He flagged down a river trip early on Sunday morning. Jeff Travis of Asta Float Trips called 911 on his cell phone.

Anholt was pronounced dead at 8:26 a.m., Sunday.

According to sheriff's reports, the Salmon River was going through the Rebar at 2,350 cubic feet per second at the time of the accident—a medium-to-fast rate for that part of the river, which can run as fast at 3,500 cubic feet per second, said Stew Albright, river ranger supervisor.

Albright said there were four rafter fatalities on the Salmon River last year.

Anholt was experienced in the sport, as he had been a river runner for many years, said his stepmother, Mim Anholt, also of Stanley.

In addition to his stepmother and brother, Anholt is survived by two half sisters, both of Ketchum. He was predeceased by his father, Lawrence Anholt of Stanley.

She poured a few more Cheerios onto Andrew's tray. She loved his precision. He used his thumb and forefinger, very carefully, to pick up each one, his pinky extended like that of a Brit drinking tea. "What do you think about all this?" she said to him. He looked up and smiled at her. "Your family, Andrew. What can I tell you?"

While the article printed out, she watched the line of sailboats on the lake. It was Wednesday, race day. Andrew dropped his spoon on the floor. She picked it up, handed it back, and called William. "I read it," she said.

"Honey," he said, taking her up short. He'd never called her that. "Keith was Patrick Anholt. He was my brother. He's the one who died."

She slid down the wall and sat on the floor.

"Say something."

"Like what?" She made a face at Andrew, and he laughed.

"What do you want to know?" William asked. "I'll tell you what I can."

"Yeesh," she said, and shivered. "It's what I don't want to know. This is way too weird, William. Even for me."

"It wasn't your fault," William said.

"I always thought there was something off," she said. "We never were an item, if you know what I mean."

"That's my girl," William said.

"I want to get off the phone."

"Call me," he said.

She clicked off the phone. "Guess what?" she said to Andrew. "Keith's your uncle."

Andrew happily banged his metal tray. Cheerios jumped and then fell onto the floor.

"It's not funny," she said, and then reconsidered. "Well, maybe in your world. Anyway, he's dead."

Andrew kicked his feet hard against his high chair. "My feelings exactly." She unfastened the snap that held the tray down and lifted it. He slid down and ran from the kitchen. She followed him to the porch and down the steps to the lake. It all looked bright and surreal, the water too black, the sailboats artificially white. Andrew's new playpen was on the lawn, filled with bright toys. She hoisted him up and over. He started picking blades of grass through the mesh of the playpen and examining them with that tidy little pinky-up gesture of his. He twisted his hand this way and that, then let the grass fall. When a blade of grass drifted onto his chubby bare foot, he laughed out loud.

She'd once read about a woman in New Hampshire who'd had nine children, all by the same father, and put every one of them up for adoption at birth. Years later, a brother and sister fell in love, not knowing they were related. When they found out, the boy was unperturbed, but the girl freaked out. Mira was definitely in the boy's camp. It wasn't his fault. He hadn't sought that out. They both described the attraction as familiarity. And she knew what they meant. She hadn't actually liked Keith Brink that much, but he'd been familiar and easy the same way.

"It should bother me, right? If I'd known, well, another story altogether. But I didn't know. So what's the big deal? We came close a couple of times, Andrew, but you know? It just never felt right." She made a face at him and whispered, "When Tinker finds out, run for cover."

The screen door banged. "Speak of the devil," Mira said.

Tinker was up at last, looking out at the lake in her bathrobe and pajamas. She smiled at Mira and Andrew, waved a hand in greeting.

It was early for Tinker. Since the day their father collapsed, she had been logging thirteen, fourteen hours of sleep a day by Mira's calculations, plus naps. And when she was awake, she moved about on little cat feet with her cups of hot tea and her nightly phone calls to Mark. Mira was left to watch Andrew and drive Isabel to her morning swim lessons at the town beach. She didn't mind this at all. Isabel had always been an enigma to Mira, and now she understood that this was because Tinker kept the child on a short leash. Left to her own devices, Isabel was insightful and curious. There was so much she wanted to know. Which is closer, the sun or the stars? *The stars.* What makes electricity? *Who knows.* Is Grandpa sick because he misses Aunt Pony? *Yes.*

Mira pulled two chairs from the beach up to the lawn. Tinker came down and settled into one of them, Mira into the other. The day was warm and quiet.

"You talk to Mark again?" Mira asked. She felt as if she were still floating, part of her drifting over the water, the other part here with Tinker, acting normal. As normal as she could anymore.

Tinker nodded. "For hours."

"You two okay?"

Tinker sighed. "We're working on it."

"Long-distance dialoguing," Mira said. "Maybe it's better than face-to-face." She waved to a solitary canoeist paddling by close to shore.

Tinker smiled. "He's not sleeping with his secretary. But he came close."

"He *told* you?"

Tinker nodded.

"That's honorable," Mira said. "To admit it."

"You think?" Tinker had lost some weight. Her features were sharper, better defined. Her hair was loose at her shoulders. In profile, her face held echoes of Pony.

"God, yes," Mira said.

"He said the difference between me and her is that she always has time for him."

"Well," Mira said. "She's paid to have time for him."

Tinker smiled again. "Donna is a tart."

"Maybe that's the point," Mira said.

Tinker glanced sidelong at Mira. "I should tart it up a little, is that what you're saying?"

"Wouldn't hurt. You look good, Tink."

"Anything yet from William? I heard the phone."

"It was him."

"Why didn't you say? Where is he?"

"Idaho," Mira said.

"What's he doing there?"

"Looking for his other family." In the days after the family gathering, Mira had told Tinker pretty much what she'd told William, leaving out the part about her own abortion. "His father's dead, but he found the widow." She handed Tinker the printout of the story.

Tinker read it. She put it down. "They must mean his half brother, not his brother."

Mira winked at Andrew. "He wants us to have a meeting on Labor Day. All of us. He'll explain the whole thing then."

Tinker let the paper fall. "What happened to us, Mira? We used to be such a great family."

"Great?" Mira said.

"You know what I mean."

"No, I never saw us as great."

"Sure we were." Tinker pulled up the collar of her bathrobe. "We were one of the old, established families. We had values, standing in the community. We had a name to uphold."

"We had a ball-bearing company, Tinker." Mira shielded her eyes from the sun. "It's not like we were great humanitarians or anything."

"We were *some*body," Tinker insisted, but not with all the old fire. She rose, walked a few paces down the lawn, then turned, still clutching the collar of her robe. "We can still be once this settles down. I want that for Isabel. For Andrew. We can still have continuity."

"We have a big fat dangling thread out in Idaho."

"Why are you so negative?"

"Sometimes it seems you're more invested in this family than in your own. Maybe this is what Mark's talking about," Mira said.

Tinker sighed once more.

"We're dishonest," Mira said.

"You shouldn't say that," Tinker said.

"Mom and Dad never even told William he had a different father. That's about as dishonest as it gets."

"I don't know that he was hurt so badly. He has a pretty good life."

Mira felt sorry for Tinker for the first time. She saw her older sister as someone who was being ground down by the truth, resisting every inch of the way. When the whole truth came out, it was going to be rough on her. "I love you, Tink," she said. "You try so hard."

Tinker opened her mouth and was about to say something, then decided against it. Probably *Somebody has to*, which was her standard response to any compliment. She smiled at Mira and looked pretty and young for the first time in years. "Me, too," she said.

In the days that remained before the meeting, Mira sunbathed on the raft and got the first tan of her life. Sometimes, if Andrew was taking a nap, Tinker would come out to the raft, too, and the two of them would loll around, drinking in the last of the summer sun. Mira thought a little about Keith. Poor guy. He could have just told her who he was and lived.

In the evenings she prepared for her fall course, freshman composition, with lots of outside reading. She decided they would read stories about the consequences of betrayals and secrets. She knew for a fact that if she'd taught this class last year or the year before, she'd have felt obligated to include her own secrets. She'd have thought it was necessary to provide them as her bona fides, as if to prove that she knew what she was talking about. But not anymore. Her job was to make her students better writers, not to stand there naked.

Chapter 20

Tinker

Labor Day Weekend

Tinker sat on the porch, waiting for people to come. The meeting was scheduled for four o'clock. William wouldn't say anything beyond what they'd read in the newspaper clipping. He wanted everyone to hear it at the same time, something she had to smile about. William was always the one who resisted Daddy's meetings and here he was, holding one himself.

Her father had been out of rehab for about ten days. He'd come home knowing how to steam vegetables and broil fish. He spent a morning programming numbers into the telephone. He shopped for his own groceries. He spoke in terms of economy, not of money—amazingly—but of motion. He washed his plate after using it; he stored things in clusters on shelves according to use. When he first came home, she tried to do everything for him, just as before, but he would raise his hand and say, "I can do this myself." She felt at a loss.

On top of that, while her father was in the hospital and Tinker was making all those trips back and forth, Mira had taken over the care of Andrew, and Isabel had gotten all caught up in the two of them. Tinker watched them now as she waited for everyone else to arrive for the meeting. Mira and Isabel lay on their backs down on the lawn, with Andrew between them, all looking up at the sky and talking. *About what?* Tinker wondered. What was there to talk of for so long with children?

Time weighed on her. She wanted William to come. She wanted the whole story of what had happened in Idaho and about Patrick Anholt. William was her half brother now. She'd been having so much trouble with that. The term was cutting. Half a brother was like half a person. What did it even mean? It felt as though William was becoming lost to her.

Minerva was on her way by taxi. William had wanted her there. God, how the taxi trips used to irritate Tinker! She had seen them as waste, as showmanship on Minerva's part. And she'd felt that she, Tinker, must correct Minerva's extravagance. Now she felt resigned. Minerva would always be Minerva, would always pull up in a taxi whenever she came to visit. It was her money and her business. If it caused a stir in the town, so what? Minerva's arrival was the least of Tinker's worries, and it was a relief, she realized, not to have to fret over it.

Normally, an empty space like this, waiting for something to happen, would drive Tinker into the kitchen. But now she preferred it here on the porch, watching Mira, Isabel, and Andrew on the lawn. Eating was less interesting. Such an odd thing had happened to her in the last few weeks. Something she wasn't able to tell Mira or even Mark about because it meant admitting to the way she had been.

Just the day before, Mira had fed Isabel and Andrew early, and Tinker had been alone at the table on the porch, exactly where she was now. On her plate were some peas and a slab of lasagna. She ate slowly and quietly, thinking about the night her father had collapsed, the spectacle she'd made of herself. That night had been the subject of her phone calls to Mark every night. Well, not at first. At the beginning their calls had been cautious, mostly about Daddy and how he was doing, but as time wore on, Mark had ventured into her behavior that night. It had taken some time—days, actually—for her to tell him (face it, to admit it to herself) that she had seen Mark go into the lake with Pony and William on the night of Daddy's seventieth birthday. She had planned to go in, too, but then had felt unwelcome. He'd rather swim with Pony, she'd thought. For a whole year, she'd barely been able to look at Pony without being so jealous she couldn't stand it. It had festered and finally erupted when she'd basically blamed Pony for her own death. "You could have come with us, Tink," Mark said. "I wanted you to. I even told them under the raft how you and I used to skinny-dip all the time."

And after remembering what he'd said, she'd just had enough to eat. She found some Tupperware, and put the lasagna she hadn't eaten into one container and the remainder of the peas in another. She thought, *I'll have them for lunch tomorrow or perhaps for dinner.* Only then did she realize the change in herself. What she'd eaten was enough. When she needed more, there it would be. It was so simple. And she no longer awakened in the morning and set about reviewing the vast amount of food she'd eaten the day before, the accompanying guilt over it. The burden was lifted. She didn't care what was left in the kitchen. She felt as though a vast new landscape had opened up before her now that she was free.

Minerva's taxi was approaching, scraping along the center hump of their two-track. It was a low-riding old yellow cab. The driver parked, and the taxi idled for a minute or so. Tinker assumed Minerva was busy settling up. What would it cost? She had no idea. Hundreds, anyway. Minerva slid a booted foot out the rear door. She swiveled. Her face blazed into a radiant smile when she saw Tinker. Tinker embraced the old woman, feeling how tiny Minerva was, how fragile, and yet so bright, and smelling of fresh gardenias.

Her father was on the porch. He'd let his hair grow so it curled at the nape of his neck. "Minerva, you old sinner," he called out. Tinker could hardly believe it; she had always thought them adversaries.

William, Ruth, and Mark arrived so soon after the taxi that Tinker knew they must have passed each other on the narrow driveway.

She felt butterflies seeing Mark, shy as a schoolgirl, grateful that Isabel leaped into Mark's open arms to give Tinker a moment. "Hey," he said. She felt a hot blush on her face. He pushed her hair back and kissed her ear, letting his tongue slide over the lobe. She hugged him harder. She'd missed him so much and held tightly to his hand, feeling the familiar oozy warmth of desire at her center.

So much happened at once. William strode to the porch to give his father a kiss. It had always been Jasper who came down to the driveway to greet people if he was at home. And Ruth! As usual, she looked sensational, in a halter top the color of her hair. She busied herself getting the luggage from the trunk, then turned and gave Tinker a warm smile, and Tinker forgave Ruth for being all that Tinker was not and would never be.

They were about to hear what William knew. *Right away*, he'd said, *let's not delay*. They brought chairs down to the lawn at the water's edge. The sun was already behind the mountain, and there was a hint of chill in the air. Tinker brought out an armful of coats and blankets in case people needed them. Mark brought down a wicker chair for her father, one with arms. Tinker sat on the ground with her back against the chair where Mark sat, leaning against his legs, Isabel at her side.

William sat cross-legged on the grass, with Ruth beside him. "What I know now explains everything of the past years. Everything is interconnected, and the best way is to tell it as straightforwardly as possible and in chronological order." William's voice was soothing and low, reminding Tinker of Mira reading a story to Isabel and Andrew. As William talked, Mark massaged her neck.

"You've all read the news report in *The Challis Messenger*, so you know how this thing ends. But the start of it was that two years before I was born, Mom had another son with my biological father, Lawrence Anholt. His name was Patrick Anholt. He's the one who died in the river. He was my full brother."

Tinker sat up sharply. She shot a glance at her father and then at Minerva. "How can that be?" she said.

"What evidence do you have of this?" her father asked.

William said there was a letter. It was still in a metal box buried in the floor of a cabin out west, and one day maybe he'd go back and get it. His mother, their mother, had written it to his biological father when she left him. It was in her handwriting; there was no question. She left because Larry Anholt had become cruel to her and to William. He was ashamed to have a weak son. Patrick was the stronger child, his father's boy. "My father turned Patrick against me and against Mom," he said. "From what she said in the letter, she could leave with me and not be found. But I think if she had taken us both, he would've come after her. I think she was afraid, really afraid."

"Minerva, did you know about this?" her father asked.

"I did not," Minerva said.

William described the life their mother had had in a small desert town in California. For Tinker, it was as far-fetched as being told her mother was a circus performer. The desert was such an unlikely place. She pictured the Sahara and its shifting sands. She pictured her mother and daddy as young people, with tiny William, traveling across the country, fleeing the wicked father, leaving another child behind.

"Patrick Anholt came east to find us," William said. "Three times, anyway. He came to each of our houses. He did drive-bys." Tinker shuddered at the thought. She pictured a man who looked like William but older, driving around in a rental car, slowing before their houses. "Patrick knew Pony," William added.

Tinker raised her head. William was moving too fast. She could barely digest the next thing he said. Pony and Patrick Anholt had had an affair. Very brief. Maybe only a night. Andrew was very likely conceived. Patrick Anholt was probably Andrew's father.

Mark's hands stopped massaging Tinker's neck. She looked up. Her father had let the blanket slip to his feet. His hands dangled between his thighs.

"So Andrew is the child of—" Tinker began. She couldn't say it out loud, that Andrew's father was William's full brother. Andrew was amusing himself at the center of the circle. The child glanced up at the sound of his name. Everyone was looking at him. He grinned with pleasure.

William continued before anyone had the chance to speak. "It was back when Pony was drinking, and we all know about that. Pony had no idea who he really was, but Patrick knew who she was. It's the kind of guy Patrick was, so don't anybody feel sorry he's dead. He got what he deserved." William cleared his throat and said he was getting ahead of himself, that what he had to say next was hardest of all, and he asked them to bear with him and let him get it all out before they spoke.

"How could this get worse?" Tinker asked.

"What I got from Patrick," William said. "I'm trying to be clear here about who he was, his motivation. He felt cheated. He wanted to be accepted into our family. He saw all of us as one big happy family with nothing to worry about. He was resentful about the life he had and unstable as hell." William drew in a breath. "Okay, now, look. He didn't know that Pony had become pregnant. He didn't find out about that part until just after Memorial Day this year. It all snowballed. It got out of his control. Pony had the true facts about everything for about two weeks before she died. And here's the part you have to remember. The pith of it all. Pony asked him up to Fond du Lac to tell him she was going to tell us everything. There were already too many secrets. She planned to talk to him first and then tell me next, since it affected me the most. You all know I left. We all know that if I'd stayed, Pony would still be alive. I'm having a very hard time with that one, but that's my cross. I'm here to tell you the rest of it. Pony thought the honorable thing was to tell this to Patrick before she brought it to anyone else.

"But Patrick panicked. If it got out—his reasoning was that a family like ours would crush him. Legally. Deny custody, sue him, bring charges. I don't know. Hire a hit man. In his mind, we were powerful people. A tribe. So when she told him she was planning to make it an open book, he lost it. He panicked. She almost got the best of him. She did her best lifesaving maneuvers, and she would have bested him, but her hair became caught."

Tinker hung tight to Mark's hand. William leaned over and pulled the blanket up over Jasper's legs, tucking it in at his sides to keep it from falling. He read aloud from some e-mails Pony had sent Katherine Nicely about incest. They said the incest taboo was mostly cultural.

"But what about all the problems?" Mira asked. "Incest kids have hemophilia, they're retarded. All sorts of awful things."

William said not necessarily. He read another e-mail. Apparently, if problems with Andrew were going to show up, they'd have done so by now.

All eyes were on Andrew. The child must have felt the attention again. He got to his feet and toddled to Jasper. "He wants to sit in your lap," Tinker said. Her father raised the child with some effort.

"Here's the hard part," William said. "Patrick *was* part of the family. He used a pseudonym. He came to Pony's funeral, and he entered our family as Keith Brink."

The name seemed to float on a distant memory. There'd been that man Keith, the one with Mira. If ever Tinker had known his last name, she'd forgotten it. He'd taken over Pony's apartment. He'd told her and Mira that Pony had told him William was angry. She'd wanted to believe him. "Mira's Keith?"

"Mira's Keith," William said. "Tell them, Ruth."

"Denny Bell tried to reach William. He left a message, but William was already in Idaho, so I called Denny back. When Mira and Keith were here that one time, Denny thought it was the same guy he'd seen when Pony died. He tried to get close so he could make sure, but Keith caught him and threatened him. Denny was terrified. He finally got up his nerve to call William."

Tinker was remembering something familiar and unpleasant, something she'd tried not to think about, but there it was. There had been a man parked in front of her house the day Pony's body was found. She clapped a hand over her mouth at the realization that it had been Keith that day, watching her and talking to Isabel.

"How did Keith die?" Mira asked. "I would very much like to picture it."

"Isabel," Minerva said. "Let's you and I go into the house and see what we can find for an old lady to drink. Shall we?"

Once Isabel was gone, William described what had happened out in Idaho. "He thought he'd be able to come back here, claim paternity, and be welcome in the family as Andrew's father."

"We never had sex," Mira said. "I want that one on the record, in case anybody's wondering."

It was all something out of a nightmare. It would take Tinker days to understand all that had happened. "Nobody can ever know," she whispered. Andrew had fallen asleep on her father's lap.

"We can't not tell him," Mira said. "Look what it did to all of us."

"But people will *judge* Andrew. The kids at school will be so cruel," Tinker moaned, remembering how she'd been teased, and she was only fat.

"We don't have to publish it in the *Burlington Free Press*, Tinker," William said. "He'll be told the truth when he's old enough to understand. The shame isn't his. It was Pony's, Keith's. It was Mother's. He shouldn't suffer for it the way I did. The way we all have."

"Why does anyone outside the family ever need to know?" Ruth asked. "It will become Andrew's information to divulge or not. In time."

William read from another of Katherine's e-mails, cautioning them not to alert the pediatrician.

"Maybe Katherine can be his pediatrician," Mira said.

"But what is the truth?" her father asked. "We have only this Keith's word that he's the father. Perhaps he's not."

"Pony seemed pretty sure," William said. "According to Keith, that is."

"Oh, man," Mira said. "How are we going to find out?"

"DNA," Tinker said. "There must be a way."

"Do you need to do anything?" Ruth asked. "Maybe you just leave it alone."

"But look at all that's happened!" Mira wailed. "And all because Mom kept her mouth shut about having another baby and about William. If we'd known, none of this would have happened. Right?"

"I'd like to speak." Jasper sounded weary. "Your mother had reasons for not speaking of that other child. I don't know them. None of us does. But I'll assure you of this: She did it out of love. Misguided? How can we know?" He smiled at them. "As far as Andrew is concerned, do we tell him the truth? And if so, what *is* the truth? What we know for sure is what Pony told William, that Andrew was conceived in a liaison with a man that lasted for only a matter of hours. We have no evidence that the man was Keith, beyond his claim. Tinker spoke of DNA, and of course it's a possibility, but we would need to approach that with great care. We need to consider Ruth's suggestion. But in any case, I think William is correct. We'll know what to tell Andrew when the time comes, many years forward. We have so much of importance to consider in the meantime. We've lost our beautiful Pony. We've been deceived and betrayed. We very nearly lost William in Idaho. We have Andrew to raise. So many events have occurred, and so much energy will be required. But can I point out . . ." He made an all-inclusive gesture that took in the family and the house. "Here we all are. We'll go forward. We're a family."

Chapter 21

William

To the east of Lake Aral, a drive of perhaps twenty minutes, Mount Pisgah rose steeply. It was a densely forested foothill, spiked with rocky outcroppings, and had a flat, bald top. The trailhead was difficult to find. Like so many of the special places around Lake Aral, this one was unmarked. The access wasn't written up in any hiking guides or touring books. But William and Jasper had been there many times. He knew to slow at a boulder on the left side of the road, drive another hundred yards, and park in a scant turnout. Their car was the only car. They had Mount Pisgah to themselves.

It had been years since William had made this climb. A short but steep distance with tricky footing. Roots crisscrossed the trail, and there were sections of difficult traprock. William wasn't sure if doing this hike was a good idea, given Jasper's recent hospital stay. It was possible he'd suffered some small strokes, and if that was the case, he would no doubt continue to have them. He was to be watched carefully. Tinker had wanted to come along today, but Jasper had said no. He wanted to make this trip with William. Only William.

Jasper walked with a cane now. One that had for years been in the umbrella stand at the front door. A cane with an ivory handle that generations of Carterets had used in their old age. When he was a child, William had used it as a sword, sparring with it. Now Jasper walked slowly, painfully, from the car to the woods. William let him take the lead and set an easy pace.

The trail rose immediately. William kept an eye on Jasper's feet, in sneakers, ahead of him, his khaki pants ballooning out. Neither of them spoke, saving their breath for the walk. William listened for Jasper's breath, for signs of wheezing or strain, but heard nothing unusual. He'd brought a cell phone, although it was doubtful that there was service here. If Jasper collapsed—well, he wouldn't worry about that.

It took them forty-five minutes to reach the top, which was barren of trees. The view brought to William's mind the climb he'd made with Keith, with its sweeping views of the Sawtooth Mountains, the river below. Here, the view was gentler. Maples and oaks darkened for winter.

A fallen tree at the edge of a clearing served as a seat for Jasper, who leaned on his cane and patted the space beside him for William. But first William did what he always did when he reached the top of Mount Pisgah: He forced himself to walk to the edge and peer down the sheer stone cliff that fell sharply, a thousand or so feet. He could see the tops of the trees below, the narrow gravel road where their car was parked. The sheer expanse of air between him and solid ground made him feel almost light-headed. He breathed deeply to will himself calm and to will away the fear. And it worked. Breathing always calmed him.

He took a seat beside Jasper. "Okay," he said. "Here we are."

"I used to bring you here," Jasper said. "Do you remember?"

"Sure," William said.

"You always did what you did just now. You went to the edge."

"Yeah," William said.

"You weren't afraid."

"I was terrified. I did it to prove to myself that I could."

Jasper looked oddly at him, frowning so that his thick eyebrows obscured his eyes. "Terrified?"

"God, yes," William said. "I did it to improve myself." He laughed.

"But you were always so sure of yourself, William. Physically."

William looked into the old man's eyes to see if he meant it. "I'm telling you, no."

"Hmm," Jasper said. "As a boy, coming up here with my friends, my family, I was too afraid to stand on the edge." He shrugged. "I was too cautious. When you and I came, I always sat right here and watched you do what I could never do. To tell you the truth, I was envious. You surpassed me so early."

William picked up a stick and twirled it in his fingers.

"It's time for the remaining truth." Jasper stood up and took a few steps, supported by his cane, and turned to face William. "I loved your mother the moment I saw her. But it took her some time to feel anything for me. I helped her leave. I met you for the first time on the night I drove your mother from Puma Springs to San Diego. She held you in her arms. She came to love me over time, through your sisters."

"I thought you and Mom had to get married because she got pregnant with me. I figured you had to come back to Hartford because of me. Gave up some dream you had. That without me, your life would have been different. You would have done what you wanted."

"Oh my," Jasper said.

"I thought a lot of things."

"Such as?"

"I thought . . ." William began, unsure if he could say this.

"Tell me."

"You loved my sisters, never me."

Jasper shut his eyes. "I loved you, William. Then and now. Not as I do the girls, no. You're correct. But as much. Every bit as much."

He wiped a hand over his face. "Physically, you see, you favor your father. I've always known that." He took a deep breath. "Put yourself in my place. How many times I had to wonder if Olivia looked at you and thought of him, particularly as you grew into adolescence and manhood. She had loved him, you see. He turned on her, and on you, but she had loved him."

"You're shaking," William said.

"Of course," Jasper said.

"Maybe we should head back. Talk as we go."

"I'm not finished," Jasper said. He sat beside William again, closer this time. "You're partly right. I went west because I wanted nothing to do with a ball-bearing company, or a life spent the way my family had always spent it, in the business, living in the Steele Road house, here at Lake Aral. I saw it as a life already led by one generation after another. A safe, unoriginal life. I wanted something else. I didn't know what. And there I was in Puma Springs. It was very beautiful, in its way. And then I met your mother. She had a small part in a community-theater production. I went to every performance. Three in all. She was required to wear a blue scarf at her neck. Her hair tied high on her head. Do you understand what I'm trying to tell you?"

"Keep talking," William said.

Jasper laughed. "I was old for that sort of thing. I was in my thirties. I thought I'd been in love a few times, but I was mistaken. Love was when I met your mother. I knew nothing of the other child, only of you. What heartache it must have been for her to leave him behind. She needed help for you. Your father was a tyrant, she said. She was frightened. You were her reason for living, William." He looked out over the hills. "And she became mine. I would have done anything for her. I did everything I could."

"You came back east," William said.

Jasper smiled. He shrugged. "It was what I had to offer her. It was what she needed. What you needed. I did it gladly. I've never had a single regret. With you, and the girls, it's been the original life I wanted."

"I'm taking Andrew," William said.

"Look at me, son." Jasper's eyes glistened with tears. William had no memory of ever seeing him so close-up. "You'll do a fine job with the boy."

"I don't know what to say," William said.

"Nothing to say," Jasper said, rising. "Let's go on down now. We have a raft to take in."

Back at Fond du Lac, the wind had picked up, blowing offshore, smelling of fall. Red maple leaves were scattered over the black water of the lake. The sky was a spectacular blue.

William, Mira, and Tinker stood knee-deep in the water. Jasper was on the shore with Ruth, Mark, and Isabel. Andrew lay on his back in his playpen, watching the sky. Minerva sat on the porch, shrouded in afghans. The loss of Pony hung heavily over them all— the memory of so many other Labor Days when Pony would free the raft from its mooring. When she'd shoot to the surface and shout, *"Finito!"*

"Let's get this over with." Tinker looked like a child, her hair stuffed into a bulging white rubber swim cap with a too-long strap around the chin so the end flapped, her bathing suit now too large for her, so it gapped at the top. They entered the lake together. All three at once dove in and did a fast crawl to warm themselves. At the raft William went hand over hand around the edge until he found where the chain went down to the anchor. "Tell me when," he called out to his sisters. Their job was to swim to the other side of the raft, the windward side, and kick it toward shore with everything they had to give the chain some slack. "Okay," Tinker shouted. "Go ahead."

William took a deep breath, grasped the chain in both hands, and pulled himself down, waiting to feel the bloom of Pony's hair. He ran his hands over and over along the slick chain. He found the rough edge of the broken link where her hair had caught, but there was nothing. It was gone. It must have come loose over the summer and drifted out into the lake. He felt the chain slacken as the girls pushed up above. He felt in the blackness of the lake bottom for the hook, eased it from the eye embedded in the concrete block. And it was done. He swam to the surface, into the bright day.

Acknowledgments

The author deeply appreciates the many contributions of the following people in the development and publication of this book: Jane Christensen, Bruce Cohen, Chief James Dziobek, Robert H. Funk, Mary-Anne Harrington, Leslie Johnson, Terese Karmel, Wally Lamb, Dr. Edward T. McDonald, Amanda Murray, Dr. Carol Steffenson, Jennifer Rudolph Walsh, and Ellen Zahl.